'Fridlund has created one of the most intelligent and poetic novels of the year' *New Statesman*

'Fridlund's writing is **vivid**: her natural descriptions elicit a superb sense of place' *Daily Mail*

'Compelling . . . **History of Wolves stands out**' *Sunday Telegraph*

'Life offers Linda two simultaneous chances to fit in, although both – as we know from the start – go terribly wrong' *Guardian*

'Fridlund writes coldly, beautifully, like a White Queen magicking spirits from the snow . . . suspicion drips like icicles in the thaw'
The Times

'Fridlund is a fine writer and her work is cut through with moments of sparse beauty' *Financial Times*

'Beautifully written' *Literary Review*

'Reminds me of Curtis Sittenfeld . . . **so original, a beautiful literary work**' Viv Crookop

'A writer with a great future ahead of her . . . **her prose is exquisite**'
Louise Doughty

'Emily Fridlund's language is generous and precise, her story grief-tempered and forcefully moving. *History of Wolves* is **the loneliest thing I've read in years, and it's gorgeous**. These are haunted pages' Leif Enger, author of *Peace Like a River*

'So **delicately calibrated and precisely beautiful** that one might not immediately sense the sledgehammer of pain building inside this book. And I mean that in the best way'
Aimee Bender, author of *The Particular Sadness of Lemon Cake*

'As **exquisite** a first novel as I've ever encountered. Poetic, complex and **utterly, heartbreakingly beautiful**'
T.C. Boyle, author of *The Harder They Come*

Emily Fridlund grew up in Minnesota. She holds an MFA from Washington University in St. Louis and a PhD in Literature and Creative Writing from the University of Southern California. Her collection of stories, *Catapult*, was chosen by Ben Marcus for the Mary McCarthy Prize. She lives in the Finger Lakes region of New York. *History of Wolves* is her first novel.

Also by Emily Fridlund

Catapult: Short stories

HISTORY
OF WOLVES

emily fridlund

WEIDENFELD & NICOLSON

First published in Great Britain in 2017
by Weidenfeld & Nicolson.
This paperback edition published in 2017
by Weidenfeld & Nicolson
an imprint of the Orion Publishing Group Ltd
Carmelite House, 50 Victoria Embankment
London EC4Y 0DZ

An Hachette UK Company

3 5 7 9 10 8 6 4 2

Copyright © Emily Fridlund 2017

A CIP catalogue record for this book is
available from the British Library.

ISBN (Mass Market Paperback) 978 1 4746 0296 9

Printed in Great Britain by Clays Ltd, St Ives plc

www.orionbooks.co.uk

For Nick

Become conscious for a single moment that Life and intelligence are purely spiritual,—neither in nor of matter,— and the body will then utter no complaints.

—Mary Baker Eddy,
Science and Health with Key to the Scriptures

I won't be dying after all, not now, but will go on living dizzily hereafter in reality, half-deaf to reality, in the room perfumed by the fire that our inextinguishable will begins.

—Timothy Donnelly, "The New Intelligence"

SCIENCE

1

IT'S NOT THAT I NEVER THINK ABOUT PAUL. He comes to me occasionally before I'm fully awake, though I almost never remember what he said, or what I did or didn't do to him. In my mind, the kid just plops down into my lap. Boom. That's how I know it's him: there's no interest in me, no hesitation. We're sitting in the Nature Center on a late afternoon like any other, and his body moves automatically toward mine—not out of love or respect, but simply because he hasn't yet learned the etiquette of minding where his body stops and another begins. He's four, he's got an owl puzzle to do, don't talk to him. I don't. Outside the window, an avalanche of poplar fluff floats by, silent and weightless as air. The sunlight shifts, the puzzle cleaves into an owl and comes apart again, I prod Paul to standing. Time to go. It's time. But in the second before we rise, before he whines out his protest and asks to stay a little longer, he leans back against my chest, yawning. And my throat cinches closed. Because it's strange, you know? It's marvelous, and sad too, how good it can feel to have your body taken for granted.

* * *

Before Paul, I'd known just one person who'd gone from living to dead. He was Mr. Adler, my eighth-grade history teacher. He wore brown corduroy suits and white tennis shoes, and though his subject was America he preferred to talk about czars. He once showed us a photograph of Russia's last emperor, and that's how I think of him now—black bearded, tassel shouldered—though in fact Mr. Adler was always clean shaven and plodding. I was in English class when his fourth-period student burst in saying Mr. Adler had fallen. We crowded across the hall and there he lay facedown on the floor, eyes closed, blue lips suctioning the carpet. "Does he have epilepsy?" someone asked. "Does he have pills?" We were all repulsed. The Boy Scouts argued over proper CPR techniques, while the gifted and talented kids reviewed his symptoms in hysterical whispers. I had to force myself to go to him. I crouched down and took Mr. Adler's dry-meat hand. It was early November. He was darkening the carpet with drool, gasping in air between longer and longer intervals, and I remember a distant bonfire scent. Someone was burning garbage in plastic bags, some janitor getting rid of leaves and pumpkin rinds before the first big snow.

When the paramedics finally loaded Mr. Adler's body onto a stretcher, the Boy Scouts trailed behind like puppies, hoping for an assignment. They wanted a door to open, something heavy to lift. In the hallway, girls stood sniffling in clumps. A few teachers held their palms to their chests, uncertain what to say or do next.

"That a Doors song?" one of the paramedics asked. He'd stayed behind to pass out packets of saltines to light-headed students. I shrugged. I must have been humming out loud. He gave me orange Gatorade in a Dixie Cup, saying—as if I were the one he'd come to save, as if his duty were to root out sickness in whatever living thing he could find—"Drink slow now. Do it in sips."

The Walleye Capital of the World we were called back then. There was a sign to this effect out on Route 10 and a mural of three mohawked fish on the side of the diner. Those guys were always waving a finny hello—grins and eyebrows, teeth and gums—but no one came from out of town to fish, or do much at all, once the big lakes froze up in November. We didn't have the resort in those days, only a seedy motel. Downtown went: diner, hardware, bait and tackle, bank. The most impressive place in Loose River back then was the old timber mill, I think, and that was because it was half burned down, charred black planks towering over the banks of the river. Almost everything official, the hospital and DMV and Burger King and police station, were twenty-plus miles down the road in Whitewood.

'The day the Whitewood paramedics took Mr. Adler away they tooted the ambulance horn as they left the school parking lot. We all stood at the windows and watched, even the hockey players in their yellowed caps, even the cheerleaders with their static-charged bangs. Snow was coming down by then, hard. As the ambulance slid around the corner, its headlights raked crazily through the flurries gusting across the road. "Shouldn't there be sirens?" someone asked, and I thought—measuring the last swallow of Gatorade in my little waxed cup—*how stupid can people be?*

Mr. Adler's replacement was Mr. Grierson, and he arrived a month before Christmas with a deep, otherworldly tan. He wore one gold hoop earring and a brilliant white shirt with pearly buttons. We learned later that he'd come from California, from a private girls' school on the sea. No one knew what brought him all the way to northern Minnesota, midwinter, but after the first week of class, he took down Mr. Adler's maps of the Russian Empire and replaced them with enlarged copies of the US Constitution. He announced he'd double majored in theater in college, which explained why he stood in front of the class one day with his arms outstretched reciting the whole Declaration of Independence by heart. Not just the soaring parts about life, liberty, and the pursuit of happiness, but the needling, wretched list of tyrannies against the colonies. I could see how badly he wanted to be liked. "What does it mean?" Mr. Grierson asked when he got to the part about mutually pledging our sacred honor.

The hockey players slept innocently on folded hands. Even the gifted and talented kids were unmoved, clicking their mechanical pencils until the lead protruded obscenely, like hospital needles. They jousted each other across the aisles. "En garde!" they hissed, contemptuously.

Mr. Grierson sat down on Mr. Adler's desk. He was breathless from his recitation, and I realized—in an odd flash, like a too-bright light passing over him—he was middle-aged. I could see sweat on his face, his pulse pounding under gray neck stubble. "People. *Guys.* What does it mean that the rights of man are *self-evident*? Come on. You know this."

I saw his eyes rest on Lily Holburn, who had sleek black hair and was wearing, despite the cold, a sheer crimson sweater. He seemed to think her beauty could rescue him, that she would be, because she was prettier than the rest of us, kind. Lily had big brown eyes, dyslexia, no pencil, a boyfriend. Her face slowly reddened under Mr. Grierson's gaze.

She blinked. He nodded at her, promising implicitly that, whatever she said, he'd agree. She gave a deer-like lick of her lips.

I don't know why I raised my hand. It wasn't that I felt sorry for her exactly. Or him. It was just that the tension became unbearable for a moment, out of all proportion to the occasion. "It means some things don't have to be proven," I offered. "Some things are simply true. There's no changing them."

"That's right!" he said, grateful—I knew—not to me in particular, but to some hoop of luck he felt he'd stumbled into. I could do that. Give people what they wanted without them knowing it came from me. Without saying a word, Lily could make people feel encouraged, blessed. She had dimples on her cheeks, nipples that flashed like signs from God through her sweater. I was flat chested, plain as a banister. I made people feel judged.

Winter collapsed on us that year. It knelt down, exhausted, and stayed. In the middle of December so much snow fell the gym roof buckled and school was canceled for a week. With school out, the hockey players went ice fishing. The Boy Scouts played hockey on the ponds. Then came Christmas with its strings of colored lights up and down Main Street, and the competing nativity scenes at the Lutheran and Catholic churches—one with painted sandbags standing in as sheep, and the other with baby Jesus sculpted out of a lump of ice. New Year's brought another serious storm. By the time school started again in January, Mr. Grierson's crisp white shirts had been replaced with nondescript sweaters, his hoop earring with a stud. Someone must have taught him to use the Scantron machine, because after a week's worth of lectures on Lewis and Clark, he gave his first test. While we hunched at our desks filling tiny circles, he walked up and down the aisles, clicking a ballpoint pen.

The next day, Mr. Grierson asked me to stay after class. He sat behind his desk and touched his lips, which were chapped and flaking off beneath his fingers. "You didn't do very well on your exam," he told me.

He was waiting for an explanation and I lifted my shoulders defensively. But before I could say a word, he added, "Look, I'm sorry." He twisted the stud—delicate, difficult screw—in his ear. "I'm still working out the kinks in my lesson plans. What were you studying before I arrived?"

"Russia."

"Ah." A look of scorn passed over his face, followed immediately by pleasure. "The Cold War lingers in the backcountry."

I defended Mr. Adler. "It wasn't the Soviet Union we were talking about. It was *czars*."

"Oh, Mattie." No one ever called me that. It was like being tapped on the shoulder from behind. My name was Madeline, but at school I was called Linda, or Commie, or Freak. I pulled my hands into balls in my sleeves. Mr. Grierson went on. "No one cared about the czars before Stalin and the bomb. They were puppets on a faraway stage, utterly insignificant. Then all the Mr. Adlers went to college in 1961 and there was general nostalgia for the old Russian toys, the inbred princesses from another century. Their ineffectuality made them interesting. You understand?" He smiled then, closing his eyes a little. His front teeth were white, his canines yellow. "But you're thirteen."

"Fourteen."

"I just wanted to say I'm sorry if this has started off badly. We'll get on better footing soon."

The next week he asked me to drop by his classroom after school. This time, he'd taken the stud out of his ear and set it on his desk. Very tenderly, with his forefinger and thumb, he was probing the flesh around his earlobe.

"Mattie," he said, straightening up.

He had me sit in a blue plastic chair beside his desk. He set a stack of glossy brochures in my lap, made a tepee of his fingers. "Do me a favor? But don't blame me for having to ask. That's my job." He squirmed.

That's when he asked me to be the school's representative in History Odyssey.

"This will be great," he said, unconvincingly. "What you do is make a poster. Then you give a speech about Vietnam War registers, border crossings to Canada, etcetera. Or maybe you do the desecration of the Ojibwa peoples? Or those back-to-the-land folks that settled up here. Something local, something ethically ambiguous. Something with constitutional implications."

"I want to do wolves," I told him.

"What, a history of wolves?" He was puzzled. Then he shook his head and grinned. "Right. You're a fourteen-year-old girl." The skin bunched up around his eyes. "You all have a thing for horses and wolves. I love that. I love that. That's so weird. What is that *about*?"

Because my parents didn't own a car, this is how I got home when I missed the bus. I walked three miles down the plowed edge of

Route 10 and then turned right on Still Lake Road. In another mile the road forked. The left side traced the lake northward and the right side turned into an unplowed hill. That's where I stopped, stuffed my jeans into my socks, and readjusted the cuffs on my woolen mittens. In winter, the trees against the orange sky looked like veins. The sky between the branches looked like sunburn. It was twenty minutes through snow and sumac before the dogs heard me and started braying against their chains.

By the time I got home, it was dark. When I opened the door, I saw my mom bent over the sink, arms elbow-deep in inky water. Long straight hair curtained her face and neck, which tended to give her a cagey look. But her voice was all midwestern vowels, all wide-open Kansas. "Is there a prayer for clogged drains?" she asked without turning around.

I set my mittens on the woodstove, where they would stiffen and no longer fit my hands just right in the morning. I left my jacket on, though. It was cold inside.

My mom, her own jacket damp with sink water, sat down heavily at the table. But she kept her greasy hands in the air like they were something precious—something wiggling and still alive—that she'd snatched from a pond. Something she might feed us on, a pretty little pair of perch. "We need Drano. Crap." She looked up into the air, then very slowly wiped her palms on her canvas pockets. "Please help. God of infinite pity for the pathetic farce that is human living."

She was only half kidding. I knew that. I knew from stories how my parents had ridden in a stolen van to Loose River in the early eighties, how my father had stockpiled rifles and pot, and how, when the commune fell apart, my mother had traded whatever hippie fanaticism she had left for Christianity. For as long as I could remember she went to church three times a week—Wednesday, Saturday, and Sunday—because she held out hope that penance worked, that some of the past could be reversed, slowly and over years.

My mother believed in God, but grudgingly, like a grounded daughter.

"Do you think you could take one of the dogs with you and go back?"

"Back into town?" I was still shivering. The thought made me furious for a second, wiped clean of everything. I couldn't feel my fingers.

"Or not." She swung her long hair back and swiped her nose with her wrist. "No, not. It's probably below zero out there. I'm sorry. I'll go get another bucket." She didn't move from her chair, though. She was waiting for something. "I'm *sorry* I asked. You can't be mad at me for asking." She clasped her greasy hands together. "I'm sorry, I'm sorry, I'm sorry."

For each *sorry*, her voice rose a half step.

I waited a second before I spoke. "It's okay," I said.

Here's the thing about Mr. Grierson. I'd seen how he crouched down next to Lily's desk. I'd seen how he said, "You're doing fine," and put his hand very carefully, like a paperweight, on her spine. How he lifted his fingertips and gave her a little pat. I saw how curious and frightened he was of the Karens, the cheerleaders, who sometimes pulled off their wool leg warmers and revealed bare winter skin, white and nubbed in gooseflesh. Their legwarmers gave them a rash, which they scratched until their scabs had to be dabbed with buds of toilet paper. I saw how he addressed every question in class to one of them—to the Karens or to Lily Holburn—saying, "Anyone? Anyone home?" Then, making a phone of his hand, he'd lower his voice and growl, "Hello, Holburn residence, is Lily available?" Blushing, Lily would do a closed-mouth smile into the lip of her sleeve.

When I met with him after school, Mr. Grierson shook his head. "That was a stupid thing to do with the phone, right?" He was embarrassed. He wanted reassurance that everything was okay, that he was a good teacher. He wanted to be forgiven for all his little mistakes, and he seemed to think—because I crossed my arms and did poorly on tests—that my mediocrity was deliberate, personal. "Here," he said, sheepishly, sliding a narrow blue can across his desk. I took a few sips of his energy drink, something so sweet and caffeinated it made my heart pound almost instantly. After several more gulps I was trembling in my chair. I had to clench my teeth to keep them from chattering.

"Did Mr. Adler ever show movies?" he wanted to know.

I'm not sure why I played his game. I don't know why I coddled him. "You show so many more movies than him," I said.

He smiled with satisfaction. "How's the project going, then?"

I didn't answer that. Instead I took another sip of his energy drink, uninvited. I wanted him to know that I saw how he looked at Lily Holburn, that I comprehended that look better than she did, that, though I did not like him at all—though I found his phone joke creepy and his earring sad—I understood him. But the can was empty. I had to put my lips on metal and pretend to gulp. Outside the window, sleet was shellacking every snowdrift, turning the whole world hard as rock. It would be dark in an hour, less. The dogs would be pacing the far orbit of their chains, waiting. Mr. Grierson was putting on his jacket. "Shall we?" He never—never once—asked how I got home.

Mr. Grierson treated History Odyssey like we both knew it was a chore. Secretly, I wanted to win. I was determined to see a wolf. Nights, I went out in mukluks, a ski mask, and my father's down jacket, which was redolent with his scents, with tobacco and mildew and bitter coffee. It was like wearing his body while he slept, like earning a right to his presence and silence and bulk. I sat on an old ice bucket near the furthest fish house and sipped boiled water from a thermos. But it was rare for a wolf to be spotted here so late in winter—all I ever saw were distant logs squirming with crows. In the end I had to settle for a dead one. Saturdays, I snowshoed to the Forest Service Nature Center, where I studied the stuffed bitch in the lobby, with her glass eyes and coral nails, her sunken black cheeks pulled back in what looked like a smile. Peg, the naturalist there, pouted when she saw me try to touch the wolf's tail. "Uh *uh*," she scolded. She gave me gummy bears and taxidermy techniques, told me how to sculpt eyelids from clay and muscles from polyurethane foam. "Iron the skin, iron the skin," she warned me.

On the morning of the History Odyssey tournament, I sawed a branch from the old pine behind our house. Needles poured in little *whik-whik* propellers onto the snow. I took the casino bus to Whitewood after school, lugging my wolf poster and branch past the old people from the retirement home, who frowned at me but didn't say anything. In the Whitewood High School auditorium, I propped the branch against the lectern to create the crucial atmosphere. I played a tape of howling wolves on repeat. Though my mouth was dry when I began my speech, I didn't have to use my notes and I didn't rock back and forth like the boy who went before me. I was focused, calm. I pointed to diagrams of pups in different displays of submission, and quoting from a book I said, "But the term *alpha*—evolved to describe captive animals—is still misleading. An alpha animal may be alpha only at certain times for a specific reason." Those words always made me feel I was drinking something cool and sweet, something forbidden. I thought of the black bitch at the Nature Center, fixed in her posture of doggy friendliness, and I recited that part of my speech over again, slowly this time, like it was an amendment to the Constitution.

Afterward, one of the judges poked his pencil in the air. "But—I have to intervene here. There's something you haven't explained very well. What do wolves have to do with *human* history?"

It was then that I saw Mr. Grierson by the door. He had his jacket in his arms like he'd just come in, and I watched as he caught the eye of the judge and shrugged. It was the subtlest shift of his shoulders, as if to say, *What can you do with kids? What can you do with these teenage girls?* I took a deep breath and glared at both of them. "Wolves have nothing at all to do with humans, actually. If they can help it, they avoid them."

They gave me the Originality Prize, which was a bouquet of carnations dyed green for Saint Patrick's Day. Afterward, Mr. Grierson wanted to know if we should load the pine branch in his car with the poster to drive back to school. I was depressed and shook my head. The winner, a seventh-grade girl in a pantsuit, was getting her picture taken with her watercolor rendering of the sinking of the SS *Edmund Fitzgerald*. I buttoned my coat, then followed Mr. Grierson as he dragged the drooping branch out a side exit. He javelined it upright into a grainy bank of snow. "It's like *A Charlie Brown Christmas*," he said, laughing. "I want to hang tinsel from it. It's cute."

He bent down to brush stray needles from his slacks, and on impulse I thrust out a hand and brushed as well—*swish, swish*—against his thigh. He stepped back, did a little shake of his pants, laughed awkwardly. Men can be so ungainly when it comes to sex. I learned that later. But at the time, what I'd done didn't feel sexual. Let me be clear about that. It felt like grooming. Or like coaxing a dog to you, watching its hackles rise and fall, and then you have a pet.

I licked my lips, Lily Holburn–style, deer-like, innocent as anything. I said, "Mr. Grierson, would you mind driving me home?"

Before we left Whitewood High, Mr. Grierson went back inside for a wet paper towel to wrap around the stems of the carnations. Then he set the bouquet in my arms, cautiously, as if it were some kind of bracken baby. As we drove the twenty-six miles from Whitewood to my parents' house, we watched a storm blow ice in monstrous crusts off the limbs of trees—so that was part of it, too, the slow-motion sense of catastrophe. Mr. Grierson's defrosting fan didn't work very well, and I swiped at the windshield with my jacket's dirty cuff.

"This where we turn?" he asked, as he drove down Still Lake Road. He was pulling little bits of skin from his lips with his incisors. Even in the near dark, I could see a crack in his lip, bloody but not yet bleeding. That pleased me for some reason.

It felt like something I had done to him myself—with my wolf presentation, with my pine needles.

The turnoff to my parents' road was unplowed, as usual. Mr. Grierson pulled to a stop at the intersection and we both leaned forward to peer out the windshield and up the steep, dark hill. When I glanced at him across the car, his throat looked as wide and soft as a belly exposed, so I stretched out and kissed him there. Quickly, quickly.

He flinched.

"This way then?" he said, pulling up the zipper of his coat and tucking his neck back in his collar. Up on the hill sat my parents' lit cabin, and I could tell he had fixed his attention there because it was the first thing in sight. "Um, that's that ex-cult place, isn't it? I heard some strange stuff about them. They neighbors of yours?"

He was only making small talk of course—still I gripped my carnations. I felt myself split open, like kindling. "They keep to themselves."

"Yeah?" His mind was somewhere else.

Sleet popped against the windshield, but I couldn't see it because the glass was getting all fogged up again.

"Let's get you home," he said, cranking the gearshift and turning the wheel, and I could sense how tired he was of being responsible for me.

"I can walk from here," I told him.

I thought if I slammed the door hard enough, Mr. Grierson might come after me. That's what it's like to be fourteen. I thought if I took a few running steps off the road into the snow that maybe he'd follow me—to assuage his guilt, to make sure I got home all right, to push his chalky history hands under my jacket, whatever. I headed for the lake instead of going uphill. I darted out onto the ice in the prickly sleet, but when I looked back, his car with its brights was turning around, doing a meticulous U-turn in the trees.

The Grierson scandal broke a few months after I started high school the next fall. I overheard the gossip while I was pouring someone's coffee, working as a part-time waitress at the diner in town. He had been accused of pedophilia and sex crimes at his previous school and was promptly fired at ours—a stack of dirty pictures had been confiscated from some former apartment of his in California. That day after work, I took my tips to the bar down the street and bought my first full pack of cigarettes from the machine in the vestibule. I knew from the few I'd stolen at home not to inhale fully when lighting up. But as I ducked into the wet bushes behind the parking lot, my eyes started watering and I coughed, an ugly fury thumping at my heart. More than anything else I felt deceived. I felt I'd perceived some seed in Mr. Grierson's nature, and that he'd lied to me, profoundly, by ignoring what I did to him in his car, pretending to be better than he was. A regular teacher. I thought about Mr. Grierson zipping his wide, warm neck back inside his jacket collar. I thought of his rank scent when I got close, as if he'd sweated through his clothes and dried out in the winter air. I thought about all that, and what I felt for him, finally, was an uncomfortable rush of pity. It seemed unfair to me that people couldn't be something else just by working at it hard, by saying it over and over.

When I was six or seven, my mom sat me down in the bath basin in my underwear. It was midmorning, midsummer. A shaft of light caught her face. She dribbled water on my head from a measuring cup. "I wish I believed in this shit," she told me.

"What's supposed to happen?" I shivered.

"Good question," she said. "You're a new pot of rice, baby. I'm starting you all over from scratch."

I didn't want to go home the night Mr. Grierson dropped me off. I thought—with pleasure, feeling a necklace of hooks in my throat as I swallowed—how I might break through the brittle lake ice and just go down. My parents wouldn't worry for a long time, maybe not till morning. My mother nodded off each night sewing quilts for prison inmates. My dad spent his evenings scavenging wood from the cleared property that was for sale across the lake. I never even knew for sure if they were my real parents, or if they were simply the people who stayed around after everyone else went back to college or office jobs in the Twin Cities. They were more like stepsiblings than parents, though they were good to me, always—which was worse than anything in a way. Worse than buying cereal with dimes and quarters, worse than accepting hand-me-downs from neighbors, worse than being called Commie, Freak. My dad hung a swing when I was ten from a giant cottonwood; my mom cut cockleburs from my hair. Even so, the night Mr. Grierson dropped me off, I kept thinking, viciously, waiting for my body to plunge through ice: *There goes the rice, Mom. There goes the whole pot.*

After I went to community college and dropped out, after I had been temping in the Cities for some time, I found a national database online into which you could type any sex offender's

name and track them around the country. You can watch someone's little red trail on a map of each state as they go from city
to city, as they go from Arkansas to Montana, as they search for
bad apartments, as they enter prison and come out again. You
can watch them try to give new names and get called out, a flurry
of angry posts erupting online every time this happens. You can
watch the moral indignation. You can watch them try again.
You can follow them to southern Florida, to the marshes, where,
among the mangroves, they set up a little out-of-the-way antique
shop, selling whatever, selling junk. Hawking rusty lanterns and
stuffed ducks, fake shark teeth, cheap gold earrings. You can see
everything they sell because people update their posts and give
all the details. There are so many people watching. People are
updating all the time. "Should I buy a map from a convicted
sex offender?" people write, and it seems an ethically ambiguous
question. "Don't I have a constitutional right to tell him I don't
want him here, selling his postcards at half price?" People write,
"Don't I have a right to tell him to his fucking face?" People
write, "Who does he think he is?"

2

PAPERS PASSED ALONG IN A PILE. That's what high school was. They went down one aisle between desks, came back around the next, looped slowly to the back of the classroom. The gifted and talented kids—transformed now into the Latin Club, the Forensics Team—licked their fingers to extract their portion. They always set to work like the swim team doing laps, breathing from the sides of their mouths, biting down on their pencils. The hockey players had to be prodded awake when the stack came down their aisle, had to be treated with great deference—or else we would lose the District Championship. Again. They woke from their naps long enough to take one paper and pass the rest on, long enough to dump open bags of chips into their mouths, wipe the salt from their lips, and return to their dreams of Empire. What else would hockey players dream about? It was their world we lived in. When I was fifteen, I figured this out. They dreamed it into fact. They got teachers to forgive their blank worksheets, they got cheerleaders to scream out their names at pep rallies, they got Zambonis to stripe the world as far as you could see—ceaselessly—in perfect swaths of freezing water. We were in a new building that year, a bigger classroom with pale brick walls, but outside it was the same thing it had been since we were children. Winter boomeranged back.

Outside: four feet of snow sealed in a shiny crust.

Inside: European History, American Civics, Trigonometry, English.

Life Science came last. It was taught by our old eighth-grade gym teacher, Liz Lundgren, who trudged over from the middle school at the end of the day in her Polartec parka and camouflage snow bib. Ms. Lundgren had a tic. Whenever she got irritated or inspired, she switched instantly to whispering. She thought that would make us listen better; she thought it would make us pay attention to protists and fungi; she thought we would try harder to understand meiosis if we couldn't quite catch all the words in her sentences. "The spores . . . in absence of water or heat . . . maneuver in great quantities," she would murmur, and it was like hearing some obscure rumor that, due to over-telling, no longer held any relevance we could make out.

In that class you could always hear the clock tick. From every window, you could see snow blow away in gusts, then drift back the next day in piles as high as houses. One day near the end of Evolution, a late-season storm brought a huge poplar branch down in a *wumff* of ice. Through the window, I watched it cascade to the ground and narrowly miss a small blue car pulling out from the grocery store across from school. At the board, Ms. Lundgren was chalking out the pros and cons of natural selection in squeaky cursive. The window fogged as I leaned toward it. I leaned back. Someone in a huge hooded parka got out of the blue car, dragged the branch from the road, got back in. Then the Honda drove a wide arc around the perimeter, crunching a few twigs beneath its tires.

Minutes after that the sun came out: brilliant, stunning us all. Still, it was no surprise when we were let out of school a half hour early due to the windchill. I made my way home from the bus stop at a rigid trot. I crunched along the snow-packed trail, felt the wind come off the lake in blasts, heard the pines groan and creak overhead. Halfway up the hill, my lungs started to feel raggedy. My face changed into something other than face, got rubbed out. When I finally got to the top of the hill, when I slowed down to brush ice from my nose, I turned and saw a puff of exhaust across our lake. I had to squint against all that white to make it out.

It was the blue Honda hatchback from town. A couple was unloading the car.

The lake at this point was extremely narrow, not much more than eight hundred feet straight across. I watched them for a few minutes, nursing my fingers, scrunching them into inflexible balls.

I'd seen the couple once before, in August. They'd come to oversee the construction of their lake house, which had been built by a team of college students from Duluth. The crew spent the summer clearing brush with backhoes, arranging plywood walls, stapling shingles to the vaulted roof. The house, when it was finished, was unlike anything I'd seen in Loose River. It had split-log siding and enormous triangular windows, a broad blond deck that jutted out over the lake like the prow of some ship. From their hatchback, the father had hauled Adirondack chairs and docile cats: one black and fat, the other white and draped ornamentally over his arm. I'd seen them out on their new dock one late August afternoon, bundled head to toe in towels. Father, mother, tiny child. The child's towel dragged on the wooden planks, and the mother and father had knelt down together, at once, arranging the folds. They were like attendants to a very small bride, doting, hovering. They seemed to be saying something very sweet to the child, who had a high, frightened voice that carried across water. That was the last I'd seen of them.

That winter day, though, they returned. I saw the father in the evening whisking away at the snow on his deck with a pink broom. Smoke drifted from their chimney. Out came the child and mother the next afternoon, waddling in their boots and snowsuits. The boy moved unsteadily across the fresh crust of snow, walking on the surface of it for a few steps before breaking through. When the mother lifted him under the armpits, he was plucked clean from his boots. As I watched, the mother dangled the poor kid helplessly aloft, unsure whether to set him down or carry him like that, suspended in socks over a universe of snow.

I thought, scornfully, what the hell had they expected? But I felt sorry for them, too. Almost nothing on the lake moved or breathed. It was the worst part of winter, a waste of white in every direction, no place for little kids or city people. Beneath a foot of ice, beneath my boots, the walleye drifted. They did not try to swim, or do anything that required effort. They hovered, waiting winter out with driftwood, barely beating their hearts.

We were prepared for another month of winter at least. Each night, I fed the cabin stove before climbing the ladder to my loft, and each black morning I scraped the embers together again and, with sluggish fingers and some cedar shavings, coaxed up a new flame. We had a cord and a half of wood stacked against the cabin that I was parceling out very slowly. We stuffed more rags in the window casings to hold in heat, kept big pots on the stove for morning meltwater. My dad had drilled a fresh fishing hole through ice that was close to eighteen inches thick.

But then, in the middle of March, the temperature shot up to fifty and miraculously stayed there. Within a couple of weeks, the south slope drifts had eroded to stalagmite pillars. A wet sheen appeared across the surface of the ice, and in the late afternoons you could hear the whole lake pop and zing. Cracks appeared. It was warm enough to gather wood from the pile without mittens, to unfreeze the latches on the dogs' chains with the heat of your fingers. Across the lake, the family set up a telescope on their deck—long and spear-like, pointed to the heavens. Beneath the tripod was a footstool where the child sometimes stood in the evenings clasping the eyepiece to his face with two mittened hands. He wore a candy-cane scarf and a red pom-pom hat. Every time the wind started up, his pom bounced on the air like a bobber.

Sometimes his mother came out in a ski cap and readjusted the tripod, raising the tube and peering through it herself. She rested one gloved hand on the boy's head. Then, as the evening turned its last shade, I watched them go inside again. I watched them unwind the scarves from their necks. I watched them cuddle the cats, wash their fingers in the tap, heat water in a kettle. They didn't seem to have blinds on their enormous triangular windows. I saw their dinner like it was done just for me. I sat on the roof of our shed with my dad's Bushnell binoculars, turning the sticky barrels, warming my hands against my neck. The kid sat in his cushioned chair on his knees, rocking. The mother barely sat at all. She went to the counter and back, she sliced things on the boy's plate. She made wedges of green, triangles of yellow, discs of something brown. She blew on his soup. She grinned when he grinned. I could see their teeth across the lake. The father seemed to have disappeared. Where had he gone?

Early spring brought more icicles. They oozed blue-black water from the school roof. They dripped away the afternoons, synced to the ticking clock, then going as fast as my heart, which I could feel when I pressed my fingers to my clavicle. I was doing poorly in school, as always, and as the hockey players dreamed us backward toward December, and the debate kids memorized the reciprocal identities, I watched Lily Holburn get abandoned—one by one—by her friends. She'd always been Number Two in a group of four, but since the start of winter she'd become Number Five. It was hard to pinpoint what had changed. It was hard to say exactly when the rumors about her and Mr. Grierson had started. But by March, a space had been cleared around her—like a forest after a fire—and her silence no longer seemed particularly dumb. It was unsettling. *Skank*, her old friends sneered, under their breaths, behind her back. It was the same thing they used to say to her face when they were joking with her after class. Because of her ripped-up jeans, because of her cheap tight sweaters. Now they were strictly sweet when forced to acknowledge her. They didn't laugh when she showed up to class without a pencil, or give her grief for forgetting her lunch. They loaned her money when she asked for it. They handed her toilet paper under the bathroom stall when she was out, whispering, "Do you need more? Is that enough?"

In the halls, though, they walked right past her.

I had news for her. I wrote it on a note, which I passed to her when the stack of worksheets came gliding down our aisle one afternoon: *I don't care what they're saying about you and*

Mr. G. It wasn't that I wanted to defend her—we'd never been friends, we'd never been alone in a room together—only that her name had somehow gotten yoked to Mr. Grierson and I wanted to know why. But Lily never wrote back. She didn't even turn around to look at me, just hunched up in her seat and pretended to understand square roots.

So I was surprised to find her waiting for me by the back door that day when school let out. She wore an elaborately wound scarf, a red one, and a strange kind of jean jacket that buttoned like a sailor's slicker from knee to neck. I was caught off guard. As casually as possible, I took out a cigarette and lit it—but when I handed it to her she shook her head and stared out at the glistening, glittering, melting world.

"What a mess," I said, to say something.

She shrugged—very Lily-like, very sweet—and I felt a twinge of exasperation.

I could see her long white throat peeking from beneath folds of red. It made me glad to see that her jacket was shabby up close, the hem torn and dragging in a puddle behind her. For all her experience, Lily had always struck me as inexplicably innocent. And now she seemed inexplicably superior, drifting just past everyone. Say *Mr. Grierson*, and up she went. Like a balloon.

I took a chance. I whispered, "What'd he do to you?"

She shrugged again, eyes widening.

"Where?"

"*Where?*" She seemed confused.

I took a step closer to her. "I knew something was up. I could have warned you." She wasn't looking at me, and I could see that her hair had been barretted back so one ear was exposed. That ear was bright red in the cold—shiny and strangely lip-like. I had a new thought. "*You* made that stuff up."

Though she didn't say anything, I knew by instinct I'd hit the mark.

"About you and him." I swallowed.

"Yep."

We might have been merely standing next to each other on the curb, waiting for the traffic to pass to go our separate directions. We might have been carefully ignoring each other: me with my cigarette, she with an open can of Coke, which she lifted delicately from her jacket pocket. Still, for the moment, I felt very close to her, and it seemed unnecessary to say anything else. The silence between us filled with possibilities. We could hear the trickling of unseen streams, rivulets coursing down the street and sidewalk. We could hear the salt crystals crunching under car tires. Then Lily shook out her Coke in the snow, and it occurred to me that she'd spoken without any sense of occasion at all. It occurred to me that she'd only told me because I had no one to tell. It was like dropping a secret into a snowbank.

My lips felt clumsy around my cigarette. "It'll pass, you know. People's talk."

She shrugged a third time. "You think so? I don't think so." She crushed a lump of slush with her boot, pulled at her scarf till she was pretty as anything, long bent arm cutting geometrical shapes in the sky.

She sounded so satisfied, almost smug about it.

I followed her the next day. After eating my peanut butter sandwich in the last stall in the bathroom, I came out and caught sight of Lily going into the counselor's office. The back of her head, the blue hump of her backpack. She didn't show up for English that afternoon, but I saw her at the drinking fountain afterward, dark hair fisted in one hand as she bent for a sip. I trailed her when she started up the stairs. On the landing, I watched her eyes move to the second-story window, out of which you could see a few purplish crows towing trash from the school Dumpster. She paused for a second to take that in. I could see the whites of her eyes when she turned her head. Then, as the last bell rang, I watched her walk the length of the fluorescent-lit hall, which was emptying out around her.

From the outside, nothing about Lily had changed. Her clothes were still gaudy and bright: clingy sweaters with unraveling seams over fraying, faded, ripped-up jeans. She still showed too much cleavage. She still walked too much on her toes, like a ground-feeding bird. Lily had always been everybody's pet. Her one fervent goal had been to please everyone. Now people turned away when she passed, wouldn't look at her. Even Lars Solvin, her boyfriend since sixth grade, turned bright red under his blond beard when he saw her coming down the hall. He was six feet tall, a second-string forward on the hockey team. But he found an ingenious way to shrink, to slouch against a nearby locker and examine his sports watch. His buddies closed around him as she approached, touching the bills on their caps, hitching up their jeans. All of them kept their eyes down—far, far, far from Lily's cleavage—but the unlucky one closest to the classroom door felt obliged to turn the handle for her.

"Thank you," she said, not smiling, but not *not* smiling either.

I followed her into Life Science, opening the door for myself.

For years I'd sat near her in class: Furston wasn't far from Holburn on the register. For years I'd felt vaguely protective and vaguely resentful of Lily, who lived in a trailer three lakes north, who was loved by everybody, whose dad collapsed each Saturday somewhere on Gooseneck Highway and had to be collected up before church. Now I scooted my chair desk a little closer to hers. I watched the green threads on her sweater sleeve quiver as she opened her notebook. She wasn't taking notes, I noticed, on the short expendable lives of protozoa. She wasn't working on a diagram of the essential role of bacteria as the decomposer link in the food chain. She was making slow, snaking spirals with her pen, then filling in the linked loops with dozens, with hundreds of smiley faces.

3

WHO'S WATCHING WHO? I wondered, when I went out to the dogs one morning and saw the telescope across the lake aimed straight at my parents' cabin. It was pointed like an arrow right into the cabin's heart, into our one window with its rags in the casings. A mold-stained tarp flapped over our front door. I felt my scalp prickle.

I looked up. Above me, a pale yellow leaf drifted in a breeze. Higher, then lower, without fully descending. I plucked the leaf from the air with a little jump. Then with one hand I slid the skin over the dogs' skulls—breathing, as I did, on their latches to unfreeze them. *Ha*, I puffed, making the dogs wiggle and spin, freeing them one by one. *Go*, I told them. I set Abe and Doctor and Quiet and Jasper loose in the woods. For a moment, I listened to their panting breaths as they loped through old snow. Then, as the rising sun bleached the treetops, I listened to the whole frozen lake groaning under their paws. It wouldn't hold out for long I knew.

It didn't. When the last of the ice was drifting ashore in jagged chunks, when the last of the snow lay in dunes on the north

slopes, I saw him again, the kid from across the lake, crouching
on the roadside not far from my house. It was the kind of day
you could leave your jacket unzipped, and as I walked home
from the bus stop, I was reading a book. I don't remember
what. At that point I was into anything with maps and charts.
Great Rescues of the Old Northwest, Build Your Own Kayak. I
was almost to the sumac trail when I saw him. A bike was
overturned on the gravel shoulder, balanced upside down on
handlebars. It took a moment before I saw a girl folded over
it, fumbling with the chain. As I approached, both girl and
child looked up. They had the same dark eyes, I noticed, the
same orange-blond hair.

I thought of deer lifting their heads in that coordinated
movement they have. I thought of anything running. But they
didn't go anywhere.

"Hi!" the boy said, enthusiastic-preoccupied, turning back
to his task on the ground.

"That's her there," he said, sidelong, to the girl.

"That's *who* there?" the girl replied. "I don't think we've
met," she said to me.

Like the boy, she was friendly but distracted. "We've gotten ourselves a bit tangled up, I guess." She laughed easily, set
a greasy hand on the boy's head. "I'm a whiz, as you can see,
with vehicles. My husband wouldn't even trust me with the car,
seriously. And he's not a patriarch or anything. That's not what
I mean."

"Patriarch," the boy said, without looking up.

"A man who is in charge of things, unfairly." She looked
at me for confirmation. "Right?"

"Okay," he said, still busy. He seemed to be stuffing snow-
flattened leaves into a black pouch.

"Like, I drove the car off the road the first day we arrived, right into a snowbank. *Wham.* So I said, I'll stick with the bike. It's better right?" She seemed to want me to agree with her. She was much smaller than I thought she'd be from watching her all those nights through the window—more skinny limbs than body. She was tiny now that I could measure her against myself. She wore a maroon U of C sweatshirt with sleeves shoved to the elbows. "You're our neighbor from across the lake, right?" she went on. "Did I say hi yet?" She turned to the kid. "Did I already say hi to her? I've forgotten what it is to talk to people."

The boy stood up. "It goes like this. How do you do!" He rushed forward, holding out a massive black hand for me to shake. The thing was bloated, weirdly twisted—fingers splayed at improbable angles.

I shuffled a few steps back.

"It's my Thirdhand Man," he said. "For survival." It took me a moment to realize the kid had stuffed a man's leather glove with leaves, and that he was now thwacking it hard against a pine trunk. After a few blows he sat down again, panting. Spent.

"He's very into that thing," the girl explained. "So, I'm Patra, the parent. He's Paul, the kid. And so far, you're Blank, the neighbor."

The kid laughed. "Blank."

Up close, she looked too young to be anyone's mother. She didn't seem to have eyebrows, and she was as skinny as I was—curveless—wearing tennis shoes, leggings, and long wool socks pulled up over the leggings to her knees. Her hair was the same wispy orange as the kid's, but frizzy, held down with a blue plastic headband. When she smiled, the headband glided backward over her scalp. "I'm kidding. You're—"

Mattie, I thought, as a breeze tugged the resins out of the trees. "Linda," I said.

The boy in a crouch on the ground pulled on his mother's sleeve. "I have something to tell her."

"Just say it."

"It's a *secret*," he whined.

"Then just go up and say it!" she urged him forward. I was on one side of the road and they were on the other. "Look before you cross. Though"—she spoke to me—"I haven't seen a single car go past since we stopped. It's marvelous. The locals here read in the middle of the highway."

Did she wink then? Was she laughing at me? Was I supposed to laugh?

To the kid she said, "Right, left. There you go."

At the trial they kept asking, when did you know for sure there was something wrong? And the answer probably was: right away. But that feeling faded as I got to know him. Paul's breathy way of talking, the way he had to sit down when he got excited—these tendencies seemed to me, more and more, just the way he was. Paul was fussy and fragile, then whooping and manic. I got used to his moods. Though he was always getting mistaken for someone older, he was four the spring I knew him. He had droopy eyelids, big red hands. He had four-going-on-five-year-old plans: visit Mars, get shoes with tics. He was building a city out of stones and weeds on his deck. Almost every piece of clothing he owned had a train on it, Thomas the Tank Engine, or nineteenth-century cattle cars, or steam engines stamped across his chest. He'd never been on a real train in his life. All spring long, he rode buckled into the plastic seat on the back of his mother's bike, to the grocery store and the post office. He carried around that old-man's leather glove wherever he went, its fingertips worn to purple, palms green with rot.

He handed it to me once he crossed the road. He gave me the glove, then put his hands in a fist at his crotch. He made me bend down to hear him. "I have to go to the bathroom," he whispered.

Oh please, I remember thinking. The sun, which had been gleaming, moved off the road into some other part of woods. What was I supposed to do about that? I looked at his mother, who was wiping her hands on her sweatshirt, righting the bike, calling the boy back to her. She walked the clicking bike across the road by the handlebars. A child's helmet dangled by the chin strap from her wrist.

"I think he has to—" I began. But it seemed obvious. The kid was holding his crotch with two hands. It seemed unnecessary to say what he said, to use those little kid words out loud. And anyway, she was already lifting him up, wedging him in his seat, buckling him down.

He seemed about to cry out, so his mother kissed him on the forehead, brushed hair from his eyes. "No luck with the bike, kiddo, but I can push you as we walk and sing. How 'bout that?" She eyed the glove in my hand, so I passed it to her, and she pressed it back into his arms. "There. What would you like to sing, hon?"

"'Good King Wenceslas,'" he said, pouting.

"Is that okay with you, Linda? Want to walk with us back?" She smiled over his head, and I saw how quickly she shifted between faces, between soothing mother and conspiratorial adult.

It pleased me for reasons I could not explain to be part of the latter allegiance. I nodded, surprising myself.

When we got to their house, the door was unlocked. Paul turned the handle with two hands. Inside, mother and child stomped on the mat. "Fee-fi-fo-fum," he growled. "I smell the blood of an Englishman," she responded. Then they both plopped on the floor, he in her lap. She took off his shoes while eating his neck.

This is a thing, I thought, as they played the ritual out. The cats watched warily from the windowsills. I stepped off the mat and into the room, and it was like wading into warm water—the heat was jacked up that high. I could feel all the layers of my clothes at once, all the weight I'd been lugging around, and then I could feel those layers sequentially, from the outside in: hunting jacket, sweater, flannel, T-shirt, no bra, sweat. Sweat dragged in a trickle from my left armpit. I shivered.

"Well, come on in," Patra said, standing up in her socks, Paul shoeless now, scrambling off to pee.

Their cabin was mostly the one big room I'd seen through the window at night. The kitchen with all its shiny knobs made up the inside wall; the lake sparkling in a million itty-bitty fishhooks came through the far windows. All the furniture was new, I could see that, all maroons and creams, all browns and yellows. Corduroy couches intersected in a corner, and a tawny table, fresh as a pine log just axed open, stood in the center of everything. Down the one dim hallway, I heard a flush. The child emerged from the hallway leaping in socks, springing from oval rug to oval rug in an elaborate game that required his full concentration. Then he was back at my side saying, "Take off your shoes."

Boots, swampy wool socks, scaly yellow toes. I shook my head.

"Take off your jacket then."

I kept it on. The room felt poured in sunlight. The uriney kind, pale and thin and hot. For a second, I worried that my mother might see me here, across the lake and through the window. Then I remembered how black those glass triangles were in daytime. There was nothing for her to see.

"Take off your shoes," he said.

"You're being a despot, Paul," his mother told him.

"Depspot," he repeated, mechanically.

"Like a patriarch, only worse. Telling everybody what to do. Without being voted into power." Patra was at the counter, filling a pot with water. I remembered how this went from watching her. Soon there'd be mugs, plates draped in steam. Soon she'd be cutting things for us.

"Let's cook something," she suggested. "Come on in, Linda."

Paul clutched at my hand. "Take off your shoes," he pleaded. "Take off your shoes. Take off your shoes."

I didn't bend down. I didn't use a voice especially reserved for talking to children. "No, thank you," I told him, but too quietly for Patra to hear. Almost hissing. "Let go of my hand, okay?"

The kid looked up at me, confused. As if I'd told him to take off his own face.

Within twenty minutes, we were eating butter on spaghetti noodles and fluffy green salads made of some kind of lettuce I'd never seen before in my life. The leaves curled up around my fork. I moved stiffly in my jacket, clumsy but careful as I lifted my mug of tea and sipped. My boots still weighed down my feet. I buttered my wedge of toast and sweat clean through my bottom layers, through my T-shirt and flannel. I didn't mind. Deep in my mug, the tea bag floated like something drowned, but it tasted bright as spring, like mint and celery. The steam made my nose wet, my eyes blurry. Patra had cut cherry tomatoes into brilliant red coins.

"I'm going to tell Leo about you," Patra said. "He was sure that it was only old hippies and hermits this far from town. He said to watch out for bears and quacks."

"There *is* ducks," Paul agreed.

"Leo?" I asked, my eyes swimming.

"Dad," Paul explained.

"He's in Hawaii," Patra added. "Doing March's numbers, looking for protogalaxies. Getting the charts started."

"Oh, *Hawaii*," I nodded. I tried to say it like I'd been there recently myself, and found the food disappointing, the locals unfriendly. I shrugged. As if I'd already wasted too much of my life looking for the so-called protogalaxies on tropical islands.

"Hey!" Patra said to me. "Speaking of which!" She'd been untangling Paul's noodles with a knife and fork, laying them out in long parallel lines across his plate. She paused. "We should call your mom, right? We should let her know where you are, in case she's thinking about fixing you dinner. Here." She reached back with one hand and pulled something from her pocket. "The Forest Service has a tower"—she gestured vaguely behind her—"and Leo put up a big booster on the roof, so! You can get reception if you go out back, next to the telescope." After a moment she added: "Sometimes."

Cautiously, I took the cell phone she handed over. It was heavier than I thought it would be for its size. Years later I would deliberately throw my cell into the river—I'd rack up a bill so high, they'd cut the service and my phone would be useless—but at the time I'd never held one before. For just a moment I sat feeling its weight, examining its rounded plastic shape and the rubbery stem of the antenna. Then, careful not to knock anything with my jacketed elbows, I pushed back my chair and crossed the room.

Outside on the deck, it was almost night. Out in the newly cooled air, my jacket felt unbelievably light, almost as if dissolved. I stood still and let my eyes adjust to the rustling darkness. Among all those shadows, the telescope seemed oddly alive. A great elongated bird—mutant heron—perched on a plank of wood and watching me. I watched the lake, ignored the telescope. Last of the ice gone, last of the sun browning the choppy surface. A bobbing loon drove down into the water.

Finally, having put it off, I set my eyes on my parents' house.

No one had turned on the lights, which was nothing special. My father, no doubt, was drinking beers with Quiet in the shed. Most nights my mother stitched her quilts at the table by the stove until it was so dark she nearly stabbed herself with the needle. And then, as if surprised, as if shocked by another day ending—yet another day handed over—she usually lit a lantern or started the generator out back, which turned on the lamp in the kitchen. She did this as if affronted. "Why didn't you tell me it was so dark?" she'd ask if I were there, if I were huddled over some last bit of homework. I don't know why it pleased me so much to let night sneak up like that. I don't know what it had to do with me at all—but it was true, I almost always *did* know it was dark, and so it felt like luring her into the same trap over and over.

Got you, I thought.

Though the lake was very narrow here, it was two miles around by foot—an hour's walk through the woods—to my parents' cabin. There it stood: half-shingled, sided with woodpiles, dark behind the pines. A muddy black path wound from outhouse to toolshed to cabin door. It was sixteen-by-twenty feet inside, including my parents' room and the loft, including the living space with its iron stove and scrap-wood table. I'd measured. In the darkening evening, I could just make out a thread of smoke pulling up from the pipe chimney. I could just barely see the shadows of dogs swimming through the shadows of pines.

Behind me, I could hear voices clearly. Forks clawing plates, dinner getting cold.

I punched some random buttons and held the phone to my ear. I imagined Patra watching from behind, so I took a big breath.

"No, Mom! I'm fine. I'll be home in a couple hours. No, they're nice! Patra and Paul. They'd like me to stay after dinner. They'd like me to play Go Fish. They'd like me to read the kid a story and watch *The Wizard of Oz* on a DVD. They'd like me to stay and eat popcorn. No, I don't know what they're doing up here. She's an astronomer or something, or her husband is. No, that's not mysterious, it's very scientific, it's the definition of science. It's stars. No they're not going to kidnap me, they're a mom and her son, not a cult, not a hippie commune or anything weird. Oh, they're pretty innocent, actually. They need guidance and help. They need someone to teach them about the woods."

4

WHICH I DID. In April, I started taking Paul for walks in the woods while his mother revised a manuscript of her husband's research. The printed pages lay in batches around the cabin, on the countertop and under chairs. There were also stacks of books and pamphlets. I'd peeked at the titles. *Predictions and Promises: Extraterrestrial Bodies. Science and Health with Key to the Scriptures. The Necessities of Space.*

"Just keep clear of the house for a few hours" were Patra's instructions. I was given snacks in Baggies, pretzels wound into small brown bows. I was given water bottles in a blue backpack, books about trains, Handi Wipes, coloring books and crayons, suntan lotion. These went on my back. Paul went in my hand. His little fingers were damp and wiggling. But he was trusting, never once seeming to feel the shock of my skin touching his.

He wasn't like animals. I didn't have to win him over.

Ten bucks a day, Patra offered, so I quit my part-time job at the diner, where I'd had to wear a paper apron pinned like doll clothes to the front of my sweater. I'd always felt an ache of reluctance, anyhow, when diners left me their mugs and plates, their half-eaten sandwiches. They left behind wet dimes caked in tiny crumbs. Patra paid in crisp ten-dollar bills.

After school I took Paul to a place on the lake where the granite was striped in great glistening tracks of quartz. A few slabs of ice still shingled the shore. Superior gulls swooped over us. We settled on the reindeer moss and ate our pretzels in silence. Usually, Paul went through his bag in seconds and then, turning the bag inside out, licked salt from the plastic. Sometimes I smoked a furtive cigarette and tossed it quick in the open water. After ten minutes or so, our butts were wet, so I ditched the backpack behind a tree, and we set off.

Away from the sun-warmed rocks, the afternoons got pretty cold by five o'clock. But it was April. Though the buds were still hard as arrow tips on the trees, we could smell the syrupy resins from the pines. We could smell the rot of leaves beneath clumps of snow in the ravines. I no longer held the boy's hand. This time of year, the woods were very empty and soft, very accommodating to little boys who wanted to jump off rocks and logs. I would go on ahead a few paces, scouting out a path through the mud and brambles. Paul usually brought along the leather glove—he only ever had the one—and he filled it now with stones, now with pine needles. Now with shiny black pellets.

"Oh, gross," I said, looking back.

"For the City," he explained.

I raised my eyebrows. "The city needs rabbit poop?"

"Cannonballs," he corrected.

He wasn't as boring as I expected. He said "watch out" to squirrels, got mad at litter, washed his cannonballs until they dissolved in a beached canoe full of water. I taught him to snap twigs back to mark the path home, to walk on the lichened parts of rocks that were less slippery. To break up the silence, for something to do, I started naming things off for him as we went. Trailing arbutus. Chickadees. When we came across some beer cans under a greenstone ledge, Paul pointed and I said "rust." Sometimes Paul told me about his father's research ("he counts baby stars") and his mother's job ("she corrects his words") and the City he was building on the deck. It had roads of bark, walls of sticks and rocks, train tracks of flattened leaves.

"Who lives in the City?" I asked him once. I remembered children from a long time ago when the bunkhouse had been full of them. They did things like build cities for fairies. They made up tiny people who came out at night.

"Nobody *lives* there." He looked frustrated by the question.

"Then why are you building it?"

He shrugged. "It's just a city."

"Just a city," I repeated. I could respect that.

He took me for granted. When he climbed up a rock and couldn't get down, he held open his arms—without saying a word—and I lifted him under the armpits. When he had to pee, which was often, he just said, "I gotta go," and I steadied him as he pulled down his pants. The first time I saw his penis, I felt a wave of sympathy and disgust, the way I'd felt, once, when I'd come upon a clump of nude baby mice in the hollow of a log. Those mice had blue bulges for eyes, pink tails wound together in a big lump. "Yuck," Paul said, when I helped him pull up his damp underwear and wipe his hands on a leaf. "Yuck," I agreed. The next time, I pointed at a log and said, "Try to hit that." Overhead each afternoon we could hear the Canada geese coming back. We could hear them giving directions, laboring through wind currents, setting down their Vs. When the sun had just about set, we turned around, Paul lagging, getting farther and farther behind, so as the day grew truly cold—miniature winter setting in, the way it does at night in April—I put the backpack on Paul, and Paul on me, and we headed back toward his house on the lake. His fingers made corkscrews in my hair and his breath heated one ear.

Once, as I was helping Paul slide off a boulder, we came upon a mallard nest so far from shore that the ducklings could do nothing but waddle in yellow, panicked circles to get away. Paul reached down to touch one. The brown mother winged a few feet back, then waited empty eyed for the disaster to play itself out. Her feathers gleamed with a faint hint of purple, unruffled and smooth as scales. She did nothing to intervene, and so neither did I, as Paul grabbed at one of the ducklings. He had good intentions: he was a gentle enough kid. At the last minute, though, he pulled his hand back as if spooked—as if he'd felt something horrible beneath all that fluffy down, something brittle and hard and unexpected.

"Oh!" he said.

"What?" I asked, newly impatient with him.

His squeamishness goaded me somehow, made me a little angry. I wanted him to take the duckling and do something heartless and boyish, so I'd have to remind him to be kind. I don't know. I wanted to be the one to stop him when he discovered the fragile contraption of bones beneath that halo of down. I wanted to intervene on behalf of animals. It irritated me that he was so careful and afraid. We stood and watched as the duckling waddled off to its mother, and the troop reconvened in a huddle under a pine.

For a strange instant, I found myself longing to lift a rock and throw it at them. I wanted to show Paul something, maybe, make him scared of the right things.

Or another time, in early evening. As Paul and I were crest-ing the last hill, as I was squinting into the darkening woods to make out the path, a couple of deer lifted their heads at once and differentiated themselves from the trees.

We stared at them, and they at us, for a full thirty seconds without moving. They multiplied as we looked at them. There were three at first, then there were four, then there were five. They were the exact color of the bark and leaves—gray brown—but the skin around their eyes was red. I felt the breeze on their backs lift the braid from my chest and set it down over my shoulder. "They're going to get us," Paul whispered. He reached for my hand.

"They're a herd," I reminded him. "They're afraid of us."

Two more appeared. Paul shivered.

"It's okay, it's okay. They're prey," I soothed.

The deer silvered under the wind. Their pink ears twitched. I knew they would take off in an instant; I could see their haunches tense. But even I had the irrational thought they were about to run right for us. They seemed ready to bear down.

Then off they went over the far ridge, white tails lifted. Hop-ping with that mechanical grace animals have—grasshoppers and birds—as if nothing, save death, could interrupt the repetitive beat of their movements. Branches rattled old rain down on us. We were alone.

Fee-fi-fo-fum. Soup from a can, lettuce from a bag. Cat hair on my sweater. The cats creeping from the windowsill to the rug, where they rolled religiously, unlatching their claws on each other. A video of a talking dog, book after book. "Slow down, Paul," who was gulping apple juice so fast it seeped down his chin. My hunting jacket hung from a hook, still holding the shape of my hunched-up shoulders. On the roof, squirrels scampering. In the ground, maple seeds and bearberry, leeching down hairy new roots. Across the lake—across the lake and beneath the pines—dogs. The dogs dragging their chains, getting hungry, waiting for me to come home. Across the lake my mother, too, forgetting to turn the light on in the evening and maybe, or maybe not, watching everything.

Patra, after Paul went to bed. She came out of the back bedroom with her hair stuck to her face, as if she'd been sleeping. She'd given me a hundred-piece puzzle of an Appaloosa horse to work on while she gave Paul a bath, and when she came out, blinking, she seemed surprised I was still at it. "Oh, Linda!" she said when she saw me at the table, surrounded by the scattered debris of the puzzle. I put my hands under the table, found a thread on my sweater's cuff to unravel and tug. "Hey," I told her.

She felt bad about forgetting me I guess, because she got busy fast fixing snacks: microwave popcorn and hard-boiled eggs. She put them into two Baggies for me to eat as I walked home—everything white and warm, one light as leaves, the other steaming up the plastic. I put them in my two jacket pockets.

"Is it too dark to walk in the woods by yourself?" she wondered then, but only idly as she glanced out the window, where a branch clicked the glass. She fished a ten-dollar bill from her wallet and handed it over.

"Nope," I said, rolling the bill into a tube, which I pretended to survey her through, like a miniature telescope. "There you are!" I said.

"Ha," Patra replied. But she wasn't really laughing.

I folded the tube in half. And then, just like that, a gust of humiliation shot through me—as if I were Mr. Grierson making the telephone joke, as if Patra were Lily humoring me to get done with things. *Ha.* Even her laugh was saying good-bye.

Why didn't I just leave? All I had to do was blink. All I had to do was lift my mind away from her, and I could already see all those old trees blowing overhead as I walked along the lake, the same old moon scraping open some clouds and laying down a path of light. Oh, I liked night. I knew it well. For some reason, though, I was finding it hard to open the door. I stashed the folded bill in my pocket with the egg and spent a long time on my jacket zipper.

"What's your husband writing?" I said, at the last minute.

"Um." She looked reluctant.

I put my hands in my pockets, weighed popcorn against egg.

"It's quite interesting I guess. It's about space."

"Duh," I said.

She offered a little smile, bending over as she did and holding out one hand to the black cat. It came across the rug and landed in her arms just like that—as if tugged by fishing line. So willingly caught. It squinted at me under her palm, gave me a smashed jack-o'-lantern look.

"I'm sorry." She let the cat rumble and hum under her hand. "It's one of those things not everybody understands. You know Newton?"

"They killed him?"

She shook her head. "That's Galileo that was almost beheaded. Newton was knighted."

"Right," I said.

"Sir Isaac Newton says that space is just space. Like, nothing worth mentioning. Then Einstein is like, no. Objects act on it, it reacts." She was stroking the cat in a way that made a tiny crackling of static under her palm. "Nothing is something after all. There's math that proves this, of course, but also observations. I know it seems like math and observations are opposites. They can seem like that sometimes, my husband gets in all these arguments. But in the grand order of things, they fit quite snugly."

"That's the book?" I was skeptical.

She laughed. "That's the *introduction*. How we have to have trust in"—she paused—"in logic, if we want to understand the true nature of reality. The whole book is more a history of the theory of life. From a cosmological perspective. For a general audience. It doesn't prove anything new, just shows that our standard of proof is questionable, and so—"

She sounded like she wanted to convince me of something she didn't entirely believe or understand herself. She was looking over my head, considering how to start over and say it again, whether to bother. She opened her mouth, closed it.

"You probably have a degree in English or something," I told her.

She theatrically frowned. "You've been spying on my past!"

I pointed at the manuscript on the counter. "I saw the way you make corrections. Like a teacher."

"Oh, my worst nightmare," she groaned. "Teaching Milton to high schoolers." She put her hand on my arm. "No offense."

"That's okay."

Then she was back to stroking the cat, and in a jagged motion I reached over to touch him as well. As I did my pocket gaped open, and a few kernels of popcorn dribbled to the floor.

"Shit," I murmured, kneeling down.

And just like that, Patra was on her knees helping me. The cat squirreled under the couch.

I watched Patra pop two stray kernels, absentmindedly, into her mouth. Then she caught my eye and her face reddened. "That was gross. Right? That was gross."

In fact she was pretty, her smile lifting me out of myself. "Not really."

I sprinkled a few more kernels on the floor and ate them. When Patra smiled for real, her lips whitened and disappeared into her face. Up close, I saw she had down on her upper lip, brown freckles merging into spots on her eyelids. She had three parallel creases on her forehead, which almost, but not quite, smoothed away when she grinned. She ate another kernel when I set it on the floor and then another and another, smiling as she did. For the first time then, for the first time since we'd met, it occurred to me that she might be lonely.

5

HERE'S WHAT I DREAM ABOUT MOST NOW. The dogs. Trying to get my numb fingers around the tricky latches of their chains. Cracking open the ice in their bowls so they can have a drink. In my dreams, I do it with a stick, or the business end of an ax, or the heel of my boot. There's a problem, I need to do this fast. In my dreams, I'm always getting back so late. I'm always coming around the last bend of the lake long after dark, pushing away branches, and there they are in a huddle by the house: too small to be dogs, somehow. They look more like rats or crows or scrabbling children—half crouching in some ditch of snow they've made. They've licked the ice from their paws, only to have the saliva seal ice again over the pads, which they've chewed until they're bleeding. They're whining, their chains are wrapped around their legs: you know how these dreams go. In reality, of course, my father brought them into the shed and fed them when I didn't come home on time. But in my dreams, I see ice hanging from their muzzles like fangs. I see them catch sight of me in the woods, and their love is ravenous. They lunge and snarl. They're so happy to see me.

* * *

It was a dog that found the stash of pictures in Mr. Grierson's California apartment, actually. I'd read about it in the *North Star Gazette* the week after Mr. Grierson was fired. He'd sublet his apartment to some college student with a cocaine habit, and, according to the article, the local police had recently started a canine program with funds from a rich breeder of English bulldogs. Everyone was very proud of the program, which defied breed expectations. The crimes editor at the *Gazette* must have made some calls to Fertile Hollow, California, because there were lots of quotes about bulldogs in the article. "We misapprehend the true nature of these dogs," the rich breeder said, "when we put booties on their feet and climb into bed with them. Give them a mission! Don't make them into Riding Hood's grandmother."

It was an English bulldog named Nestlé Crunch who, in less than twenty minutes, found a kilo of cocaine in the college kid's sock drawer and a shoebox of dirty pictures beneath the bathroom sink. The shoebox was a lucky find, not part of the initial drug investigation. Still, there was no question about what the pictures showed or whose they were. "Minors," the article said. Minors in fat envelopes addressed to Mr. Adam Grierson of West Palm Blvd. Who knows why he left them there after he came to Minnesota or why, for that matter, he used his real name. The article was fuzzy about the unsavory parts, oddly upbeat and cheerful as it went on, focusing less on Mr. Grierson and his arrest than on the triumph of the dog who found him out. In the end, Nestlé Crunch of Fertile Hollow was promoted to sergeant and given a gold shield, a week's vacation, and a police hat full of Milk-Bones.

*   *   *

There was nothing in that first article—or any of the early police reports—about Mr. Grierson and a student. There was nothing about Gone Lake or a kiss. But that didn't stop the rumors.

I kept my eye on Lily that spring. On my way to school one late April morning, I saw her slide out of her dad's pickup truck behind the baseball field. The temperature had plunged the night before, and a layer of fresh spring snow had the temporary effect of returning the road to a slurry of slush and salt. As the pickup rumbled off, I watched Lily lick her bare hand and bend over, dampen the salt-stained cuffs of her jeans with her own saliva. Her coat hung open, and her hands were bare, her head was bare, her hair was wet. As I followed her across the field to the high school, I felt I could see her long hair freeze as she walked. It swung darkly, then grew stiff. It looked like something you could crack off with your hands.

Inside, she did not go directly to class. All the bells had rung, and I followed her through the empty halls, down the dark staircase, past the closed gym door, past the trophy case with all its bronze boys pointing their nubby toes. She was quiet, but I was quieter still, setting each boot on the floor carefully—one at a time—as if walking through the woods. I made the linoleum absorb my sounds. Lily's tennis shoes squeaked.

She bought a Coke from the vending machine and stood for a moment gulping it before wedging the half-finished can behind the radiator. She yawned so wide a second chin appeared on her neck. That was a revelation to me, Lily Holburn's future fat. I thought by then I knew everything there was to know about her. I knew how Lily's mom had died in a car accident when she was twelve, how her dad dropped her off at school every

morning in the baseball field, how she went to a special teacher
for her dyslexia during homeroom. I knew that Lars Solvin had
broken up with her recently, a few days before prom, and by
then I knew what she was saying Mr. Grierson had done to her.
He had driven her out to Gone Lake last fall, she'd said, driven
her there after school in his car and *kissed* her. That's the word
I kept hearing in the halls, "kiss," and there was something all
the more perverse in this, as if she couldn't bring herself to name
anything more explicit.

I don't know why I followed Lily that day for so long, save
that it was easy. As she continued down the empty hall, she ran
her fingers through her hair, cutting open the thawing spokes
with her fingers. Her tennis shoes left a gray streak of water on the
brown linoleum. I thought maybe she was heading toward the
loading dock to sneak out, cut class—but no. She went straight
into the girls' locker room, peed in one of the stalls, washed her
hands, cleaned her teeth with a finger, then walked over to the
lost and found in the corner.

I stayed behind a bank of open lockers and watched her.
People used to say that Lily was a little deaf. People used to say
she was a little touched, that she had been left outside too long
in the cold as a baby, had never fully bloomed. Because she rarely
said more than a few words at once, because her dad's trailer
bordered the reservation three lakes north, she was called Lily
the Indian when we were kids. *Poor Lily the Indian*, the Brownies
in their sashes used to say, bestowing on her the pudding cups
from their lunches—even though everyone knew that the real
Ojibwa kids had their own school up on Lake Winesaga. Still,
the story persisted until her mom died, that Lily's grandmother
or great-grandmother was a member of the tribe, and it occurred
to me now Lily never denied it.

I was thinking about this in the locker room that day as I watched her bend in half and rifle through the box of tangled jackets and bras. She systematically sorted through the lost and found until she discovered a pair of heeled black boots, which made her look abruptly older when she put them on. Elegantly tall, casually looming. She looked like someone who might raise her eyes to the mirror and see me standing right behind her. But she did not. She twisted her damp hair with her fists and squeezed out a last trickle of water. Then, with a sigh, she kicked off those beautiful black boots and selected something no one would ever ask her about—a big pair of puffy blue mittens that she wedged under one armpit. I watched her pull her hair back with someone else's lost barrette and wrap her neck with someone else's frayed pink scarf. Before tying her tennis shoes up, she pocketed a purple vial of nail polish.

May, and who needs boots anymore anyway? Lilacs were exploding early. Crabapple blossoms covered branches the way snow once did—white as that, but poofier. Petals caught in Paul's hood as we walked. Chickadees were doing loops.

May, and Paul was getting bored of woods, just as the woods were getting interesting. Wood ducks with their glossy green hoods had come back to stay, as well as beavers. You could see them hauling whole logs across the lake with just their jaws. "Cool?" I suggested.

Paul whacked a stick against a rock. He wanted a swing set, a slide. He wanted a playground with sand in a box and public shovels and public pails, which people at the Department of Parks and Water cleaned and kept nice. He knew his business when it came to parks. He'd lived in a Chicago suburb for most

of his life, with sidewalks and such. Golden retrievers fetching
Frisbees. He wanted a tire swing, a baseball diamond, acres of
mowed grass.

"Oh, brother. Another beaver," he said.

"Oh, *brother*," I mocked him. Then I felt bad.

The upshot being that on a drizzly day in mid-May, I arranged him in his green rain slicker in the bike seat and pedaled
the six miles into town. I had to stand up on the pedals to do the
hills, and when I came over a ridge, we careened down through
oily puddles wide as the road itself. Within minutes, we were
both soaked. At the elementary school we trudged through the
piled pebbles on the playground, and I pushed Paul on one of
two plastic swings.

"This what you want?" I asked.

"I guess," he said. It clearly wasn't at all what he wanted.
Back and forth he went: I stood behind, watched his hood flap.
Some sorrow shoved around in my chest, like a stick in wet sand,
and so time passed.

Later, I could get that drizzle feeling just about any time
I saw a kid on a swing. The hopelessness of it—the forward
excitement, the midflight return. The futile belief that the next
time around, the next flight forward, you wouldn't get dragged
back again. You wouldn't have to start over, and over.

"Should I push harder?" I asked him.

After a moment: "I guess."

School had been out for hours, so at first we were alone in
these labors. My arms were getting tired, though the rain had
begun to let up. At some point a young mother arrived with an
umbrella, a baby in a plastic stroller, and a little girl. The girl
looked older than Paul: she wore yellow rubber boots and a pink
rain jacket. When Paul saw her, he lit up instantly. He dumped

all the pebbles out of his leather glove and worked his hand in up to the elbow. He wanted the girl to push him, and when she took over from me, heaving him with her hands, he got this goofy look on his face, both concentrated and dazed, as if he were trying to watch her without turning his head. I walked to the park bench—not exactly jealous, though not quite generous either. Paul never said another word after he asked the girl to play with him. He sat still on his swing, let her fall all over him from behind.

I had, then, a very complete vision of him as a fifteen-year-old. I thought I knew the sort of guy Paul would be. He'd be the kind of boy who let himself be pushed on some little kiddie swing by a girl who adored him, who wrote his name in purple pen on her palm and waited for him after school. He'd be the reluctant but radiant star of *Our Town*, or vice president of the student council in an ironic yet good-natured way. He'd be a mediocre but heroic huddler for the track team. He'd have a mysterious Chinese character tattooed on his wrist, something only he could read and slightly smeared because he'd gone to a dingy parlor in Bearfin to do it. He'd be called Gardner, probably. He'd be the kind of boy known by just his last name.

"Higher," he said to the girl, without any rancor or desire, as if he were doing her a favor by allowing himself to be pushed. Overhead, a floatplane skimmed the treetops. Across the parking lot, several trucks of senior boys were making screeching circles through puddles. They had their windows down. They were shouting, "Marco!"

"Teeth," the young mother said to me, when I sat down next to her on the wet bench.

"Um, hmm," I nodded in agreement, letting the word arrive like a cleaned fossil from another epoch of meaning. It suited my mood to believe that some words, such as "teeth" or "Marco," needed no further explanation.

Then the young woman said, "This bugger's going to bite my nipple off." So "teeth" got its tag and was filed away with all the other mindless small talk, all the obvious things you say to strangers on a park bench in the rain. I sighed and she went on, "Your brother's quite the lady-killer."

"Your girl's pretty easily killed."

We watched them for a moment in silence. The little girl with the yellow boots was standing too close to the swing, and every time Paul swung back he barreled into her chest. She looked ready to topple over.

The woman snorted as the little girl stumbled. "That one's not mine, thank God. Or not the way you mean. She's my sister."

I peeked over at the mother and saw that she had pimples on her chin and plucked eyebrows. She had spit-up on her letter jacket and a Pixy Stix straw in the corner of her mouth like some cartoon hick with his piece of hay. She could have been any one of the Karens in my class a few years down the line, and when I realized this I wanted to laugh but not because it was funny. The girls who stuck around Loose River after high school were always having babies and getting married at eighteen, then moving into their parents' basements or backyard campers. That's what happened if you were pretty enough to be a cheerleader, but not smart enough to go to college. And if you *weren't* pretty enough, you got a job at the casino or a nursing home in Whitewood.

"How old's your baby?" I asked her then, to be friendly.

"Fifteen weeks," she said. "I'm halfway there. At thirty, I'm not doing this nursing thing anymore, you know? My boyfriend's afraid of my tits! They gross him out he says."

I took another sidelong look at her, curious. I thought it was nice that her boyfriend had stuck around, anyhow. It surprised me in fact. The story didn't usually go like that—usually pretty girls got married to boys who left town for the army, for Junior Hockey League—so maybe this Karen had some secret vein of talent. From the corner of my eye, I saw her breast poking out of her shirt. It looked surprisingly *long,* with a pimply seeming nipple. "Why don't you just stop now?" I ventured.

"I'm not a bad mother! Studies say mom's milk is the *shit* for babies. Plus"—she raised a stubbled eyebrow—"my boyfriend's happy to stay *down there* for now. He calls it the better half."

I wondered what that meant. What that felt like.

"Marco!" the seniors yelled from their trucks.

"Polo!" another car returned.

"What's he doing to her?" the Karen wondered.

I followed her gaze back to the playground. The little girl was lying flat on her back in the gravel, Paul's empty black glove at her side. Had she fallen? Had the swing knocked her down? As we watched, Paul crawled on top of her, his knees spread over her stomach, palms in the rocks. He seemed to be talking to her very quietly, and though there was no obvious reason to think he was doing anything wrong, I sensed there was something predatory in his kneeling stance, something aggressive. The little girl was still, her face turned away from us. Paul looked like he might have been about to kiss her on the mouth.

But he was just talking. They seemed to be playing a sort of game. "There is . . . matter . . . All is . . . mind," he said. For a second it sounded like words from a book, from a fairy tale, the words running together so they were hard to hear. Then his singsong words became clear: "There is no *spot* where God is *not.*"

"What's he saying?" the Karen asked me. "What's going on?"

I wasn't sure. We stood up together. But for some reason we were hesitant to approach. There seemed something very private about what we were watching, something secretive and excessive that excluded us entirely. The little girl started whimpering slightly, and Paul stayed crouched over her, blond hair hanging in his eyes. "There is no spot where God is not!"

"What the fuck?" The Karen shot me a disgusted look. "What the fuck is this?" She started forward. "I sit down in a park, and Jesus weirdos just show up out of nowhere."

"No!" I said, startled.

"Freaks just flock to this town, like fucking geese."

"Wait—" I followed her.

I felt a rush of defensiveness, and then—like a leaf flipping in the wind—a rush of relief arrived right behind it. I put my hands on my hips. I felt as though I'd been hiding something from her all this time, and that she'd finally called me out on a lie I'd been surprised I could maintain so long. I had no idea what Paul was up to and, for the moment, I didn't really care. So we were weirdos. So Paul and I weren't headed for a long afternoon of Sesame Street in a basement somewhere or an eventual brain injury from a puck to the head, so we weren't headed for whatever crushing mediocrity this Karen and her boyfriend and her bald baby had planned. So *what*.

The Karen stalked over to the girl, her baby tucked under one arm. Then she grabbed the little girl by the hand and pulled her out from under Paul. For a second, the girl seemed stunned, as if she couldn't quite breathe, but then she let out the piercing wail of a much younger child, snot bubbling from her nose. She looked at Paul with a face broken open, with a look of utter love and desolation, as if she'd given him everything in the ten minutes she'd known him, and he'd taken it, oh, he'd taken it anyhow, knowing just how much it cost.

I hadn't planned on asking Paul what he'd been doing to her, but he brought it up. On the bike ride home, he was quiet for a long time. Then after a while he started saying, "That girl, that girl . . ."

So I craned my neck around and said, "What?"

"That girl . . ."

"Paul, you *hurt* her." I felt obliged to say that.

"She fell!"

"You held her."

"I healed her."

"Gimme a break."

By their nature, it came to me, children were freaks. They believed impossible things to suit themselves, thought their fantasies were the center of the world. They were the best kinds of quacks, if that's what you wanted—pretenders who didn't know they were pretending at all. That's what I was thinking as I pedaled Paul home. Rain made the breaks squeal beneath us, made the bike tires drone.

"Gimme a *break*!" Paul said.

By their nature, kids were also parrots.

6

IN FACT, PAUL AND I DID NOT ALWAYS GET ALONG. We respected each other most of the time, and in general we were pretty good at setting up compromises. I gave Paul an afternoon at the diner eating pie, and in return he gave me an hour on the lake in the canoe. We sat in the back booth of the diner, and I paid from my slowly growing savings, smoothing one of Patra's ten-dollar bills on the table when we were done. No oily quarters and dimes, no waiting around for change, no small talk with Santa Anna, the slightly bearded waitress.

"What makes pie so good?" Paul asked as we walked out. The sugar had wound him up. He was doing a little jig of ecstasy, hopping from foot to foot, flapping his fingertips.

"It's in the name," I said.

"Chocolate?"

"Mousse." I raised my eyebrows.

Paul looked up at the moose head mounted over the door, antlers wide as a man's flung-open arms, nostrils big as bowls.

The canoe ride was a tougher sell. He was fussy about it from the beginning. He didn't want to get his shoes wet getting in, so I waded through the water in my boots, Paul in my arms, and set him down on the hull near the prow. This seemed more stable than getting him to perch on the seat. Then I gave him his pretzels and a mildewed life vest to sit on, sultan-style. I told him to stay still as I paddled: don't rock back and forth, just look straight ahead. That day the water was calm and black, absorbing each dip of the paddle. Paul got so bored he fell asleep. Head down, arms crossed over the portage pads, water *clunk-clunking* beneath us. I had to carry him back to the house with his legs wrapped around my waist like a baby. I had to leave the canoe half-beached in the rocks, where it could have been carried away if the wind picked up. I didn't have a free hand to drag it.

And even then, he was whiny in my arms. Fighting me and refusing to be put down. Going, "*Stop* it, *stop* it, Linda." As if I had been tormenting him with the pleasure of a canoe ride. With the gift of a perfect day.

I'm not saying he was especially difficult to manage. But he did have a ferocious streak; somewhere in him there was a sharp line drawn between order and chaos. He did not tolerate, for instance, any break in his routine. If occasionally I lingered after I brought him back—if Patra laid out an extra plate and showed me how to whisk oil and lemon for a dressing—Paul would grow increasingly clingy. Possessive. All through dinner, he'd beg to sit in Patra's lap, and by the end he'd work his way up and nuzzle her neck. She'd fork lettuce into her mouth with one hand, pet his blond hair with the other.

There was one night in particular. Paul was whiny, and Patra was casting about for something other than trains and bath time to talk about. I remember how she pushed back her bowl, set her chin in her palm and pointed herself at me.

"O-kay, Linda," she said. There was something unsettled about her that night, a frenzy of tiny movements in the skin around her eyes. "Tell me. You're one of those girls who wants to raise horses or something, be a vet, when she grows up. I can tell. I'm right, aren't I? That's what you want to be."

I wasn't one of those girls, actually. I didn't think much about the future, but when I did, all I could come up with was the weird image of a semitruck, white and floating down the highway. Of course I couldn't say that. I couldn't say *truck driver*, so to stall I looked across the table at Paul, who was inching from his chair to the floor.

Singing: "I want to be a phy-sic-ist. I want to be a phy-sic-ist."

Patra was just teasing, though, I could tell. She didn't really care what I said, as long as I played along. She wanted something to do before clearing the table, before coaxing Paul toward bed. A distraction before the husband called.

"I could be a vet," I said, offering myself up. "Sure."

"Or, no!" Patra pulled one bent leg under her. "I've got something better for you. I'm good at this kind of thing. Let's see, you, Linda, you deserve something you haven't seen—a city to explore, you know? A bunch of people trying to get in your doors. You should be—" She snapped her fingers, flashing a grin. "A hotelier. A restaurat*eur*." She looked so pleased.

"A restaurant-er?" Paul asked.

I grunted to keep from smiling. "Like a waitress? I did that already." I swept my hand across the room, like, *what's all this then?* "I quit for you."

She widened her eyes, feigned shock. "You left the restaurant business to be a babysitter? That's a whole lot of pressure for us here, isn't it, Paul? We should give you a better title then. Where did the word 'babysitter' come from, anyway?"

I shrugged.

"An ugly word, right? Should we call you nanny instead? No, no, that sounds like an old lady. What about governess? Oooh, let's call you governess." She was laughing now. "That's so much better. A *babysitter* would never be hired for Flora and Miles. You've read *The Turn of the Screw*? Or, a *babysitter* couldn't fall in love with Mr. Rochester, right? And be the heroine. Governess you are."

"Governess!" Paul shouted from under the table. He waited for Patra to define it, and when she didn't he pulled a fist of pebbles from his stash in the glove and threw them.

"Watch it," I told him. To Patra: "I don't know. I'm not sure. Sounds like kind of a sissy thing to be. Plus, people will think you're, like, millionaires or something." I was trying to keep from grinning at her.

"You're right." Patra pouted.

"Time for my bath." Paul pouted, too. He crawled from the floor onto her lap.

Patra let him nestle into her chest while she stroked his hair. She patted his cheek, but her eyes were on me. "You're right, Linda. You're right. People here *already* think I'm a snob or something. An anomaly." She furrowed her brow, following a new train of thought. "I'm still figuring this place out, what's what. It's funny. I've been to the diner with Paul four, maybe five times? For lunch? I see the same people every time I go in, and they all look at me. They all smile and say hi. But no one has asked me one thing about myself. Not my name, not a thing. People are nice in a way, but also—"

"Not," I said.

She pulled Paul's hand away from the buttons on her shirt, so he took up her hair instead, winding his fingers in her blond curls. "Was it a good idea to come here?" she asked me now. "The idea was that while Leo was in Hawaii this spring, we'd come out to the new summer house. Go somewhere quiet and nice. Just me and Paul, as kind of a hideout—"

"A hideout from what?"

She spun her free hand around in a general way.

"You on the run?" I teased. "You rob a bank over there in Illinois?"

"Ha, ha, ha," she said. Paul was yanking on her hair—not hard, but slowly and repeatedly.

"If so, no one cares too much what you do here, so long as you keep to yourself," I joked. "And don't, like, take all the good fishing spots."

"Hmm."

I winced at how lame a line it was. But that didn't keep me from trying again. "And as long as you're not something really unforgivable, like divorced or an atheist or something—"

"*Gentle*, hon." Patra was prying open Paul's fingers, pulling out her hair.

"Or, or—"

"Paul, *stop*." She scooted him at last off her lap, patting his rump to offset the burst of irritation in her voice. "Go get your puzzle, bucko. Let's do the owl puzzle, how 'bout?" When he'd left, she started stacking plates and bowls, making noise, moving quickly. Then she sat down again, suddenly. "I really don't know if it's a great thing for us, all this quiet. Why did I think it would be a good thing for us? Maybe it would be better for Paul to go back to preschool, to be around people who . . . Maybe it wasn't such a good idea to come here in the first place?"

She looked up at me then, and there was something I didn't expect in her eyes.

"It's still a pretty good idea," I said, unsettled by her guilty expression.

On the walk home that night, I kept thinking about Mr. Grierson. He used to come into the diner fairly often by himself—I discovered this after I started waitressing there in the fall. Like Patra, he had always been left out of the small talk at the counter. The few times I waited on him he'd ordered the Eggs Special, scrambled, and he read fat paperbacks with spaceships on the covers as he forked his food down. He called me Miss Originality, for the prize I'd won in History Odyssey the year before. "Thank you, Miss Originality," he'd say, holding up his white mug for more coffee. I hadn't known what to say to that. Sometimes he'd ask me a few questions about my new teachers at the high school before he went back to his book. Usually he'd just ask for cream, his finger on the sentence he longed to return to.

The last time I saw him, though, in early November, I wasn't on the clock. I'd only stopped by the diner to pick up my check, so it was probably a Friday evening around five. The first blizzard of the year had been predicted for that weekend, and I'd just come from Mr. Korhonen's grocery store. I had a backpack full of last-minute winter supplies—kerosene, salt, toilet paper, that sort of thing. Flakes so big and wet they looked like elaborately folded pieces of origami hung in the air outside all the windows. As Santa Anna tallied my wages at the register, I'd brushed snow from my hair and pretended not to see Mr. Grierson in the back booth. I never knew if the Miss Originality thing was mocking or friendly. I never knew what to say to him once the History Odyssey competition was over and I stopped meeting him after class. I remember the diner was unusually empty that day, everyone at home preparing for the storm. The frayed vinyl booths looked especially lonely and cold with all the snow whitening the gray evening outside. Did Mr. Grierson see me standing there? I don't think he did. He was dividing his food with a fork and knife, dumping half his eggs onto a second plate, and only after I'd left with my check did it occur to me that maybe someone had been sitting across from him in the booth, back to me. And only much later, when I was walking home from Patra's that warm May night, the night she first called me governess, did I wonder if it could have been Lily.

Occasionally Leo the husband called before dinner was over, Patra's cell phone startling us all with its *Star Wars* ringtone. On those nights Patra pushed back her chair and mouthed *thank you* in my direction as she headed toward the deck with her phone. *Thank you* meant Patra wanted me to put Paul to bed. So I did, reluctantly, herding him into the bathroom, pleading with him to brush his teeth, threatening him if he didn't stay under the covers.

"You're supposed to count to a hundred!" he'd yell, when I tiptoed for the door.

"You're supposed to be out cold," I countered, turning back, pushing him down.

"You're supposed to be *nice* to me!" He squirmed under my hands.

"You're supposed to be sweet and cute," I whispered. "You're supposed to be a lovable little boy. You're supposed to be lots of things you're not always."

*   *   *

Once, *Star Wars* lit up the phone on the table just as Patra was finishing Paul's bedtime bath. Patra dashed out of the bathroom to answer it, a towel slung over her shoulder and a naked Paul tearing out from behind her. He darted around the house dripping, scaring the cats, clambering over the couch and under the table. I must have grabbed his arm harder than I meant because he cried out as though stabbed. When I pulled him toward me, he spun around and slashed a fingernail across my face. I could feel the bright stinging trace of it in an arc from eye to ear. I looked for Patra, but she had already gone out onto the deck with the phone. Something revised in me at that point, changed course, and I simply lifted Paul full body—wiggling, naked, everywhere arms—and carted him to bed. I tossed him down, load-of-logs-like on his mattress. He looked pathetic, dampening his sheets in his naked crouch. He couldn't breathe around the phlegm in his throat, dragging a few long, gurgling breaths as he glared up at me.

"That's an education." I felt like my dad. That's what he said when I'd carried the canoe on a three-mile portage through the mud. I felt like my dad, and at the same time like the kid who'd carried that canoe, who was desperate and aching and crying from exhaustion.

"Be quiet!" Paul yelled.

"You want *me* to be quiet?" I asked him. I could still feel the long scrape his fingernail had made across my cheek, the wet shape he'd printed on my flannel. "You want *me* to be quiet?"

His face was marbled white and red. "I'm a perfect child of God," he said.

"What did you say to me?" I grabbed at Paul's arm. There was something in the singsong lilt of his sentence—like when he'd spoken to that girl on her back in the playground—that made the back of my neck prickle unexpectedly. "*Who* are you?" I found myself hissing at him.

I must have truly scared him I guess, because when I let go, Paul pushed his hands in under his butt, sucked in his cheeks, and hunched up his shoulders. He was so naked his skin looked like clothes to me. He seemed sealed up in a very tight pink suit, without a wrinkle or a seam to be found. Wet and unfathomably opaque. Smelling of baby shampoo. Of urine.

I heard Patra whoop with laughter all the way out on the deck—then add something and start laughing again. I walked over and closed the bedroom door.

"You cut your face," Paul noticed.

"You wet the bed." I'd noticed, too.

He started crying then, crying as I'd never seen anyone cry before. His face was clenched and he made no sound, but for high-pitched suck of air every time he took another breath.

"Calm down," I told him. "Let's get you dressed."

"I want my mom," he whimpered.

"Not yet," I said.

"My *mom*," he begged.

"You don't want her to see this." I pointed at the dark stain on his sheets.

He set his wet eye sockets over his knees and wouldn't look up.

"Come on," I said. "Come on, *okay*? Let's put you in your pajamas."

He dragged his face away from his knees. "The choo-choo ones?"

"The train ones, yes."

He lay back as I worked his feet into the footed fleece.

Bit by bit, I got him dressed. Then I stripped the sheets, threw the comforter over the bare mattress, hid the wet sheets in the closet for the time being, and turned on his night-light, which was a caboose shining a warm red light. Together, we lined up his stuffed animals again the way he liked, in two rows against the wall. We opened *Goodnight Moon*. All the while, Paul was winding his wet hair with one finger into a worried horn on his forehead. All the while, I was thinking about where my hunting jacket was, which hook it was on, so I could put it on and get out fast. Both of us guilty and ashamed. Both of us wanting comfort of a kind we could not give the other. I was trying to figure out what to tell Patra, who would come in any minute with what would be, I feared, a confused, disappointed look on her face. I could say Paul had been a tyrant, and he *had* been: he'd scraped an arc on my face that stung still. But of course I was eleven years older and had everything on him—age, weight, education (as my father would say)—and all he wanted was a half hour with his mother before bed. And all he had in the world was the ability to throw a tantrum.

We sat stiffly apart on the rumply made bed. Paul pretended to be absorbed, and I pretended to be amused, by the little mouse in the great green room. I turned one page, then Paul turned the next. We waited for Patra.

But she was distracted when she came in. She opened the door, and I saw that her face was flushed, her lips wet. She bent down and kissed Paul on the mouth, shoveling his damp hair back with her hand. Then she kissed me as well, a feathery little peck on the scalp. I felt my heart do something to the skin at my throat, which I hoped she didn't see.

"Guess what?" she gushed.

We said nothing.

"Your dad's coming up for the long weekend."

I looked at her. She scooped up her hair in two hands and held it above her head for a moment before letting it go. I could hear it come down in the dark, a little *whoosh* of hair against her neck.

Then she leapt into bed with us.

There were eleven years between us all. We were four, fifteen, twenty-six. I'm not particularly superstitious. I never went in big for horoscopes or anything like that, but at the time that number became significant to me. I started to see it everywhere. When we had our spring pep rally there were eleven red EXIT signs spaced evenly between bleachers. I noticed that in blackjack the ace could be counted as a one or an eleven, depending on which was better for your hand. My father reminded me of this rule when we were playing cards one night, generator off, the lantern making huge shadows of our cards on the table. That night I won from him one of his precious hand-rolled cigars, which I promised not to smoke until I was eighteen. Or try this. After Judas Iscariot betrayed Jesus, the remaining apostles were called the Eleven, the chosen. My mother, repeating some sermon, reminded me of that.

I felt almost spooked when I remembered that the husband— the astronomer who was always gone—was thirty-seven. Though I never got very far past algebra in school, it seemed that such a fixed pattern should have some meaning beyond mere coincidence. It should, shouldn't it? At the time, I thought about this a lot. I tried rearranging the variables, keeping the constant constant. I wondered what Patra was like at fifteen. I imagined her in high school: shorter than me, even skinnier, better liked. She'd be the kind of girl who had one close friend, someone who moved away when she was twelve and left her disconsolate at first, then sweetly, tragically distant. She'd have really excellent pens and extremely legible handwriting. I imagined myself at the husband's age, thirty-seven (I'm thirty-seven now: I have a car payment, a PO box), and I made the husband into a child. A belligerent four-year-old with Velcro shoes, a milk moustache, and a temper. I sent Paul into his twenties by himself. I gave him a college degree, maybe a master's, and I set him loose in the world with his golden hair, with a degree in architecture and maybe an admirable ear for music or foreign languages. I gave Paul time to be a lady-killer for real, to regret his Chinese tattoo, to begin to regret lots of things. You know. To be twenty-six.

7

THE HUSBAND WAS SCHEDULED TO COME JUST BEFORE MEMORIAL DAY. His return coincided with the unofficial start of the season. Walleye fishermen had been trickling in for weeks, but ahead of the long weekend they began arriving in caravans. They drove up from the Cities with their campers and boat hitches, their pickup beds overflowing with tackle under tarps. They set up in campgrounds and rented cabins around the biggest lakes—most out-of-towners back then were still renters and weekenders. Some were summer regulars, many had read about Loose River in a glossy fishing guide, and they all tried to get a bait-shop clerk to slip up and reveal secret local spots for walleye. All of them were optimistically but predictably dressed in T-shirts and fleece vests, in elaborately pocketed cargo pants. All of them were squinting when they slid from their trucks in town to buy gas, to stock up on beer and bug spray. Pretending to know each other, because maybe they'd fried muskie together once, last Fourth of July. Pretending to know us.

"Got the spot this year?" they'd ask J. D. in the hardware store, or Katerina the Communist when they were paying up at the gas station.

Katerina would simply shrug and smile. "Do I look like a fisherman?" she'd ask, batting her heavy-lidded eyes. She *did*—she wore gray coveralls and a camouflage cap—but no one ever wanted to say so. J. D. would sell them venison jerky and out-of-date maps, making broad ambiguous circles in unlikely places with a ballpoint pen. Tipping his cap, crossing his arms.

"Well, thanks. Thank you—is it Jay?"

The out-of-towners had a thing about calling everybody by name, preserving some ritualized belief in small-town hospitality. They called Mr. Korhonen the grocer—who wore an ironed plaid shirt every day of his life—Ed. They called Santa Anna at the diner Annie, Anne, *sweetheart*.

"If it isn't Jim's girl," they said to me, "all grown up!" Approaching me at the bank when I was depositing bills in the checking account I'd opened up, or waving at me when I came down the road with my backpack. Complete strangers said this to me, people I'd met maybe twice or three times—years ago, when I was a little kid—back when my dad had occasionally picked up summer work as a guide. As if they weren't interchangeable to me, like geese, like birds with their reliably duplicate markings. I marveled that I could seem so particular and durable to them. So distinct.

We took our final exams the week before Memorial Day, all the school windows propped open with rulers. The occasional dragonfly died against the pane. May was such a dissociative time. Everyone had that underwater look in their eyes, especially teachers. It was so hard to care—if anyone ever cared to begin with—about the law of cosines told the twentieth time. About

the sum of the area of the square of the hypotenuse. Even the
debate kids were in a frisky state, giving up cosines for poetry
and mix tapes, for arguing over the secret meaning of Oasis lyr-
ics. Lily's desk, by then—by the end of exam week—was empty.
Last I'd seen her, Monday afternoon, she'd been handing Ms.
Lundgren a pink slip from the principal. Ms. Lundgren had
frowned when she read the note, and Lily left without waiting
for her response, tugging her long black hair out from her jacket
collar, pulling it up and over her head, letting it slither down
her hood. The rest of the week she was gone.

Friday afternoon, I wrote the essay portion of my Life Science
exam in less than twenty minutes: three paragraphs on the cel-
lular basis for reproduction. Then I scratched my name on the
cover, slipped my blue book into the pile on Ms. Lundgren's desk,
and took off into the blissfully mild afternoon. I stopped on the
way out of town to buy licorice and cigarettes, and I smoked two
in a row—strolling through milkweed along the highway, watching bees and monarchs rise—and then, on impulse, I chucked
the pack into the bed of a red pickup as it passed. As I did, three
pelicans floated overhead like a reward for good behavior. *Go,
go*, I thought at them, exhilarated. They flapped their enormous
wings in unison, disappeared over trees.

From four to six that day, I sat with Paul on the warm wood
of the Gardners' deck, watching ducks arrive in droves, watching
geese skid into the lake and snake black necks beneath the surface.
I pointed them out to Paul as they came, though in my heart I kept
hoping for more pelicans. Or for something even rarer to arrive,
like a falcon. I gnawed my licorice as Paul got busy stacking piles
of stones. He shuffled around on his sweatpants knees, arranging

strips of bark into lanes. He was changing his city from a medieval village into the modern capital of Europa, Jupiter's sixth moon.

"Most likely place becept Mars to have life," he explained.

"How do you know?"

"In the Goldilocks zone."

"The what?"

"Not too hot, not too cold."

"Ah, I see." I nibbled a twist of licorice. Then I remembered: "But no one lives in the City, right? Isn't that what you said?"

He nodded without looking up. "Hasn't been discovered yet."

On the deck, he'd pulled apart all the geometrically intersecting walls and roads, all the towers and moats, and made what looked like a random assortment of leaves and stones—what the wind might have left, or a big rain. He kept picking up a certain pocked maple leaf and setting it down somewhere else, perfecting a design only he could see.

Which is why when Patra returned an hour later from errands in town, she walked right over Europa's capital. Paul howled for exactly one second—"*Mooom!*"—then laid on his back in the ruins of his city and refused to speak.

"What is it?" Patra asked, at first amused. Then exasperated. She crouched down and kissed at his chin. "Kiddo, what is it? What did I do?" but he wouldn't open his eyes. She looked over at me, sitting with my knees to my chest, and though it would have been simple to say what she'd done wrong, I kept quiet. I wasn't sure how to explain Europa's capital to her without it sounding condescending, without speaking as if Paul weren't there. I shrugged. "Okay," Patra said. "Paul the kid is taking a time out. This kiddo here is having a rest, because he's so excited that his dad's coming tomorrow. Right?"

It was clearly Patra who was so excited. That afternoon, she'd biked into town to pick up extra groceries and cut her hair instead of working on the manuscript. She'd made an appointment with Nellie Banks—who'd gone to beauty school—and it was strange now to see Patra's hair feathered and short, curled up under her ears. It moved with a different gravity than it did before, Europa's gravity perhaps, shifting complexly in the late afternoon light.

Slowly, deliberately, I put on Paul's leather glove and had it walk on two fingers over to him, sniff his knee like a tiny animal.

"Hee," he said, sitting up.

When he did, I saw that his face was pouring with sweat. It gathered in a big drip at his chin. His pupils had taken over his eyes, flying saucers coming in. He swayed.

"Okay, then," Patra said. As if Paul had made some argument to which she'd given in. She scooped him up in her arms, and her voice scrabbled up an octave—"Feefifofum"—then it came back down slowly on stairs. "I. Smell. The blood—" She chewed his neck, and when he half smiled, she said, "Hey, little man. Hey, kiddo. What does CS tell us?"

"*I* smell the blood."

"There is no spot where God is—"

"*You're* the Englishman," he told her.

Patra nudged open the sliding door with one knee and went inside, Paul in her arms like an excess of infant—all dangling limbs—and the white cat darted out just as the door closed. Patra didn't notice. The cat made a break for the far side of the deck, then stopped abruptly, as if coming to an unseen boundary. The end of Europa. The start of the woods.

"What?" I asked it. "May as well try the world."

The cat turned around to look at me. Ears back, whiskers trolling the air.

I menaced it. "What do you think I'm gonna do?"

It was already evening, already six o'clock. But as I listened to a running faucet, snatches of a song through the screen, the whole day seemed to bare its open jaws at me. There was nothing to do now that Paul and Patra had gone inside. The sun overhead was still high enough in the sky to feel fixed forever. The white cat made a wide slow circle around me on the deck, then sat stiffly at the sliding glass door, waiting to be let back in. Meowing plaintively, going like a clock alarm, without pause. I should have just gone home. I should have clomped down the steps and found the trail, headed for the ridge of red pine, followed by the stand of old birch. Loon nest, beaver dam, sumac trail, dogs. I should have gone home to the dogs, who would have slobbered all over my face and hands with happiness.

Instead I stood up, snuck around the side of the house, climbed up the spoke-like branches of a spruce near Paul's window. Patra lay on the bed with Paul reading a book. I could see their bodies spooned together, Patra's arm wrapped around him, her face pressed into the sweaty hair at the back of his head. He held a sippy cup, half-tipped, in his hands. As Patra read to him, she kept kissing his one exposed ear, that raw little flower rising up from the bedclothes. *There, there.* Her tenderness was breathtaking. I could feel it—even from outside the room, even in my treetop perch—making everything disappear. There goes the world. There goes the house. *Poof.* There goes your bed and your body, too. There go thoughts. His eyes fluttered a few times, closed. The wind gave up rustling the trees. The sky clouded over. When Paul's mouth opened up and he was asleep, Patra carefully stood, extracted the cup from his hands, and left the room.

She came back and undressed him as he slept. I watched her uncoil his legs from his pants and put him in a diaper.

His soft belly puckered beneath the plastic waistband. I'd never seen him in a diaper before. I don't know why that got to me, but up came a curl of saliva in my throat—something I didn't expect, a liquid claw—and as it did, the black cat pounced to the inner windowsill. Nonchalantly, not even looking out at me, licking one paw. Still. I was startled, so I left.

I thought that would be it till Tuesday because of Memorial Day weekend. But the next morning, I was sitting on the roof of the shed, reading a *People* magazine I'd stolen from the school secretary's trash, when I saw Patra's blue Honda coming up my parents' road. The whole woods droned with motors—weekenders on the lake testing their speedboats—so I didn't hear the car until it was halfway up the sumac trail. Popping gravel and snagging trees.

I came down from the roof in a single leap, just as the dogs started getting nervous, hauling their chains from the dirt and peering down the road. *Shhh*, I told them. I trotted a little way through the dense corridor of sumac and then stopped Patra's car by patting it softly on the hood.

"Linda! Careful!" She rolled down her window and leaned out.

Patra didn't look at all like herself. Her lips were pink as earthworms under rocks, wrinkling up under lipstick. Blush glittered on her cheeks, giving her the look of the Karens, of girls despising themselves in mirrors—scratching open pimples, then sealing up the wounds with foundation. She looked both older and younger at once. A kid dressing up, or a middle-aged lady trying too hard to look young.

"Listen," she went on. "I didn't have your mom's number. I went through the whole house this morning, but couldn't remember where I wrote it down. The thing is Leo's coming today. Paul and I were planning to meet his plane in Duluth. We were going to drive there together, but Paul's—"

"But Paul's—" I wanted to help her out. I wanted, by instinct, to finish the sentences that gave her trouble. To ease her load, to do her dirty work. "Paul's—"

"*Fine.* He's sleeping in. He's actually still at home—"

"Alone?" That made her eyes change, a gleam coming over them.

"Come with me," she begged. "Just for the day. Just while I'm away, stay with him."

I had a take-home trig test to finish, a big blowndown branch I'd promised to chop up. My dad was on the lake even now catching walleye I would need to clean before nightfall. I knew, though, that I'd do what Patra asked. Here she was, after all, gripping the wheel of her car so tight her veins popped up in her hands. From the corner of my eye, I could see my mother coming around the hilltop path where she'd been hanging laundry. I told Patra, "Hold on."

"I can come in, talk to your mom." She turned off the engine, started to open the door. I could hear the dogs' chains rumbling across the dirt, the *flap-flap* of the tarp on the front door in the wind.

"Hold *on!*" I told her. I must have yelled, because she put two hands up. In surrender.

"*Okay.*"

I saw my mother squint over at the car, once, before she went inside.

I followed her in.

*   *   *

The sunlit room swirled with sooty dust. My mother was folding laundry on the kitchen table, a great pile of sun-crisp clothes in a crazy jumble. "That the girl from across the lake? The one you've been spending so much time with?" She had a propped-up look on her face, hopeful and suspicious both. Her long dark hair latched to the staticky sheets as she folded rectangles in half, then in half again.

"Yeah."

She nodded, not meeting my eyes. For years she'd said she wanted me to be more like other kids my age. She'd always told my dad that she wanted me to spend less time on the shed, have more regular girl experiences. So here I was, satisfying her. She said: "She's *nice* then?" But she meant: *She's not from around here, right?* Because at the same time, I think, my mother always wanted me to have loftier ambitions than the local girls, to be just a little superior to them.

"Yeah."

"Good. Then have fun." She went to the shelf over the sink, opened an old mason jar, fingered four crumpled dollar bills from her stash. She wrinkled her nose at me when I waved her away. "I'm serious."

"Mom—" The bills felt soft as cloth in my hand. They didn't feel like money.

"It's important." She was smiling knowingly now.

I had a flutter in the back of my throat. A warning. "What is?"

"Having a little adventure."

"*Mom.*" I didn't like how she put that. Like she knew what I was up to when she didn't, and wouldn't ask. Like I'd run off to the casino, get high, go off the rails on her four fucking dollars. Like she wanted me to. "I'm just telling you I'll do the fish tomorrow, okay? I'm telling you to tell Dad, all right?"

She tossed me my blue flannel from her pile, still warm from the sun, still smelling of detergent and cedar. "Go." She went back to folding. "I'm not going to pry. I'm not going to ask you what she's doing up here alone with that kid. On one long vacation. Go on and be free."

In the car, Patra drove with one foot on the gas pedal and one foot on the brake. The whole car shuddered as it ground through gears, then shot forward in rapid bursts. She was trying to rub a spot off her skirt as she drove, and she was listing more instructions than usual: give him two glasses of water before he eats, four crackers at three, tuna on toast at five. I listened but didn't reply. I was busy thinking about the bills in my pocket, about the mason jar of money on the shelf above the sink. I was thinking about the fishing lures we'd made to sell but never did, the jars of jam we'd filled to peddle at the diner on weekends, the clothes my mother folded that were made from other clothes.

When I stayed silent, Patra's eyes flicked over to me then back to the road.

"This okay with your mom?"

"Is Patra your real name?" I felt like accusing her of something. I don't know why. I was suddenly angry at her niceness. And I was angry at the skirt beneath the spot she was rubbing with her finger, at its byzantine floweriness.

She was surprised. "No, actually. I'm Cleopatra, my whole life Cleo for short. Why?"

I snuck a peek at her. One black beaded earring lay flattened across her cheek like a slug. "No reason."

"After I met Leo, I changed it. Who could be named Leo and Cleo?" She sounded defensive. "In what world would that work?"

It would not. She was right.

"Listen, you'll like him," she promised. "He's one of those people you can *hear* think. You can see him making all these calculations when he talks. He's that smart."

I wondered. I wondered if I could hear him thinking right now all those miles away, up in the air, in his plane, making his calculations, keeping track of his baby stars and their magnetic fields, charting galaxies so far away they were billions of years old before we knew they existed, and arranging the movements of Patra and Paul and me and this car, which, I'd noticed, Patra had rinsed clean of salt for his arrival.

"Sure," I said.

Patra was nervous about having left Paul asleep in his bed. But when we got back to their house, he was up and making himself a sugar sandwich, which he wanted to pack in his Tonka truck and take to his cabin in the woods. His cabin was a chair overturned, so I suggested we set up a real tent—one from their garage they'd never used—on the living room rug. Only a grayness in his skin made me think of how he'd been the day before, with that engorged drip of sweat on his chin. Patra was thrilled. Before she left, she kept kissing his head, rubbing her face in his hair, taking in his scent, like a dog. "Your dad's going to be so proud!" she gushed. "So happy to see you. Good job, hon."

We spent the day setting up camp. I'd promised Patra not to take him out of the house, so to kill the long hours indoors, I taught him everything I knew about fighting off bears, about surviving on bark and berries, about living with just a knife if you had to. Never follow a creek expecting it to lead to civilization, I told him. That's a myth. Be sure to find a clean water source before two days are up. If you have to, tie your jacket sleeves around your ankles and walk through tall grass to gather dew on the sleeves. Suck it off. (We practiced this, Paul dragging his jacket across the rug.) Don't be afraid to eat grasshoppers. Avoid plants with milky sap. Avoid white berries.

I taught him how to crawl across the ice when it was thin, how to distribute his weight, how to go like a soldier on his elbows.

"Here comes a bear after you!" I told him.

He crawled for a minute, took a rest.

"Here comes a wolf!"

"Nothing to worry about." He was panting. His cheeks were bright red. "They're. Nice."

"Good," I said. I lay down on my stomach beside him.

At five on the dot, I gave Paul his tuna on toast. Just exactly that: tuna from a can, the brine squeezed out, beige meat mushed with a fork over a dry field of bread. Paul scarfed this down, then went in big for a dessert of broken animal crackers. Crumbs caught in the folds of his shirt and sprinkled to the floor when he stood up.

At seven, I gave him his bath. I filled the water first with stirred-up shampoo, making a boatload of frothy bubbles. Then I pretended to examine a bug bite on my ankle as he tugged off his pants and droopy diaper. Absentmindedly, I pulled the cap off my scab, which let out a trickle of blood like a brand-new wound. I took my time swiping my skin clean. Eventually, I peeked over at Paul in the bath, where he was briskly stacking two towers of bubbles on his knees. We did not talk. Only after I set out his pajamas, only after I'd tossed away the awful diaper and handed him his underpants, did he initiate a conversation. "Are you an explorer?" he asked.

The farthest I'd been on a bus was to Bemidji on a school trip to the Paul Bunyan statue. The farthest I'd been in a canoe was a six-day trip up the Big Fork River to the Canadian side of Rainy Lake. "Not really," I told him, regretfully.

"Oh. Are you married then?"

I put my chin in my collar. I thought I knew what he was asking now. He wanted to know what category to put me in, whether I was adult or child, whether I was more like his dad or his mom or himself—or something else, some novel discovery. My fingertips felt heavy on his pajama buttons as I did them up. "No. Not really."

At that, he looked so unreasonably dismayed.

I thought of Lily then. I thought of how she went from being seen as a stupid girl to being treated like a possible threat, how she did it in two months flat, and as I did I stole a look into Paul's dark eyes, which seemed sometimes gray, sometimes green, sometimes almost black. I shrugged at him. "There was a guy once. Named Adam."

"Was *he* an explorer?"

"He was from *California*," I said, expecting to impress him a little. "He was an actor. Well, no. Actually, a teacher."

"Sounds like my dad. He was a teacher to my mom in college."

I would have liked to hear more about that, but Paul—now dressed, wet hair dripping down his neck—ran off to slay a bear and drink some dew and start the campfire.

At eight, Patra was still gone, so we crawled in the tent we'd set up on the rug and zipped the fly.

"Shoes off?" I said.

"Check."

"Hatchet by your head for defense?"

He touched the wooden handle of the hatchet. "Yep."

He made a ball of his body in his sleeping bag, tucked his leather glove up under his head, and then, like a stone tossed in water, sank straight into sleep. I lay down on the other side of the tent: it was very warm and quiet in there, it had an underground feeling. I meant to stay awake until Patra and the husband came back, but the tent inside the house muffled all the regular night sounds, so I couldn't hear the crickets or the owls or anything. All I heard was Paul's breath against the nylon, a very hushed sound. And I heard the black cat leaping off the windowsill, bell jingling across the room.

Sometime later—a few minutes? a few hours?—I heard Patra whispering. She was on her knees, halfway in the tent, hanging over us. She was a shadow and a scent, not much more than that, jacket drooping from her haunches.

"Everything okay?" she asked.

"He's fine," I said.

She crawled in on her hands and knees and kissed Paul's cheek, then, sighing, lay down between us. Her jacket smelled of fast food and wet woods. She must have come quickly from the car, because I could hear her heart pounding and then, little by little, settling down, getting back into its routine.

Though maybe it was mine I heard. Maybe I'd woken up afraid of something.

"Cozy," she said. "So much better than being alone in a car for five hours. Or sitting in an airport parking lot."

I turned toward her: "Where is he?"

She released a big breath. "Delayed. Delayed, then canceled."

Patra hadn't zipped up the tent fly, so I crawled over and did that for her. Lay back. When I did, I could feel Patra's dry hair against my ear on the pillow. I could smell the cool woods in her hair, even over the scent of her coconut shampoo. She was still wearing her jacket, and every time she shifted I could hear it, the synthetic fibers crunching under her weight.

"I should take him to bed," she whispered.

"Okay," I said.

She didn't move. She lay so still even her jacket was quiet. "I'm exhausted," she whimpered. As she spoke, her voice did a U-turn in the dark. It drove right from exhaustion into despair, right off some invisible bridge between us.

I didn't wonder what made her sound like that. I didn't have to guess what upset her.

"He's really okay," I said.

She began to cry. She was breathing and then it was something else. She put her palm over her mouth, trying, unsuccessfully, to stop up the sound. *Sorry*, she might have said between breaths, or, *for God's sake*, or *stay here*.

"Hey," I said after a moment. "No shoes in the tent."

So I crawled to her feet and plucked open the buckle on her little ankle boot. I slipped my fingers in and felt the bony knob of her heel, hot and damp in my hands, in her sock. Then I slipped the bootlet off, reached over and undid the other. Her feet in her socks seemed so vulnerable to me, so ridiculously small. I set her heels down next to each other, and the crying stopped. I heard it turn back into regular breathing.

Before I lay back, before I pulled up my sleeping bag, I checked the hatchet out of habit. The wooden handle under my fingers was like a promise fulfilled. I knew, before touching it, everything there was to know about it. Which made me confident and glad.

Later when I woke up, I found Patra had curled up around Paul. Back to me. But I could feel her curved spine through her jacket when I pushed in closer, all those little vertebrae linked up, all those bones laid out, like a secret. The night had come down hard, finally. Thunder was rumbling far away. Wind had kicked up waves, and they were loud enough now that I could hear them on the shore of the lake, shoving pebbles forward and back. I could hear pine needles whipping the roof of the house. I could hear Paul and Patra, breathing in syncopation.

Happy, I was happy.

I barely recognized the feeling.

So who could blame me for wishing that the husband's re-scheduled plane would drift into a low-lying thunderhead? That it would shunt in sudden turbulence, lose elevation fast? Who could blame me for hoping his pilot would be young and scared, that he'd turn around and fly back over the ocean? The husband had his own baby stars to watch over and his own mountain to do it from, in Hawaii. I longed for straight-line winds between him and me, for hurricanes off the California coast. Downpours and lightning. The thunder was getting louder now. I felt the tent I'd built gather us in, Paul and Patra. Patra and me.

I slept and woke. I dreamed of the dogs. I dreamed of taking Patra and Paul out on the canoe, currents like underwater hands thrusting the boat around, so we had to fight to go forward. My paddle guiding us toward shore. Or maybe guiding us away from it, maybe we were leaving after all. I slept and woke. Slept.

Eventually, just after dawn, I heard scuffling outside. It sounded like a slow-moving mammal, a possum or raccoon, unsettling the driveway stones. Then I heard a car door thump. Very gently I sat up and pulled the hatchet from under Paul's pillow. I unzipped the tent, tiptoed across the braided rugs, crept to the front window. There, in the driveway, in the early morning light, stood a man in a blue slicker next to a rental car. He held a brown sack of groceries, a duffel bag. He looked bland and harmless—so when he opened the door I let the hatchet hang in my hand where he could see it. And Patra was right: I *could* hear him think. I could hear him taking in the dark room and the tent on the floor and the tall, scrawny kid coming out from the shadows, with a good-sized weapon.

Here's how the story about Lily went. It was simple at first, but as time passed, as the rumor was repeated and spread, it grew more and more detailed. Mr. Grierson, last fall, had taken Lily out on a canoe. Gone Lake was the largest of four just outside town. It was so round that in the center the bank looked like a ribbon of black, and in the gloom of a mid-October afternoon, it no doubt disappeared altogether. Everyone could imagine this. It was a good choice, Gone Lake. They both paddled because, Mr. Grierson said, a little exercise builds trust between people. He sat in back and steered, though Lily, of course, could have gotten them where he wanted to go much faster. Like all of us, she could paddle a boat like she could ride a bike. Mr. Grierson, the Californian, splashed and tottered. Got his pants soaked, got his shoes wet. By the time they reached the middle of the lake, the day was gone and the water was oil black. The sky, clear, was thick with stars. And though it was chilly—though most of the aspens had let loose their leaves already—they didn't wear gloves or hats. They had to set their dripping paddles across their laps, had to warm their hands, in turns, on a thermos lid of steaming coffee.

At any point along the way, Lily could have tipped the boat and stranded Mr. Grierson. All it would have taken was a hard lurch to one side. She knew this lake like her own pretty face. He knew nothing at all. When he pulled out a disposable camera and aimed it at her, he acknowledged as much. He said he wanted Lily to know how vulnerable he was, how his fate was in her hands. He said if he were lucky enough to get back to the car, it would be because of Lily's kindness and mercy. He wanted her to know how grateful he was—in advance. Before he unzipped his pants, before he said *just a kiss* and pushed her down, he wanted her to know she had a choice.

8

LEO'S PANCAKES HAD CHOCOLATE CHIPS AND RAISINS. His orange juice was thick, boggy and sweet with pulp. He played word games as he cooked, Liar Liar and Mental Hangman. Paul's guesses were the same every time. N-O and P-A-U-L. As he made our breakfast, Leo found lots of excuses to touch people, Patra of course—who was grinning like an idiot, still in yesterday's clothes—and also Paul, whom he high-fived as he cooked, as he flipped things with spatulas. And also me.

"Here, Linda," he said, his palm on my shoulder as he ushered me to the table with a plate of pancakes. When he'd first come through the door that morning, he'd hesitated only an instant before holding out his hand for me to shake. Under his rain slicker, which he'd draped over a chair, he wore a bright blue T-shirt and a matching fleece vest. But his shoes were real enough. Red Wing boots. No one made him take them off at the door.

"Sit, eat!" he said, though I kept threatening to leave, kept saying that I needed to get home, that I needed to brush my teeth and get started on homework.

"Sit! Eat!" Paul yelled. He pounded the table with his utensils.

Patra had been sitting at the table for a long time already, legs drawn under her, red eyes blinking. Her newly cut hair was a frizzy halo of yellow and gold. All her makeup was gone, save a tiny wedge of mascara on one eyelid. She wiped syrup from her plate with a finger, sucked it off. She lifted the hatchet with sticky hands, pretended to take a swipe at Leo when he said all the orange juice was gone.

"Fee-fi-fo-fum!" Paul screeched.

"Patty!" the husband scolded. But she seemed surrounded by a force field of pleasure and just grinned up at him. She set down the hatchet, rubbed her hands on her skirt.

"Who needs napkins?" her husband asked, handing Patra one first.

I left when the sun came over the treetops, when it bore a shaft of light and dust into my skull and turned everything else in the room into shadows. Paul was shouting about Europa's capital, and Patra was saying something about Paul's "demonstration" the day before, so no one noticed much when I got up for more milk and slipped out the door. Last night's rain gave the sunny woods a squinty newborn look. It seemed fizzed, fermented—everything shimmering and throwing lights. I was almost out of sight of the house, almost to the tasseled pines, when I heard someone behind me on the path. "Linda, wait!" Patra called.

I turned and saw her running awkwardly, stumbling over roots and pinecones. She was still in her socks. I held my breath when I saw her coming like that. Long wrinkled skirt caught between her legs, hair shot through with sun, like a mane.

"Thanks!" she said, handing me four ten-dollar bills.

My heart sank. I already had four soft, unspent bills in my pocket from my mother. I already had enough money from a month of Paul to buy a kayak, or a bus ticket to Thunder Bay, or a purebred malamute if I wanted.

The problem was I couldn't bring myself to want any of these things quite enough.

"No, thanks," I mumbled, refusing to hold out my hand.

"You've got to take it, Linda. I'll feel bad." She mock pouted. Mock stamped her foot.

"Okay." *That's not my problem,* I meant. I turned to leave.

"I'm going to bury it here under this rock if you won't take it. I'm not kidding!" I could see she was still buzzed from the conversation inside the house—the back-and-forth of it, the pointless frolic. "Here I go, burying your wages!" she said. "Dig, dig."

She really did. She got down on her hands and knees in the dirt, in her skirt. She went ahead and lifted a piece of granite, revealing, in the wet soil beneath, a clump of earthworms writhing skyward. It was like the guts of the woods were showing.

"Seriously!" she called.

I shrugged.

"Here goes your money. Under a rock with the bugs."

"Bye," I said.

Finally, she stood up and shook her head at me, unable to keep from grinning. Hands on her hips. "You're a pretty funny kid, you know?"

Her socks and palms were black with dirt. "You're a weird adult."

I arrived home muddy from my walk through the woods. The dogs reared against their chains as I made my way to the door. "Mongrels," I told them, bending down and making sure to

touch them all the exact same amount, even old Abe who was
my favorite. Two pats on the side of each ribcage. Then I straightened up. I could just catch the rumbling voices of my parents
through the screen window. I thought maybe I'd hear my name—
Madeline—but no, they were talking about a groundhog in the
garden. I turned impulsively and went the other direction.

The shed was cool and dark, the roof beam awhirl with
startled sparrows. I stood still and listened to them flap. I glanced
at the fish cooler but couldn't bear the idea—not after last night,
not right now—of slicing ribcages out of walleye. The day-old
fish would be on the edge of spoiling, but I didn't check the ice.
There would be so many tiny bones for me to deal with, if I did,
a bucketful of gleaming skins. Doing my take-home trig exam
would be no better—would be worse, probably—so I stood
in the musty shed a long minute, wavering, before filling my
backpack with a few things, tying a crushed rain slicker around
my hips, and dragging the Wenonah down to shore.

The minute the canoe touched water, it moved on its own.
Every stroke with the paddle was almost excessive. There wasn't
a ripple on the lake, not a wave. You could see clear to the bottom. You could see bluegill rising, lily pads sinking under the
prow. You could see air bubbles winding away in a trail behind
the boat. At the far end of the lake, I pulled the canoe ashore,
bent down, and rolled it up to my shoulders, my head inside
the hull. It took me a second to get the balance right before I
set off on the rocky portage.

The next lake over, Mill Lake, was much larger than ours,
its shore studded with RVs and pickups at the national forest
campground. Speedboats wrecked the surface, leaving behind
thirty-foot troughs. They didn't slow down when they saw me
coming. They were in a hurry to get to the next fishing spot,

engines gunning, green awnings rippling as they passed. I was surprised to see a woman in a red bikini bumping in an inner tube behind one of them. The water was still pretty cold. She screamed hello to me over the roar of the engine, but I didn't try to respond. The boat flew by too fast.

I kept paddling. After another half hour, clouds hunkered down over the treetops, and a breeze nicked the lake's surface, giving it the look of old skin. At that point, all the weekenders headed in, fearing a return of bad weather. They were always confusing clouds with danger, seeing all clouds as interchangeable. They turned the lights on inside their RVs, making two o'clock look like dusk.

I wound my way through the little stream that connected Mill Lake to Lake Winesaga.

From there, Winesaga lay in front of me like an arrow— long and narrow, pointing north. The reservation was on the far end. When I'd been there last, years ago to get muskrat traps with my dad, the reservation had been just a few buildings. It had one paved road and maybe a dozen mobile homes, a pack of roaming Lab mixes. Now, as I drew closer to shore, I saw that all the dogs were behind chain-link fences. There was a Dairy Queen, a parking lot the size of a football field, and a stoplight. The new casino on the highway had done well. I saw a Heritage Center made from prim, narrow logs and a fish-shaped sign that said MINO-O-DAPIN! Welcome.

I beached the canoe and shunted it discreetly under a balsam fir. Then I set off down the asphalt streets, which disintegrated into the front lawns of prefab houses. All of them: white, aluminum-sided. All of them: bookended with porches and two-car garages, crowned with satellite dishes, fronted with pickup trucks.

The reservation seemed deserted but for a group of boys who came out of the woods in their bright Sunday school sweaters. They carried Popsicle-stick crosses they were using as guns. "Pow," said one of them. Another held up his cross and shouted, "Stay back, Leviathan."

"Hey, you know where the Holburn place is?" I held my ground. "Pete and his kid, Lily."

By then, she'd already missed four days of class.

"Why should we tell you?" one of the boys—their Leviathan-hunting leader—asked.

"I'll give you money. I'll give you a dollar each if you tell me where her house is."

They paused for a moment. Then they agreed as if by telepathy, barely lifting their shoulders.

"Down that way." One of them pointed to an overgrown gravel road at the end of the paved street. So I handed over my mother's bills, flat and warm from two days in my pocket. The moment they were paid the boys turned on me. They held up their crosses and harangued me: "What do you want from Lily the Polak? She's a wee-wee sucker homo freak. You a homo, too, or something?"

I sighed. I'd fielded this question from boys like these all through grade school. It was often the worst accusation eight year-olds could muster, and I was amply prepared from years of being taunted on the playground. "A *Homo sapiens*?" I asked, suggestively.

They shrugged, uncertain.

"I am. Yes."

"Barf! Gross! Yuck!" they squealed.

They were delighted, though.

I left them gagging themselves with their Popsicle-stick crosses and headed down the road where they'd pointed. I walked for a while through switchgrass and mud before I saw a rusted-out trailer in the pines. I didn't approach Lily's house from the front. I went around back, where the grass was unmowed and woods encroached. Fir and more fir. But there was a swept concrete patio under a faded blue awning, and when I looked in the back window, I could see dishes stacked neatly in the drainer. I could see a Formica table with the chairs pushed in, a lit fish tank whirling with bubbles. It was an old trailer, but tidy and aspirational, with a new carpet sample on the floor and a crocheted blanket over the tiny bench couch. I saw the pink scarf Lily stole from the lost and found—tassels trembling in a draft—on a hook by the door. As I watched it move in the breeze, I realized the hook was in fact a horn, centered on a mounted deer head.

The thing had its wide mouth closed, its white nostrils flaring.

From behind me a man's voice said, "Lily?"

I turned. Someone lay in a lawn chair in the shade under a far fir. "Lil, you back?"

It was Mr. Holburn, and as I watched, he took a deep breath and pushed himself up straighter in the frayed nylon chaise. I tried to think of something to explain myself—I'd been picking early Juneberries, I'd lost my way—but then I saw the tallboy in his hand, the pile of empties overturned in the moss. It was Sunday afternoon, Memorial Day weekend, so it probably didn't matter what I said. He wouldn't remember once I left.

There was a bright yellow pine needle hanging from his gray beard.

He swung his legs off the lawn chair and started to stand. "You back now? I've been waiting here—"

His aggrieved expression drained the moment he stepped out of the shade. That's when he understood a mistake had been made, and forgot he'd made it just as fast, giving in to a long, laden blink of his eyes. When he opened them again, he was squinting so intensely he looked like he was in pain. "You?" he asked. "Excuse me," he added, all politeness. "Do I know you?"

"Nope," I said, though it wasn't quite the truth. I'd poured his coffee at the diner more than once, and years back, when I was twelve, I'd competed against his two nephews, and won, in the Two Bears Classic Dogsled Race. He'd given me a slap on the back at the finish line.

He put a palm to his gut, sliding it up his Forest Service T-shirt to his throat. A sliver of belly grinned out at me. "It's like a tree is growing from my chest, you know? I don't feel right. It's like my mouth don't fit on my face or something." He rolled his jaw. "Don't mind me," he apologized.

He turned from me, found another can on the ground to crack open. When he turned back again, his brow was creased. "You still here?"

I reached for my backpack, unzipped. Pulled out a pair of boots.

"This is private property," he explained then. But sadly, as if it couldn't be helped. "No hunting or fishing allowed."

Did he think I'd pulled out a tackle box or something? A gun? "I'm not *hunting*."

"No—" he had to search for the word. He had to look at the black-and-orange sign posted to a tree in their yard and read it. "Tesspressing." He giggled.

"Where's Lily?" I blurted.

"Lily?" He shook his head slowly, as though he bore the weight of all the world's mysteries. "Gone with that lawyer son-of-a-bitch. She said to me when she left, 'Keep the house nice.' And look! I've had all my fun outside, like she asked. I did dishes, right? I kept it up good." He sat back down in his lawn chair, grunting, as if the mere mention of these tasks had drained him.

As he slumped down, he pointed warily at the boots now cradled in my arms. "What's tha—?"

"It's—" I was trying to think of some way to explain. Before I could answer, though, he brought his palm over his face like a lid.

In front of the trailer again, I hesitated for a moment near the door. Then I set down the black suede boots I'd taken from my backpack. I wondered if there was any way to leave a note and decided immediately there wasn't. Bending down, I arranged the boots under the awning on the front step: toes pointed forward, heels lined up. I gave one of them a quick stroke on the flank before I took off running down the road. I'd collected them from the lost and found last Thursday after class, carried them in my backpack in the canoe across three lakes, brought them all the way here for Lily. I think I'd meant them as a kind of gift. I think I meant them as some token of secret understanding or agreement. But as I hurried down the gravel road, as I headed toward Lake Winesaga and my boat, I glanced back once, and there they stood—the boots I'd stolen for Lily. Their effect on the trailer step was very different from what I expected. They looked like an invisible, implacable person standing watch at her door. Accusing, blocking the entrance.

*   *   *

The lake, when I got back to it, was rough with waves. My stomach rumbled. There was nothing in my backpack now save my Swiss Army knife and the rain slicker. I'd brought no provisions. I plucked a small unripe raspberry from a bush near shore and rolled it over my tongue before spitting it out. It was haired and hard. I thought of Paul. I thought of Paul in his cabin—taking down the tent with Patra, Leo presiding with the spatula—and I decided to practice survival, right then and there. I practiced being starving, stranded, a hundred miles from civilization, from people. I shoved off with my paddle in the canoe and headed straight to the center of Winesaga, where waves crushed against the prow and mist wetted my face. The boat bobbed, and I dug in deeper with the paddle to straighten my course. To my right, to my left, the black-arrow faces of loons appeared over and over. Or maybe it was the same loon, diving under my boat, trailing me. Loons have been known to do that.

This time around the three lakes ran together. All the RVs on shore looked alike. Clotheslines whipped with towels, fishing boats nodded on ropes. The occasional beer can or milk carton skated across the water. To pass the time, to distract myself, I counted eleven (plus one) RVs and eleven (plus one) boats. I counted eleven minus two ducks on the bank, eleven strokes of the paddle to the portage: it's easy to make a pattern if you fudge. You can take eleven breaths and then hold it. You can see eleven stars appear over the horizon if you don't look for more.

I only have one real memory from when I was four. It involves Tameka, who was a year or so older, who slept with me in a bottom bunk in the bunkhouse until the commune broke up. Tameka had a drapey orange sweater with big alphabet letters, which she rolled into fat donuts at the sleeves. The scar on her left elbow was purple. Her hands were a deep brown on the backs, white on the heels. Of course, there were lots of Big Kids around, faster and older than both of us, who moved in a pack and hit. But Tameka was quieter, lovelier. Mine. She bit her nails off into a pile, saved them in a clear plastic Baggie she squashed into a ball and put in her armpit. *Her stash*, she called it. *Don't tell*, she whispered. Of course I wouldn't. Of course not.

"You're so lucky to live like this," everyone was always telling us. The Parents, as they went by with axes.

"Lucky ducks?" Tameka wondered.

Ducks, I agreed. We flew away into the woods.

Here's what I remember best from that time. For a few weeks when I was almost five, Tameka and I were sick together. We lay in our bed and slept, we swam into dreams and out, we woke up coughing at the same moment. I remember the heat, the endless strangling blankets. I remember sucking the tip of Tameka's braid. I remember Tameka deciding that we didn't have to speak to each other anymore: we knew each other's thoughts just by being in the same world together she said. The way loons did or the sneaky pike—you know how they always dive down at exactly the same moment? They're mind readers, they see into the future and avoid disasters, that's what being sick is. Okay?

In bed, Tameka pulled the tip of her braid from my mouth and waited for me to agree.

Okay then, I thought.

After that, I watched Tameka like I was a loon, with a flat button eye that didn't move, that saw everything across the lake and never blinked. Whenever she lifted her spoon to her mouth, I lifted mine too, and we both swallowed mushed-up rice down into our bellies. Later, when Tameka wanted to scratch her scab,

I wanted to scratch mine too   until it bled down my leg and
into my toenail cracks. And when the Parents started fighting
at Meeting, waving their arms and holding their heads, Tameka
and I decided at the same time to sneak out the back door and
down into the cattails—that empire of green stalks—and when
we came out on the other side we had to squint in the bright
sun. We ran up the Big Rocks together, ripping up little swaths
of moss with our calloused feet. We scrambled up the far bank to
the Road, and walked all the way to the Highway by ourselves,
collecting the good pinecones and leaving the stupid ones, carrying armloads, and—amazed at our newfound strength, our
endurance—we kept right on going toward Town. We weren't
afraid of the trucks that blew past us.

Gnashing their terrible teeth, I thought.

Showing their terrible claws, Tameka thought.

One of those truck drivers slowed down as he passed, waving a long white arm from his rolled-down window. "Hey, watch
it!" he called, but we waited until he was close enough to shoot
with a rifle in the head, and we did—with our trigger fingers,
bam—and screamed, "Be still!" We weren't worried about him
or his little white hand, waving, waving, waving at us from up
high. We knew where we were going. We knew in a way we
would not say to anyone, a way past explaining, a way like the
pike or the loons—who dove beneath the surface at the exact
same moment and appeared as tiny points on the far side of the
lake. One, two. We blew kisses at the deer. We threw pinecones
in the road.

We watched trucks swerve.

One of the big boys eventually showed up, yelling at us,
coming down the road behind on his bike. We liked how his
greasy black hair had blown back and made two funny bulges

over his ears, like the beginnings of antlers. Tameka and I laughed. He stopped when he neared us. He had a face like he was chewing something he couldn't get his lips around, and only later did I wonder what it must have been like to be fourteen in that crowd, all those shrieking little kids and whining hippie songs, and not an empty room anywhere, ever. There were always too many of us, too few beds and clean spoons, too few rolls of toilet paper.

What was his name? Did somebody send him after us?

What he didn't like was little girls laughing. He was pissed off and he made that clear to us, yelling, "Are you two crazy? Get the hell out of the road!" Then he paused, calmed himself. With two hands, he smoothed his baby antlers, one after the other, and drew his hair into a stubby ponytail. Then, at last, he got his mouth to say the thing he was supposed to say: "You're detracting from our overall positive experience." He sighed.

"We're lucky," Tameka reminded him, tapping her own lucky forehead. Twice.

"You're in deep dog doo," he corrected.

The year I was twenty-six, I totaled my car. I was heading back to Duluth after my father's funeral when I swerved around two deer and skidded into a stand of cedar. I bit open my lip on impact, but other than that I was fine. I was maybe two miles from my parents' cabin, three and a half miles to Loose River, and I kept trying my cell phone—even though coverage was spotty there, and even though I was pretty sure my service had been cut because I'd failed to pay my bill on time. I kept opening my phone and saying, *Please.* A few cars drove by, and every time one did I ducked down. I didn't want to have to go back to the cabin. I didn't want to have to explain to my mother why I was still around, so when those two deer came creeping from the woods again, when I saw them drop their heads to nibble shrubs, I retrieved my backpack from the trunk and headed off down the road.

It was three when I started walking, long past dark by the time I hit the first gas station. I went in the opposite direction of Loose River, aiming for Bearfin, which was eleven miles north.

At first as I walked I kept going through the numbers, making a dozen different plans to pay for the car repairs and the phone bill and the boots that—as I went—lost one of their heels. Then at some point I stopped making plans. Plans just stopped coming to me. The Bearfin mechanic who drove me back to look at my car offered $750 for parts on the spot. I took the cash, got a room at Motel 6, threw my phone in the river behind the parking lot, and bought a rusted used motorcycle the next morning. I called and quit my Duluth retail job from the garage pay phone. I didn't call my mom, who'd installed a landline by then. I let her think I was on my way back to Duluth.

It was six hours on the road to the Twin Cities, and the whole way I kept telling myself that I liked the Kawasaki, that I loved the speed. But I thought it would be more like driving the ATV, and I had to clench the handgrips at all times to keep from swerving from my lane. It was exhausting being a biker I realized. So in Saint Paul, I sold the bike to another mechanic, one with a pierced tongue and a pierced navel, which I found out about later because I started sleeping with him after I used the bike money to rent an apartment in Minneapolis. That felt good, taking the mechanic home to the studio apartment I shared with a roommate I found through a Starbucks posting. I liked sneaking him in, fucking him quickly and quietly on my futon

bed, seeing nothing in the dark, getting rid of him by morning. By morning, by seven, my roommate was always up doing
stretches, doing yoga before job interviews, improving herself.

Once during this period, I woke up to her singing as she
opened the curtains, and in my groggy state I called her Patra.
"Morning, Patra," I said, surprising myself. As if Patra were
not a proper name, but a feeling I'd once had—a lost feeling
come back, something not unlike happiness. My roommate,
Ann, who was from a Manitoba wheat farm, studiously ignored
this eccentricity along with all my other oddities, my snuck-in
boyfriend and empty closet. She'd recently gotten a tattoo of a
heart on her ankle, the most aggressive rebellion she could think
of against her Lutheran parents, and she sat on our carpet, still
humming as she cleaned her infected ankle with a folded baby
wipe. Only after she finished this task did she set the wipe in
the trash and look over at me again: "Good morning, *Linda*."

As if we hadn't gone through these same pleasantries five
minutes before, as if she could, with discipline, deal with my
distressing peculiarities the way you dealt with an unfortunate
accent or a child chewing her nails.

"Good morning, *Patra*," I said, to freak her out, to mess
with her a little.

Not long after I turned thirty-seven last fall, it occurred to me
that I could probably look up Patra online. I don't know why
this came to me after so many years, but once it did I spent
several hours tracking her down. She'd changed her last name so
she wasn't easy to find, but eventually I remembered that she'd
been called Cleo before I knew her. I found a Cleo McCarthy
who might have been Patra, though there was so little about her

available. Aside from all the old articles about the trial, which I didn't read, there was a current address in Tucson and a recipe submitted to a baking website for popcorn balls. *A little too sticky*, one reviewer said. Dissatisfied, I poked around the University of Chicago website for a while and eventually, finding nothing more, I decided to look up Tameka instead. I looked up Tameka and saw her life like she'd left it there for me to find, every step laid out in the kind of narrative detail you rarely find on the Internet. Tameka Luna Trevor graduated from Perpich Arts High School in Saint Paul, went to Wesleyan, became a probate attorney, married a pediatrician from Doctors Without Borders named Wayne. She had athletic twin daughters, photographed playing basketball in the Wesleyan alumni magazine. She bought a ranch house in Edina, Minnesota, an upscale suburb of Minneapolis, which was the home of the Hornets. Her house, pictured in realty shots before she bought it, was flanked by a man-made pond.

We'd know each other's thoughts just by being in the world together, she'd once said to me.

I was back here in Loose River when I thought to look her up. I had been taking care of my mother for years, had already subdivided the property to pay off debts. By then, Tameka had long since left our world. Or I had. I couldn't imagine even one of her thoughts.

On the Tuesday after Memorial Day, I arrived a few minutes early at Patra's house. The weekend's rain had subsided. All the out-of-towners had cleared out for the week, and the minute they were gone the temperature had shot up to eighty. That plus the rain brought out the first mosquitoes. They descended in any patch of shade. As I made my way down the highway after school, I tried to stay in the middle of the road, in the sun, to avoid them. I slapped at them as they floated in their doddering newborn way from the woods. I was wiping blood from the back of my hand when I spotted Patra at the end of her driveway.

She waved. She was wearing her U of C sweatshirt and her husband's big boots, untied.

"Hey," I greeted her, smiling.

She came across the gravel, eyebrows up, as if in prear-rangement of some agreement she wanted me to make with her. "Thanks so much again for your help this weekend."

"Sure," I said.

Then we just stood there. I could see mosquitoes thread-ing their way to us from the woods, and I wondered why Patra was out here on the road by herself, if she'd come to intercept me. I hoisted my backpack higher on my shoulder. "Um, I was thinking maybe Paul and I could try swimming today," I told her. "It might be warm enough."

"Oh, that would be wonderful. Yes. Thank you." Her most functional smile flashed into place. "But, actually. That's what I wanted to say. I think we'll be okay for a couple of days."

Without me, she meant.

I glanced at the house behind her with its pulled shades, its closed door, its sealed-log façade. All the good windows were on the other side, the direction that faced the lake. And all weekend, those windows had been black with sunlight (the days were get-ting long now), except for an hour or two in the evenings when Patra and the husband ate in dim lamplight. I hadn't seen any of them out on the deck for days. I wondered if they'd driven somewhere together—to the Forest Service Nature Center, or to Bearfin to return the rental car, or to the diner in town for a piece of chocolate mousse pie. I wondered if they'd gone as far as Whitewood, where there was a playground with two slides. A minigolf course. A movie theater.

Patra was still smiling intensely. "I mean, we'll be okay with both Leo and me around, for now. But thank you, Linda."

"Sure."

"I'll definitely call."

"Great." There had never been any way for her to call me.

Mosquitoes were all over Patra now, flickering at her hands and neck. She was waving at her ears. I stood still and let them get me if they wanted. I could feel a dozen or more probing the hair on my arms, and as they did I felt some measure of relief. It felt right, now, to give in to the mosquito feast, to do nothing to avoid them. "Tell Paul I say hi!" I said, pointing my cheerfulness straight at Patra. Aiming precisely. "Tell him I hope he's feeling better!"

Did a look of panic catch on her smile? Maybe I'm only remembering it that way now.

"Of course! Sure! He says hi, too!"

But when I turned to leave, Patra stopped me. She took a few clumsy steps forward, nearly tripping on her bootlaces. "Hey, Linda"—she touched my elbow—"there's something else."

I waited for her to say what it was. She was very close to me now, chewing her lip, sweating a little. "It's Drake." She brushed a mosquito from her eye, waved another from my neck. "Have you seen him?"

I thought of the white cat as I'd seen him last, Friday afternoon, meowing like an alarm clock at the sliding door.

"No," I said.

9

LESS THAN A WEEK LATER SCHOOL LET OUT. There were four long days of war movies to watch first—*Glory, Doctor Zhivago, M*A*S*H*—while teachers hunched in the dark back of the class and calculated grades. Lily's desk still sat empty. All the unclaimed items in the lost and found were confiscated by the student council for charity. All the goose shit was cleared off the football field for graduation ceremony, the bulletin boards in the halls stripped down to exposed pushpins, to itty-bitty holes in the cork. The last day of school began with someone pulling the fire alarm during homeroom, so we went out to the parking lot—and stood for ten minutes on the puddly concrete—then shambled back inside again. When the final bell rang that afternoon, the seniors flung their notebooks out the open windows one story up. We could hear them pushing back their chairs, thudding around. Everyone rushed from Life Science to join them, the freshman hockey players and the Karens, but I stayed put at my desk and watched all that paper come down outside. It fell surprisingly slowly, catching drafts. You could see exams and tests and notes and graphs. You could see years of education sailing down, whirling over parked cars and across Main, landing in gutters and papering fences.

When I stood up, there was just Ms. Lundgren left rewinding *Project X* on the VCR. "Have a good summer," she said, crouching in front of the TV console.

"Summer doesn't technically start for another two weeks," I told her.

"True," she acknowledged, glancing up. "Have a good spring, then."

The days gaped open after that. No school, no job, daylight going on and on like it would never quit. I cleaned two perfect northern pike and did the north-forty wood the first day, then I dithered about in the boat for a few more, catching crappie near the beaver dam. I filled the net without trying, sorted all the tackle one morning, took a comb to the dogs and teased out the mats left over from their winter coats. One afternoon I walked the five miles into town and bought toothpaste and toilet paper from the drugstore. My mom gave me a rubber-banded roll of ones for this purpose, and afterward I went to the bank, where I filled out a pink slip at the counter and withdrew two twenty-dollar bills. The woman at the counter asked if that was how I wanted it, and I said yes. At the market, I splurged on a bag of hard green pears for my mom ("Argentina," the label said) and a jar of Skippy for my dad. Then I went into Bob's Bait and Tackle, lifting glittering lures from his bins, unhooking them from my sleeves, leaving with nothing. I paused outside in the sun. After a long moment, I pushed open the door of the diner, where I bought a pack of grape Bubble Yum from Santa Anna before I could ask to bum a cigarette. I stuffed gum into my mouth as I started home, chewing until my jaw hurt.

Twilight and more twilight. By then the stars were already doing their summer bit, the Summer Triangle sliding north, as well as Scorpius, with its splay of pincers and curled hook. After dinner I sometimes took the canoe out and lingered until dark—especially on overcast nights, especially after nine, when twilight finally halved, and then halved again, sliding the sky through epochs of orange, then epochs of blue and purple. Then epochs of violet. The days just never seemed to get done. I huddled low in the boat and listened to the water tut at the hull. Sometimes, at last, a lamp would go on inside the Gardner house. I'd see Patra through the window at the counter, Leo with his arm around her, and not much more. With Leo home, Patra went to bed earlier. With Leo home, Paul didn't spend time anymore on the deck or the dock, though the water had warmed up enough to go swimming.

I tested it out one evening after the Gardners' lights went dark. I wadded up my T-shirt and jeans and underpants in the boat, then slipped into the water so fast it was like being gulped. Stirred-up rotten algae from the bottom of the lake congealed around my left leg. I kicked away from the canoe and floated, dismally, on my back, my tiny hard nipples pointing up at Scorpius. Scorpius pointed back at me. I was bright white from six months of winter: my chin and nipples and kneecaps all floated atop the water. After a moment, the moon slunk out from under a cloud, sprouted a tail of light across the lake. It wouldn't have been hard to look out any window in the house and see me. I was right there to be seen.

The mucousy thickness of the water slid beneath me—how many years of summers had I lain on this lake? I felt the exact indentation in the water my body made, skinny girl-print, and after bobbing for a moment on the surface I took a deep breath

and dove down. I moved through warmer and cooler columns
of water, kicking hard, finding the silky cold mud at the bottom
with my hands. I thought of Mr. Grierson in the diner again. I
could see Lily with him one minute, but not the next. I could
see the black back of her head over the vinyl booth, Mr. Grierson
looking across at her. But then it was only Mr. Grierson alone
with his book, with his paper napkin and eggs. Outside the
diner windows, snow had been falling. The fluorescent lights had
been buzzing, the coffee machine clucking away. At the bottom
of the lake the water grew colder, and I put Lily in that booth
and I made him beg her. *Don't tell, don't tell.* I felt the shiver of
air bubbles I'd created, beetling up around my arms and legs.
I felt them rising from the roots of my hair. Then, after a dark
interval, my body followed.

Teeth chattering in the canoe, I got dressed again. I paddled
across the lake, washed the muck from my feet with a splash of
well water, climbed the ladder to the loft over my parents' bedroom, and masturbated, miserably, my wiry pubic hair catching
between my fingers. I slept soundly then. By morning, order had
come back to the woods. The rising sun had set down predictable shadows, long and straight as bars. All that remained of the
night before was the damp underside of my braid, a miniscule
fleck of algae on my thigh.

You know how summer goes. You yearn for it and yearn for
it, but there's always something wrong. Everywhere you look,
there are insects thickening the air, and birds rifling trees, and
enormous, heavy leaves dragging down branches. You want to
trammel it, wreck it, smash things down. The afternoons are so
fat and long. You want to see if anything you do matters.

*   *   *

One day, maybe a couple weeks after school let out, I went to check the Juneberries along the lake path to see when they'd be ready to pick. I wanted to get to them before the summer people did, before the bushes were stripped bare by half-assed day-trippers. I'd been walking around for about an hour, finding no good berries, when I heard the sound of a gunned motor coming down the old boat-launch path toward the lake. There was a long, anxious rustling in the trees. I stopped, waited to yell at whoever it was for going off road and trashing the wilderness. But it wasn't a tourist. It was my dad who appeared in a cloud of dust and leaves. He was riding the ATV he'd traded the dog sled for last spring, and he lifted an orange-gloved hand as he approached. Hello. He was in shirtsleeves and his face was bright red. Sweat flowered in dirty lines around his neck.

"Hey, kid," he said, releasing the throttle.

I humphed at him. Got on.

Though half the time that summer that ATV didn't work at all, half the time it *did*, and for ten minutes that afternoon, I sat behind him on the hard leather seat as we rumbled along the overgrown trail destroying everything we touched—smashing ferns and goldenrod and baby white pine and sumac fronds—and it was wretched, and it was so delicious, too.

The next afternoon, after the fish cooler was restocked, after the last of the spring's blowdown was chopped and stacked, I decided to take the dogs out in the woods. I'd been busy after school for months, so it had been a while since I'd gone very far with them. Jasper and Doctor sprinted ahead, pouncing on every trembling leaf and fern. Abe and Quiet—both almost as old as I was—were slower and more selective in their chases. I took them up the ravine, where I'd taken Paul all spring, and the younger dogs leapt clean over logs and boulders. The older dogs hopped up and off. I lingered atop, looked around. All around me, dogs were rolling and sniffing, squatting and urinating, scarfing down scat. Their pleasure at being off their chains gave me an ache in the chest. It was so simple to please them.

But even the older dogs in early summer could be unpredictable. By the time we'd walked for an hour, they were disappearing in the woods for longer and longer periods. Tearing off after a scent, coming back for a pat, going farther, taking risks. Before long, even old gray-muzzled Abe had found a squirrel to tree. For long stretches, I could only hear the scuffling of leaves. Time after time, I thought about shouting after them, calling them back. And time after time, they returned on their own in twos and threes, tongues lolling, grazing their wet noses against my knuckles.

Once, they were gone for more than five minutes. Long enough for the woods to return to its predog state, for birds to settle again on branches. Then all four came thundering back at once as if they'd made a plan of it, as if they'd organized at last into a real wolf pack, and I saw they were chasing something small and white. The creature shot up a spindly birch and bent it down double, silver leaves dropping in a *pat-pat-pat*.

"Oh, Drake," I said. The bristling cat hissed from its branch. "How did the world go for you, then?"

The world, it appeared, was going crazy below, all four dogs leaping and nipping. I shushed them with a few choice words. There was nothing for me to do but shimmy up a rock beside the tree and retrieve the cat. He arched up when I grabbed for him, but then twenty claws sank like twenty hooks into my neck and shoulders. It wasn't so bad being caught like that. My hands around Drake's scrawny chest, I slid from the boulder and started walking. The dogs followed behind. They spun circles of ecstasy, panted miserably, did their endless orbits of triumph.

So when I knocked on the Gardners' door, there we all were. Four panting dogs, one freaked-out cat, Patra looking a little shocked, and me—trying to keep from grinning.

"Found him," I said.

I turned and, tightening one elbow around Drake, lowered my other hand to the dogs. They lay down on the gravel, reluctant but happy now, because they thought this meant the cat was theirs. "Stay," I said, feeling like some mini-god, some deity of dogs. I wanted Patra to see this, the control I had.

Then I slipped past her with the cat and went in.

10

THE INTERIOR OF THE CABIN WAS DARKER THAN USUAL.
The summer foliage was out in full and shaded all the west
windows. Though it was midafternoon, there wasn't a patch
of direct sunlight in the main room, so it took me a moment
to see Leo in the easy chair in the corner, and a moment more
to see Paul there, too, on his lap. Leo's chin was balanced on
Paul's head. Paul was wrapped in a quilt, his orange-blond
hair parted over each of his eyes. Something about those two
inverted Vs of hair exaggerated an especially childish look Paul
had. Had he always been so young? Nestled in the quilt on
his father's lap, he looked barely past toddlerhood, barely past
being a baby.

Patra moved behind me, closing the door. At that, Drake
wrestled free from my arms. No one said anything as the cat
crept, ears back, around the couch, then flattened and disappeared underneath. With Drake gone, with the door closed,
the room fell into a hush. That was Leo, I could tell. That was
his influence.

"Well, thank you, Linda," he said.

And Patra from behind: "That's a relief—isn't it, hon?" To
me: "That's such a relief."

She wasn't whispering exactly. She was just speaking carefully. She was wearing the same thing as when I'd seen her last, her U of C sweatshirt and leggings. In one hand was a browning apple slice, which she set so tenderly in the trash it was like she was finding it a nest. "Want a glass of water or something, Linda? Want some juice?"

In his cocoon of blankets, Paul said, "Some juice?"

I looked over at him again. "Is he still sick?"

I learned in that moment that this was not a question I was allowed to ask. From his chair, Leo frowned up at me, as if I'd said something rude or inept. Paul, as if prompted to mimicry without even having seen his father's face, frowned too. They really looked nothing alike. Paul was round faced and blond haired, like Patra. Leo the astronomer was gaunt and gray haired, bushy browed. His thick moustache made him look somehow like a man from another century. He wore glasses, which had slipped to the tip of his nose and made him seem, though he was sitting, like he was looking down from a perch. He wore black slippers. His khaki pants were rolled up once at each cuff.

Patra put her hand on my arm, a gesture that might have been a friendly warning. "Paul's *fine*," she said.

Leo nodded. "He's had a demonstration, in fact. Right, kiddo?"

There was that word again, with its curious ring of accomplishment. But before I could wonder about it out loud, Paul was pulling one arm out from under the quilt and waving it in my direction. His arm was buried to the elbow in the leather glove, which he moved like a puppet. "We're going to see the tall ships tomorrow," he said.

"The tall ships?" I asked, confused.

"You know those old-fashioned boats with the sails?" Patra asked.

"The maritime festival in Duluth?" Leo added.

Patra continued, "We thought we'd do a little trip. We thought a trip to Duluth would be nice. A change of pace, right? Have you been, Linda?"

"To Duluth?" I hadn't, but I didn't want to admit that.

"To see the tall ships?"

That was an easier question to answer. "No."

Later, in preparation for the trial, they kept asking why I didn't pose more questions from the beginning. What was your first impression of Dr. Leonard Gardner? How would you describe the couple as parents? What kind of care, exactly, did they provide? It was hard to explain that I didn't ask questions because they were both only exceptionally, almost excruciatingly, kind. When Paul started talking with such excitement about the tall ships, Patra came over with a glass of amber-colored juice and kneeled in front of him. He slurped down the juice within seconds, handed the glass back to her. But she did not stand just yet she lay her head down on his quilted lap. Leo stroked her hair and Paul did, too, with his one gloved hand. I felt ashamed to see this, and at the same time I couldn't take my eyes off them. I could do nothing but stand there silently, tracing the rough cat scratches on my arms. Finally one of them murmured something, and Patra scooped up Paul, carried him off into the bedroom. I went into the kitchen and found a pot in the drainer, which I filled to the brim with water for the dogs. As I was doing this, Leo stood up too. I could hear his knees cracking from across the room.

He walked silently, though. He moved on padded soles across rugs.

Not a single window was open, though it was hot this time of day and very humid. There was a strong smell in the house I hadn't noticed a week back, when I'd been there last. It was not a bad smell, just intimate and particular—faintly sweet, full of unexceptional secrets: ripe fruit, kitty litter, laundry detergent, maybe the slightest whiff of sewage from the bathroom. Leo made his way toward the kitchen, sat at the table, and asked a few distracted questions about my family. "Twenty acres along the east shore," I said, when he asked about the range of our lot. "They're mostly retired," I hedged, when he asked what my parents did for a living.

"Good for them!" he said, cheerlessly. Tucking a piece of graying hair behind his ear, like a girl.

At the trial, the prosecution asked, did you ask any questions in return?

The prosecution asked, weren't you curious about *him*?

I was and I wasn't. It was hard to explain how ingrained a habit it was to pretend I understood what was happening in other people's lives before explanations were offered. How I took in information differently, how carefully I watched Leo pour a glass of apple juice for himself and swirl it around without taking a sip. I watched as he set the glass down on a magazine, as he lifted the juice container Patra had left behind and wiped the sweat from the bottom with his sleeve. I learned fast that he was finicky and earnest, his mind was not the marvel Patra had made it out to be, but exceptionally well organized, exceptionally disciplined. He could make small talk with me about my parents, ask a reasonable series of questions, without seeming to take in my answers. The pattern of the conversation, the rhythm of small talk he knew by heart   better than that, even. He put me on guard, without seeming very interested, without ever giving away his true aim.

"Do you have many siblings, then?"

"None."

"But you're fond of children?"

"Well—"

"*Some*, surely." He raised his eyebrows, offering the correction to me. Then he smiled. As he did, his moustache changed shape, spread out across his face. "Paul says you've taught him to eat grasshoppers."

"Ummm."

"He's grown attached to you it seems."

"He's gotten used to me," I said.

"You're being modest."

I shrugged. "He doesn't really have a lot of options."

"He's a pretty particular kid." Leo swirled the juice around in his glass. "And Patra says you've been a big help to her, too. She says she can't imagine what she would have done— "

I waited for him to finish that thought, but he was finally drinking his juice, drawing it down in restrained swallows. As his throat worked he seemed to be turning something over in his head. "How about this?" He set his glass down. "Why don't you come with us this weekend to Duluth. It would be nice for Paul, and it might even give Patra and me a chance to have dinner out or something. I think she might need a little break. What do you think?"

By the time I went out with the soup pot of water, not even old Abe was waiting for me on the driveway. I'd been inside for more than twenty minutes. I'm not sure what made me think the dogs would just stay. I placed the pot on the front step for Patra to find and headed for the shore trail. I didn't bother to go back inside to say good-bye. I'd already made arrangements with Leo for the morning, and home was an hour away. Even in the shade of the dense pines, the day was hot, so by the time I got back, I could feel sweat on my neck and in the wet patches of T-shirt beneath my armpits. My mother came out of the house wearing a smock that was smeared black with dirt. She was twisting a bud of loose skin on her elbow.

"Oh, here comes Madeline! Oh, she decides to come back!"

"They're here?" I asked.

But I could see the dogs for myself, chained to their stakes by the shed. They were standing up stiffly as I approached. Four bushy tails wagged low and fast.

"You know how traffic is on the 10 in June, don't you?" She squinted at me, let go of her elbow. "It's lucky none of them got hit. What happened that you lost control of all of them at once?"

I was about to tell her about Drake—about rescuing the cat and returning him safe—but when I opened my mouth something else came out. "I was having a little adventure, *Mom*." I watched her brown eyes squint at me. "And this is part of it, actually, but it's the boring part between the exciting bits, where the girl does the same predictable dialogue with her mother."

I got down on my haunches and roughed up Abe's neck. I heard my mom go inside—a single flap of the tarp—and guilt swooped over me and away, like one of those birds of prey blacking the sun for an instant. Then I was just angry at the dogs, which felt better. I could see that their legs were covered in thistles and burrs. Their coats had dried in front with spikes of mud. "You're getting wild," I told them. Which was true I felt.

I waited until I was done drying the dishes that night before I told my mother I was going with the family across the lake to Duluth for the weekend. "Tell your dad," she said to that, giving me a look I couldn't read. So I went out to the shed after the dishes were put away and sat with my dad for an hour listening to a ball game on the radio. Twins versus Royals. As we sat together on overturned buckets, my father drank three Buds, methodically, measuring each sip, making them last to the final inning. Then he crushed the cans into disks, one after the other, as the announcers described the weather in Kansas City, the heat wave that was followed by a thunderstorm, which had knocked out so much power they'd almost canceled the game. Almost, but not quite.

I told my dad about going to Duluth just as he was standing up.

He nodded, turned off the radio, and then pulled one more dripping can of beer from the cold lake water inside the cooler. As if reconsidering his prospects for the evening, as if changing his mind about something. "That front'll be coming east by tomorrow night."

"I know."

"I thought we might get some walleye up in Goose Neck tomorrow."

"I know."

"The out-of-towners will be taking over soon."

"I know."

"Superior sure is pretty in a storm, though. Have you seen that?"

Never.

They picked me up at ten the next morning. I'd thought a long time about what to bring the night before, had laid out my second pair of jeans and rooted through my mom's thrift-store bag for something besides an old T-shirt to sleep in. I found a baby-blue slip my mom had collected for scraps, and though it was musty and wrinkled and too big in the chest, I thought it might pass for pajamas. I'd also packed my toothbrush and comb, and right before bed—pumping well water in the dark—I tried shaving with my dad's razor. The hair on my legs was fine and long, and the first stripe that was gone felt magical beneath my fingertips, a track of shorn skin like silk ribbon from ankle to thigh. I'd finished most of the first leg before I realized there was blood from a cut I hadn't seen or felt in the dark. I could tell it was blood from the greasy way it slid between my fingertips, and how it smelled. I was too disheartened to do the second leg. Instead, shivering, I washed my hair with the last of the shampoo and a little bit of lemon dish soap. I rinsed caked mud from the soles of my tennis shoes and set them near the outhouse to dry. Peed in that plywood hole, closed the door on the flies. I squeezed out the wet rope of hair that hung on my chest.

When I slipped into the backseat of the blue Honda the next morning, Paul was asleep in his car seat. As Leo did a three-point turn, Patra twisted around and whispered from the front, "Good morning!" She handed me a bran muffin, still warm, crumbling as I peeled open its waxed paper cup. "Mmm. You smell good," she added.

My mouth was already full of muffin. The moist crumbs filled up every bit of space between my teeth and tongue, every empty place available.

Patra grinned. "Good, eat up. Leo never likes to stop. He'll drive straight through anything. Tornadoes, floods. Breakfast and lunch."

"I stop! When we get there. Just say where 'there' is, in advance, and I'll stop."

"Then 'there' is lunch. 'There' is sometime before two o'clock."

"That's when there is, then. It's agreed."

Once we got to the highway, all the familiar points disappeared within minutes. I saw the lake in flashes between the trees, blue gray showing through cracks of green. In Loose River, we drove past the high school just when the sun broke over the tallest roadside trees, turning every surface into a flat knife of light. Stop signs and windows flared as we drove past them. Leo and Patra both wore dark sunglasses, but I just squinted, feeling dizzy and excited. Then we were on the interstate, going seventy, and Leo and Patra were talking quietly about something I couldn't quite hear. I wanted to roll down the window, feel the speed on my face, but I held back.

Late morning, Paul woke up sluggishly stretching. I gave him one of Patra's bran muffins, which he held between his knees but didn't eat. His eyes were slowly unpinking. "Are we there?" he asked. "Hmm mmm," I said. Outside, the pine forest was unstitching, opening into aspen groves and grassy farms dotted with hay bales. We played a halfhearted game of Rock, Paper, Scissors. We played I Spy with My Little Eye. At one point I

said, "I spy a purple water tower," so Paul craned his neck to
look out his window. His pale, sleepy face had a sunken look.
"I don't *see* it," he complained, setting his forehead against the
window. "Let's do *mental* I Spy."

"Okay."

He closed his eyes and spied his own purple water tower.
He spied his own iron-ore train and Mars. After that, there was a
long, indecipherable silence—while Patra fiddled with a car vent,
while Leo drove through a brief rain shower—and somewhere
just past the last farm it occurred to me that Paul had dozed off
again. I couldn't blame him. The car was warm and rumbling.
Quietly, I ate Paul's muffin and watched the pine come back,
rising up along the roadside in a long corridor of green.

We hit construction outside Duluth. After an hour of sitting in traffic and dust, windows up, Leo pulled off the highway
for lunch. "See?" he said to Patra. "I stop." We ate at Denny's,
where I opened the huge glossy menu and ordered—after long
deliberation—soup. I was nervous about chewing, about cutting up my food with a fork and a knife. Leo sat with Patra on
one side of the booth, and I sat with Paul on the other. Patra
guffawed when my French onion soup arrived in a bread bowl
as big as my head. Warily, I prodded the thick boat of cheese
that floated atop the brown broth. All around the restaurant,
there were other families like ours, booths with two parents on
one side and two kids on the other. Paul gulped down his glass
of milk, so Patra ordered a second, shaking her head, laughing
at me as I struggled with my soup.

"Want a bite?" I asked, when she finally reached out and
plucked the string of cheese that webbed from my bowl to my
mouth.

She wrinkled up her nose, bringing the freckles together into a brown smudge. "Who could manage to eat that without looking like a—a baby bird or something?"

"A baby bird?"

She smiled. "Sucking up worms."

Leo was a more focused eater, tucking his BLT into his mouth in careful sections. But once he was finished, he turned to me, wiping his moustache with a folded napkin, and within three minutes had asked me more questions than Patra had in three months. I let my soup cool as he spoke. I licked the salty spoon, but did not attempt another bite of the cheese. It suddenly seemed too treacherous.

"What grade will you be in then, Linda?"

"Tenth," I said. The question felt like a rebuke—of the way I ate my soup, of my childishness.

Leo pushed his plate to the edge of the table. "What college are you considering?"

"College?"

"Or, well, what subject do you like most?" He crossed his arms on the table.

"History." I couldn't, at the moment, think of anything else.

"Ah. American or European? What historical period do you like?"

"The history of *wolves*," I said, but the minute the answer was out, it sounded foolish. I sipped the tiniest bit of broth from my spoon.

"You mean natural history?"

"Yep."

"So biology actually?"

"Biology, I guess."

His two elbows scooted forward, bumping his empty plate. "I had to take some molecular biology courses in graduate school. In my line of work, everyone is always looking for extraterrestrials, as if the universe matters only when endowed with a narrowly carbon-based definition of life."

"In the Goldilocks zone," I tried. Repeating what Paul had said—Paul, who'd just left to go to the bathroom clasping Patra's hand.

"That's right," he said, surprised. He folded his hands on the table, and you could see the straight planes on his fingernails where he'd cut them. "I'm not saying the molecular biologists are *wrong*," he went on. "That's not exactly what I'm saying. But I'm a scientist, too, and I think those folks tend to hone in on an extremely limited set of questions."

He had a way of watching me very closely, and not seeming to watch me at all. He was a teacher, of course, probably a good one. He was one of those teachers who set up hidden traps. Like all teachers, he wanted me caught, but he wanted to lead me there first; he wanted me to go on my own accord; he wanted me to feel like I'd made the discovery myself, that I hadn't been lured in.

His chin was in his palm. "Let's do a thought experiment."

My parka slithered off my lap.

"A scientist always starts with premises, right?" He twisted the wedding band on his finger. "But so often they start with unsound premises and go awry, like the world is flat, or the human body is made up of four basic humors."

I wanted to reach for my parka, but resisted.

"But of course we've learned that if you want to be a real scientist, Linda, you have to be more rigorous than that. You have to figure out what your premises are first, before you decide what's true. A good biologist should always start by asking, for instance, what are the conditions we assume are required for life? And why do we assume that and not something else?"

It seemed to be my turn to speak. He was waiting. "You mean—"

"I mean, you have to ask yourself, from the beginning, what do you *think* you know?"

The twenty acres of land on the east side of Still Lake. That's what I knew. That's the one thing I'd always assumed I'd understand. I knew the red and white pine on the hilltop, the quaking aspen and birch closer to shore. I knew the honeysuckle and chipmunks and sunset views of the lake that weren't worth very much in the end to developers. When I had to sell off pieces of the lot at last, I got less than sixty grand, even though the market wasn't bad. We only ever had the ten feet of pebbly sand to beach our canoes. The old commune bunkhouse—under a collapsed pine by the road—had long since returned to woods. For years my dad had pilfered its decent boards to patch his shed, fence the garden, repair the outhouse. The cabin was more substantial than the other buildings at least, with its stone foundation and old-growth logs clear-cut in the twenties. We had a rocky meadow behind the cabin and, in summer, a working garden, my mom's lettuce and potato plants enclosed in rusty globes of chicken wire. We had a cinder block smokehouse and a good well. But the acres of woods were what I knew best, the big trees with their stippled trunks, red pine bark coming off in plates, white pine gouged by age into yawning furrows. We had six perfect black ash. We had one massive cottonwood. We had sumac blanketing the roadside hill, encroaching on the garden, arching over the dirt drive, until the county required that we widen the road and we cut most of it down.

Our hotel rooms in Duluth had bay windows and views of the lift bridge and the harbor, green hills rising up behind. The carpets and walls were a uniform white, and in each room a red silk poppy stood in a vase on a lacquered desk. A mirrored bathroom connected our two rooms, with columns of creamy towels and soaps wrapped like candy bars.

I didn't have anything to unpack. Instead, I climbed with my backpack onto one of the high, soft beds and watched as Leo and Patra moved between rooms unzipping bags. They were searching for Paul's socks, for his panda puzzle and hat, and as they did I found my gaze drifting to a book on the bedside table. *The Big Fitz* it was called. A hotel book. I pulled its cool weight onto my lap, began reading about the taconite ship that sank in 1975. For a half hour, I turned the book's slick pages, studied black-and-white photos of the ship rising up from the waves, and its eroded lifeboats recovered years later. I was especially interested in a huge diagram of the broken ship, the bow shown upright and turned the other way from the facedown stern.

A lamp clicked on—the afternoon was darkening. I could hear Lake Superior lapping the shore outside, enticing, so I slid off the bed and moved across the room to where Patra was transferring yogurts from her cooler bag into the minifridge. I convinced her to let me take Paul for a walk by promising to be back before five thirty.

"Five fifteen," I revised, when I saw her glancing anxiously at the clouds out the window.

"Let me get his jacket on, though," she nodded. "Let me zip him up in case it rains. Let me get his hat."

Behind the hotel parking lot, I found a rickety wooden staircase that led down the steep, barren bank to the water. As Paul and I descended, step by step, I could see brown waves dragging stones in and out of the rocky cove. Gulls hung overhead. At the shore, lake water misted our knuckles each time a big wave broke. I tried teaching Paul to skip stones, but he just lobbed them in so they sank. "Like this," I said, curving my wrist and sending one out. Watching it bounce on the water four times. Five. Six. Farther out, away from shore, Lake Superior was a deep blue, almost black near the horizon. The Wisconsin side of the lake was hard to see. My dad was right. Night was arriving early because a thunderhead was advancing to the south. There was the trawl of stones and then a hiss, as a wave withdrew between the tiny pebbles on the shore and another one came in. Paul had his hands in his jacket sleeves, and even so he was trembling. His face was drawn and gray, the color of carp. It occurred to me then, as the waves picked up, that I hadn't really looked at him since morning. He'd been sleeping in the car. And when he was awake, he'd been turned into something of a pet by Leo, who'd carried him around, who'd talked over his head, who'd given him Lego bricks to play with.

I bent down and looked at him. "Everything okay?"

"Everything okay," he repeated.

"We should go in?"

"We should go in," he said. His breath against my face smelled fruity, sweet.

*   *   *

Inside again, Patra fed us dinner. She'd ordered room service for two, grilled cheese sandwiches and chocolate milkshakes with bent red straws. Each of our rooms had a pair of queen-size beds, so there was a football field of bedclothes between us, a dozen blood-red pillows, bowls of peppermints in plastic twists on the nightstand. I sucked my shake in bed and watched the Weather Channel on the big-screen TV, the storm front a pixelating haze passing to the south. It would just miss us I saw, with the tiniest jab of dismay. Patra lay in the bed opposite, Paul snuggled in her arms. Eventually, Leo came in from the other room and tapped his bare wrist with a crooked finger. They had a reservation at the hotel restaurant downstairs, so when Patra glanced over at me—beached on my private shore of blankets and pillows, across the room—I whispered, "Go." *Thank you*, she mouthed. She kissed Paul, tugged at her drooping socks, and left the room.

A moment later, Leo poked his head back in and said, "We'll be right downstairs if you need something."

As if I didn't already know that.

I crawled off the bed and crossed the room to where Paul was dozing. Brushed crumbs from his covers, clicked off the lamp. Then I went into the bathroom and scratched open one of the tiny bars of soap with my fingernails. I didn't know how much time I'd have before they returned, so I didn't risk taking a bath—though I was tempted. Instead I stood under scalding water in the shower for one magnificent minute, letting needles of water pluck open some feeling of woe, some feeling of desolation I hadn't known I'd felt. A capsized feeling, a sense of the next thing already coming. I toweled off, wriggled into the cool thrift-store slip. I couldn't see myself in the mirror for the steam. I couldn't make out whether I looked more like a little kid trying too hard or a teenage girl with secret worries, like boys and college. Back in the bedroom, Paul was sleeping with his mouth open. I arranged my limbs on my own bed so they were splayed out, exposed. After a moment, I changed my mind and put my legs in a coil, and I waited for Patra to find me like that. Curled up in my nightie, facing the wall. Unconcerned about anything.

I didn't sleep of course. I listened to the unfamiliar sound of traffic on the road, and real waves, Superior surf crashing into real Superior boulders. I could hear the squeals of girls at the bar across the parking lot, and the elevator humming up and down through the walls. When Leo and Patra returned at last, they left the lights off, so I never knew for sure if they looked in on us. The cool slip barely covered my thighs, and I was shivering by the time I heard a thump in the other room, followed by a stiff muffled cry. My newly shaved leg scratched with goose pimples. It felt like someone else's prickly leg in bed with me when I brushed against it with my hand. "Ah!" someone said through the walls.

That's when I slid from the bed and crept through the bathroom in my bare feet. I nudged open the far door, waited, then looked in through the crack.

It was dark, but the window blinds were open. A streetlight was shining in. At first I saw Leo all alone on the bed, sitting up at one end and looking out the window—as if waiting for some signal, some comet or celestial appearance in the darkness of the heavens over the city. Then I saw Patra on her knees on the floor in front of him, Leo's hand on her head, and so I thought of Lily and Mr. Grierson. They morphed there in the

dark as I watched them. They were Lily and Patra, and Leo and
Mr. Grierson at once. They were husband and wife, they were
student and teacher—they were frightened bully and beautiful
Lily. They were both. She looked so small on her knees on the
floor, hunched over his lap. She gasped when she raised her head.
"Come on, please," she panted, so I might have gone in, I might
have interrupted them, if I hadn't seen him push her head away,
gently, the way you push an overly affectionate dog. If I hadn't
heard her say to him, just as gently, "Stop being a baby, Leo."
She was playfully mean: "Relax. I know you like that."

I found out later that Lily had left town in May to testify at Mr.
Grierson's trial. She'd gone to Minneapolis, where there was a
federal court, but when she got on the stand, when the prosecut-
ing attorney prompted her to tell the story about Gone Lake,
Lily finally confessed she didn't know Mr. Grierson very well at
all. She confessed she'd never spoken to him alone, except for
once, when he'd given her extra time on an exam because of her
dyslexia. According to court documents, the attorney pressed her
on this. "Didn't he take you out on the lake?" the attorney asked.
"Didn't you say that in your original statement?" He was flustered,
no doubt, and had little patience for a victim who was going to
take it all back at the last moment. He tried to convince her that
she was afraid, that she was lying now, on the stand. He asked
the judge, "Why would she say what she did if it wasn't true?"

Lily didn't answer that. It was a rhetorical question for the
judge to consider, not her.

Here's the statement Mr. Grierson made in his plea bargain:
"I have done many, many things. Let me start again. I can't face
my own thoughts. They are not thoughts I want to face, and it's

Just a relief—how do I put it? It's just a relief to have what I've feared the most said out loud. I'm ashamed, no argument. But I'm relieved, okay? I didn't touch that girl, but I thought about it, I thought about it, I thought about it, I thought about it. I thought out worse things than she said."

In the morning when I woke up, Paul was gone. The door to the bathroom was shut tight. I slunk out of the slip and into my jeans and shirt, opened the bathroom door. Saw through the tile-and-mirror corridor to where Leo sat in a cushioned chair in the other room.

"Good morning," he said, glancing up from a book.

"What are you reading?" I asked. To stall, to give me a chance to look around. I saw Patra's open suitcase on the closer of the two beds. The white strap of a bra draped out, along with the mauve sleeve of a sweater.

"*Science and Health*."

"Is that for your research?"

"No. Well, yes, in a way." As he spoke, I moved deeper into the room. I thought Patra and Paul might be huddled over a puzzle in the corner. They were not. Leo watched me eyeing the beds, eyeing the door, eyeing the suitcase. "Linda," he said, "do you believe in God?"

I looked back at him.

"Just a question. Did you think at all about what we discussed yesterday? I'm especially curious about that. What is it you believe—that is, assume—to be true about your existence? That's the question to start with, of course. What are your premises of self?"

"I don't know."

"You do."

I crossed my arms.

"You *do*. That's the definition of an assumption. For instance," he coaxed, "are you an animal or a human?" His legs were crossed, and he was jiggling one foot. He was wearing his black slippers, I saw, so he was the kind of man who packed slippers for a night in a hotel. He was a man who couldn't be without slippers, which made me sad and maybe a little repulsed by him. "Or do you take for granted that you have a body? What age do you think that body is?"

One slipper dangled. "Fifteen."

The slipper fell to the ground and he scooped it back on with a snout-like toe. "So then you assume your life began fifteen years ago and that it will end at some unknown point?"

"I guess."

"You assume that is a biological fact?"

I nodded, then shook my head—unsure what he was getting at.

"Now ask yourself, how do these assumptions about yourself change if you take as your premise that there is a God?"

His slippered foot stopped jiggling. He'd gotten back around to where he started and could afford to linger. "A thought experiment. Okay? It's just logic," he murmured. "If God exists, then what kind of God makes the most sense? Either God is all good, or he is not God. Either God is all-powerful, or he is not God. So logically, if God exists at all, then by definition He must be all good and He must be all-powerful. Right? That makes sense, doesn't it? That makes the most sense."

It did for an instant. A gap slowly opened between his slipper and his heel.

He pressed on. "And if we're saying that God exists—if, that is, God is by definition *God*—then there would be no place in the universe for evil, for sickness, for sadness, for death. There is only one premise that even makes God possible. So we've reasoned our way to the only possible answer. If, in the thought experiment God exists, then how would that premise change what you assume about yourself?"

"Where's Patra and Paul?"

"They're fine. What's the most reasonable answer to the question, Linda?"

"Where are they?"

"We'll meet them at the harbor at ten. Let's get back to the question—"

"Did something"—I took a step forward—"did something happen?"

"Lin-da." He parted the syllables very slightly, as with a comb. He pushed up his glasses with a touch of testiness. "Maybe we'll have to talk more about this another time? That's fine. Maybe we should start thinking about getting ready to go?" When I didn't move, he went on. "Patra tells me you're very mature, Linda, a good listener."

I watched him.

"Good company, she's always saying, and smart. But alone a lot, and I've seen that. I know that can't be easy. I know how it can make a person, a *young woman*, clingy."

I felt my face getting hot, but I didn't say anything.

"Lin-da." He spoke so kindly, now, so benignly and intensely at once. "You'll see, I think you'll see, that when you start with the premise we discussed—if you're intellectually honest and as smart as Patra says—you'll see that everything you think you know about your existence is wrong." His brown eyes did a mild blink behind glass. "You're not lonely, really."

My neck tensed up. "You know, Patra told me something about you as well."

"Is that so?" He was only somewhat interested.

"She said you're so busy with your work—" My voice slipped on a wet spot in my throat. I steadied it back into words. "She said you're gone so much that you hardly exist to her at all."

He frowned. "She didn't say that."

"Don't be dense." And because that wasn't quite enough to faze him, I sucked in a breath. "*Don't be a baby, Leo.*"

That made his eyes widen slightly. That made him stand up fast, jiggle his pockets for keys, walk across the room to the closet. He wouldn't meet my eye after that. He just mumbled, "Let's not be late, Linda. They took the car, so we need to walk." When I still didn't move, he said, more insistently, "We'll meet them at ten, okay? That's about fifty minutes from now, tops."

It was irritating how he was closing the door on me before I was even out of the room. It was infuriating the way he kept skipping over *now* for *then*—his insistence I be reassured by Paul and Patra's appearance at the harbor at ten, almost an hour after I asked about them.

But there they were, on a great wrinkled blanket on the grass, and I couldn't help it.

I was reassured.

11

THE WET GRASS IN THE HARBOR WAS TENTACLED IN SHAD-
OWS FROM THE PASSING SHIPS. Paul and Patra sat sprawled
on a blue cotton blanket with their legs open and palms back,
looking up at the ships as they went past.

Leo and I were late by mere minutes, so we didn't see the
lift bridge lift. But we heard it clanging its warning across the
harbor, and we saw the line of traffic backed up for blocks on
Lake Avenue. By the time we wound our way through the thick
crowd, by the time we made it to the knoll beneath the bridge,
the first of the ships were already sliding through the narrow
concrete channel. They passed overhead in silence—a tall, tidy
drift. I looked up and saw dozens of white sails, all gorged with
wind. The complexity of their rigging was startling, but the
boats themselves moved with gorgeous simplicity, as if, having discovered some trick—having determined the secret to
motion—hurtling into harbor at forty miles an hour was the
greatest of all forms of stillness.

There were nine ships. The whole crowd seemed to hold
its breath as they passed, the way people get when a green thunderhead looms or when a moose with a weighty rack of antlers
emerges from the woods. And then, just when the last of the

ships slipped beneath the raised bridge, applause broke out. Not cheers, but appreciative, almost nervous clapping. People started checking each other, self-conscious suddenly, as if unsure what to do next. Gulls floated after the boats, wings curved open, unimpressed. Some children started chucking bread over the water, which broke the spell the ships had cast.

We watched seagulls seize whole slices of white bread from the air.

"How many boats?" Leo asked. I knew by now it was a habit of his to make a lesson out of this—out of anything—to snatch up every opportunity for improvement. Paul and Patra twisted around, noticing for the first time that we were standing behind them. Patra smiled her welcome, a slick of relief in her eyes. Now that Leo was here, she was ready to play the part of sidekick parent again, to pull up blades of grass with her fingers.

"Did you see them?" she asked. Folding a blade of grass back and forth, making an accordion of it.

"Of course." He crouched down. "Hey, Paul. Hey there, kiddo. How many did you count?"

Paul hadn't thought to count the ships. There was a white hollow in his throat when he looked up at us.

"Nine," I said.

I felt the need, then, to defend Paul from Leo's good intentions. From above, from where I was standing, there seemed something funny about the way Paul was dressed. His steam engine T-shirt draped over him, bagged a little from the neck and shoulders. The toes of his blue Velcro shoes pointed inward.

Leo said, "Paul, do you know what time period those ships are from?"

I felt the need to jump in again, but then Patra opened a wicker basket on the blanket—revealing elaborate compartments for silverware and plastic cups, for cloth napkins rolled into tubes—and the feeling passed. That feeling was always passing. Patra swung open what seemed like a hidden door in the basket, and out came a silver thermos, which she tilted over cups, one for each of us. Lemonade. She peeled open a blue Tupperware, out of which gnarled strawberries bulged. "Organic," she emphasized, passing the container to me.

I slit open a strawberry with my teeth and sat down next to Patra on the grass. "There's room," she said, patting the blanket, so I scooted in. Leo continued his lesson:

"They're mostly from the eighteenth and nineteenth century. Do you know when that was?"

"Before rockets," Paul guessed, blinking his gummy lashes.

"Before *cars*," Leo said. "And how many sails did you see on each ship?"

"They went by pretty fast," I intervened.

"A hundred," Paul breathed.

"Fourteen," Leo said, a tyrant for facts. "Or eleven or eight, depending on type." Then he settled into an explanation about wind currents, topmasts and topsails, traditional rigging and nautical miles. He wasn't preaching, exactly, just giving numbers, just enumerating statistics and particulars. Still, there was something pontifical about the way he talked, something lulling and insistent at once, and as he spoke, I rolled a single strawberry seed over my teeth, hard as a grain of sand, gritty as that, and as unswallowable. After a while, I stopped listening to Leo, who was advancing a method for converting fathoms to meters. I set the seed between two molars and took a sip of lemonade, waiting, as I did, for Patra to notice I was wearing her headband. I'd swiped it from the bathroom counter that morning on the way out. It was hard blue plastic with rows of tiny inner spikes. It felt like having someone's teeth against my temples—uncomfortable, vaguely threatening—but reassuring, too, like when a dog closes his jaws affectionately on your wrist and does not bite down, but could. My head felt different: I waited for Patra to notice my new head.

But Patra had her eye on Leo, who, after finishing his speech about sails, had his eye on a tugboat coming into the harbor. The tugboat captain was waving from the deck at Paul, who—I noticed then, in a disconcerting flash—had his eyes on me. He was saying something garbled about Europa, where there was a sandbox with diggers, where nobody lived, where ships sailed around empty, and lawn mowers mowed.

"In the Goldilocks zone," he said.

Leo laughed, glancing at Patra in surprise. "He's doing Europa and Illinois, combined."

"He misses *home*," Patra explained, happily almost, as if she'd discovered the key to something. "He just misses Oak Park, right?" She looked to Leo for confirmation.

"Um, excuse me," said the woman on the blanket beside us.

She stood up. She had a stack of paper napkins in her hand, which lifted up one by one like birds and fluttered to the ground. It seemed oddly coordinated, like a magic show for children, in which the trick was a simple application of gravity. I wondered if she was performing for Paul, who often got little performances like this from strangers. I smiled obediently at the woman, which was the wrong thing to do. She frowned and dropped the remaining napkins on the grass in front of Patra and me. "Excuse me?" she scolded, barely concealing her disgust, and I saw then that Paul was throwing up in a bubbly white mass on the grass.

Leo set his hand on Paul's spine, patted down very gently.

The woman shook her head at us. "Looks like he's come down with something real bad."

"Thank you!" Leo said politely.

The sun kept shining and the wind kept blowing as we packed up the silver thermos and the Tupperware, the plastic cups we'd shaken out in the grass, the black cloth napkins. Patra and I put everything back in its compartment, in its loop of elastic, and shut up all the wicker doors. Patra's hands were white, but she wanted to put everything away precisely and in order, so we did. Leo carried a listless Paul to the car. As we followed across the grass, children ran in circles around us, chucking food at the seagulls. The children were hatted, shiny with sunscreen, laughing uproariously at the predatory gulls. They craned their heads back, lost their hats in the wind. More and more of them gathered in the spot we'd left open on the grass, and above them, the flock of gulls continued to grow. The birds were ravenous, undiscriminating. When I turned around for one last look, I saw the kids were experimenting. They were tossing into the air popcorn pieces and wax cups, carrot sticks, packets of gum, coins from their parents' pockets, handfuls of rock.

That was June twentieth, so summer was spinning around us in full force. The city was crowded with traffic and day-trippers, white toy dogs on leashes, flower and popcorn vendors, kids on skateboards, old people with canes and walkers, corner ice-cream carts. It was a snow-globe kind of summer day—seagulls every-where floating down, the sky a dome of unbroken blue. One day later, on June twenty-first, Paul died of cerebral edema. This, I later learned, is similar to what climbers die of at high altitudes, and what deep-sea divers sometimes succumb to after they ascend. The brain swells and presses outward against the skull, and the optic nerves are under so much pressure they smash into the back of the eye. The brain literally gets too big for the head, crowds the plates in the skull, rearranges the gray matter. In his bed at sea level, wedged between his rows of stuffed animals and stacks of books, Paul probably had a terrible headache. He probably had a funny sweet taste in the back of his throat. He had diabetic ketoacidosis, I was later told.

Later I was told many things. That Paul had likely been nauseated and incontinent for weeks before this, that as his brain had started to swell in the last twenty-four hours, he went partially blind, lost consciousness, slipped into a coma. That, while this last part was happening, he was left uncared for in his bed at the summer house—that instead of taking him to the hospital, instead of giving him the insulin and liquids he needed to survive, Leo had made pancakes and read him books, and Patra had tidied the house and emptied the litter box, and I had moved pieces around a Candy Land board. His parents had taken him for a long drive in the car, while his babysitter had hauled into his room stones and leaves and pinecones. I'd brought in *yard waste*, they said, incredulous.

What were you *thinking?* I was asked on the stand. I could not bring myself to say that it was Europa's capital, that pile of leaves and rocks on the bedroom floor. I could not bring myself to tell them what I'd meant to tell Paul—who, when I'd seen him last, had been looking out from his bed with just one open eye. Half his face had been smashed against a pillow. *No one lives in Europa*, I'd wanted to tell him when he got back home. *Not yet, maybe not ever*, but the capital has been built and there are trains that go on the ocean floor, and submarines and floating cranes, and it's not a city for people. It's not for fairies or aliens or anything cute and fantastical. *It's just a city*, I'd wanted to say. It's just a city, with trains and diggers and bulldozers and roads.

This is how I remember leaving Duluth. Patra needed help folding up the cotton blanket, which we shook free of grass, and I remember how those blades were so green in the sun they were almost blue. When we got to the car, Patra and Leo had a short discussion about what to do next, and it was decided that we head back to Loose River early, that afternoon. Leo wanted Patra to walk back and check out of the hotel while he waited with Paul in the car. They had a little argument about it, actually, the first argument I heard them have. They didn't yell at each other or raise their voices. They just stood on opposite sides of the car and squinted at each other in the sun, first disputing who should stay with Paul in the car and who should go back to the hotel and pay, and then, caught in the orbit of arguing, they switched right into bitter apology, Patra pleading, "I'm *sorry*, Leo," and Leo responding, "No, it's my fault. I shouldn't have let myself get upset over such a little thing. You stay with Paul. I'll go back."

Paul sat this out in the backseat. I stood near him in the open car door, near him but not too close. He didn't want to be touched. "The weather is under me," he said, and I couldn't help smiling.

"You're under the weather, you mean."

He was too busy drinking to respond. After taking a few sloppy sips of lemonade, and then, sweating instantly from the effort of this, taking a gulp or two from the plastic water bottle Patra produced—after dampening the whole front of his shirt with some combination of lemonade, water, and saliva, he set his head against his car seat, took a shallow breath, and closed his eyes.

Patra sat in the backseat with him. She gave me the key, so I climbed in the passenger seat to turn on the air. It blew hot as breath for a minute or two, then gradually cooled, so we rolled up all the windows and sat in the chilled car, cut off from the summery world outside. I had the impulse then, as my sweat dried, to slide to the driver's seat and pull the gearshift into drive. It would be simple I thought. How hard could driving be?

"He's not himself today," Patra said from the backseat. I glanced back at her. I assumed she meant Paul at first, but she was staring out the window in the direction of the hotel. So it was Leo she meant. She unclasped her breath the way people do when they're about to speak, then closed her mouth again, chewed on her lip.

I curled around more fully, peeped at her over the seat. "Is the temp okay?" I asked, coaxing her out. I wanted her to unload her worry, like she did in the tent. I wanted her to need me for something she couldn't do herself.

"Yes, thank you. *Thank you*, Linda." She gave me a smile that was all forehead. She was gazing down at Paul, who'd drifted off. She was petting his long bare arm with one hand.

I tested out her gratitude: "Do you want me to pull the car up a little bit? Do you want me to get out of this traffic?" Cars kept honking at us, hoping to get our parking spot.

She considered it. "Do you have your license?"

"No," I admitted.

"That's okay." She leaned back against the seat and closed her eyes, and in the bright sunlight I thought I could see her eyeballs moving beneath her pale lids. *Oh, there are her black pupils*, I thought, triumphantly, frightened almost, but then she shielded her whole face with her hand and whatever I saw was gone.

She said, "Leo'll come for us in a moment."

I didn't like how she put that. I didn't like how confident she sounded. I didn't like how she changed with Leo around, how all her gestures were stretched out of size with a touch of performance. I didn't like how deferential she was with him, but also charged somehow, confident she could draw his attention if she wanted it.

Her headband was making my head pound. I could feel its teeth in a cruel crown from ear to ear. I felt just miserable enough to take a swipe at her.

"Where'd you guys meet?"

Patra opened her eyes. She checked Paul before meeting my gaze. "Leo and me?"

I nodded. "Yep."

"He was my professor."

I felt smug. "At the University of Chicago?"

"How'd you know?"

She'd worn that sweatshirt about a thousand times. I shrugged.

"Astronomy 101." She wrinkled her nose, making the smiley rueful expression I was coming to recognize. She set her hand on Paul's sleeping forehead. "I thought it'd be easy. I thought we'd memorize constellations, learn the names of planets. That sort of thing."

"Did you?"

"We did some of that, sure." She caught my eye. "It's not what you think."

I held her blue gaze. "What do I think, Patra?"

She shifted in her seat, fingered Paul's hair so he stirred. For a moment, he looked hounded by his dreams. His face crumpled as if he might cry out. He didn't wake up, though. "*I'm* the one who stayed after class, who, you know, actually asked him out. It was me, not him."

I waited for more.

"He was, like—I don't know. He was bigger than anything else to me at the time."

I found that hard to believe. I found it difficult to imagine that slippered, thin man leaving such a mark. He seemed insubstantial to me—though stubborn, maybe, like a stain. I thought about how his heel had bulged out of his slipper, how the slipper was worn and black and ugly.

"Once, one of my friends at school ran into him on campus—she was collecting signatures or something, for charity—and she said, there's something unsettling about him. And I said, I agree! He's unsettlingly smart. He really is."

She was justifying herself. She was making a case to me, setting up her defenses. She was trying to convince me of something, and as she spoke I could see she was sitting up straighter, finding focus.

"Listen, Linda." She was attempting to whisper, so her consonants got especially hissy. "I'm not any good at explaining things. I'm not like Leo in that way. After the semester ended I got him to sit with me in the cafeteria and eat a muffin, and he had a bran and I had a blueberry, and we did that again the next week, and the next, and I remember how he tucked in his

shirt when he stood up. You know how that is? How you wait
for someone to do this thing, and then he does it? He tucks in
his shirt the same way every time he stands up, and it seems, I
don't know, like you don't have to go to all the work getting to
know him because he does this thing, this one thing, and you
can predict it. He was so smart, and I felt like I knew him better
than he knew himself, right away. That's very powerful."

"You liked how he tucked in his shirt?" I was intrigued. I
was repulsed.

"No, I *knew* how he tucked in his shirt. It's different. And
I was flattered. He was just out of graduate school, a big deal on
campus for an article he'd published in *Nature*, and he said to
me, oh, maybe, a month or so in, that he hadn't told me everything about himself. He said he wanted to tell me everything,
and, you know, I was nineteen. I was like, oh no, he's a felon or
a pervert or something! I was just a kid."

"He wasn't a pervert," I said.

"No, nothing like that. He just wanted to tell me about
his religion, he was a third-generation Christian Scientist, and
I laughed at him when he said it, I was so relieved. I was really
afraid of what he'd say."

By then I could see Leo coming down the street. He was
shading his eyes with his hand, scanning the crowd for the car. He
had two backpacks over his shoulder, mine and Paul's together,
and the big rolling suitcase in one hand. He was half trotting
as he went, khaki shorts bunching in the crotch, exposing his
pale thighs.

"What happened then?" I asked Patra, feeling urgent about
it now.

What I meant was, what are you trying to say to me? I felt
that I'd missed something along the way, that the essential part

of the story had already come and gone while I'd been looking out the window.

"Oh, I don't know!" She must have seen Leo too, then, because her voice changed—lowered and glazed over, got sweet and cool, almost arch. "I laughed at how serious he was. Then I married him. I liked that he was serious, and I thought I stood apart."

Together, we watched as Leo caught sight of the car. He went around back and loaded the trunk. Clearly he couldn't see us inside, staring right at him, because when he came back around, when he saw his reflection in the car window, he took a deep breath and flattened down a tuft of blown hair at the top of his head. He plucked his shorts out from between his crotch with two fingers. But that wasn't all.

"Watch," Patra whispered.

An instant before Leo opened the door, he slid his flattened hands an inch beneath his belt and shoved his blue cotton shirt in deeper. It was an automatic gesture, and he looked a little flustered, as if he wasn't sure whether he'd be welcomed back in the car—or what he'd find when he opened the door.

Patra said to me, "You think you're as old as the ages when you're nineteen, that you're years past being grown up. You'll see."

"Everything okay in here?" Leo asked, sitting down hard in the driver's seat.

Patra leaned forward, kissed the lobe of his ear.

He swung around to study Paul's sleeping face, then Patra's.

"We're okay," I answered for her.

The car ride home reshuffled things. The whole way Leo asked me polite but absentee questions about lake fishing and iron ore,

and it was Patra who whispered games to Paul in the backseat.
We sat in the construction traffic outside Duluth even longer
this time around. Through it all, through the orange dust and
the black exhaust, Leo spoke to me without turning his head,
nodding and noncommittal about my answers. I stopped answering with more than a few words, and finally he stopped asking.
An hour, two hours of silence opened up between us. Nobody
suggested we stop at Denny's on the way back. Once the construction ended, I started looking for landmarks I remembered
from the day before—the purple water tower, the tunnel blasted
through the hillside—but everything looked different from the
other direction, and I couldn't anticipate when these landmarks
would appear. I only recognized them in retrospect, the moment
we passed, and I had to turn around and watch the water tower
receding in the window.

"Almost home!" Leo cried triumphantly, when the tunnel spat us out. He seemed resolved to this idea long before it
was an accurate description of our circumstances. By the time
we got to the old familiar highways—the ones I'd walked for
years—Leo had been saying "Almost home!" for more than an
hour. Then Loose River appeared in the dappled sun of the deep
woods, and Leo was so elated he broke into a round of "Good
King Wenceslas." Patra joined him in an obedient soprano. My
heart disobediently sank. "We're back!" Leo announced when
Patra trailed off in the middle of the second verse, so I slid my
hands under my butt and imagined the car breaking down or
a wretched deer in the road or any kind of calamitous barrier.
I didn't offer to get out and walk up the sumac trail. I let Leo
scrape up his car driving through that dense corridor of trees in
the early evening shadows.

Slowly, slowly, I retrieved my backpack from the trunk.

"'Night!" Leo called through his open car window, turning the Honda around as soon as I slammed the trunk. I didn't hear if Patra or Paul said anything. The backseat window was rolled up tight.

Surely, they said to me later, surely by then you sensed something was off?

Maybe. Maybe there is a way to climb above everything, some special ladder or insight, some optical vantage point that allows a clear, unobstructed view of things. Maybe this way of seeing comes naturally to some people, and good for them if it does. But I remember it all, even now, as if two mutually exclusive things happened. First it goes the way the prosecutors described it—nausea, headache, coma, etcetera—and then it comes back to me the way it actually was with Patra and Paul—tall ships, car ride home, Good King Wenceslas, bed. Though they end the same way, these are not the same story. Maybe if I'd been someone else I'd see it differently. But isn't that the crux of the problem? Wouldn't we all act differently if we were someone else?

"Back early?" my mother asked when I pushed open the cabin door.

She was waiting for an answer even though I'd killed some time before coming inside, even though I'd sat against my backpack behind the shed for more than an hour with the dogs. I'd hoped to avoid this exact question.

"Madeline?" I couldn't see her clearly, though. She was a hunchbacked shadow at the table. She had been stitching something or trying to read. I couldn't tell. I didn't say anything to

her, just found my way across the dim room with my backpack
and climbed straight up the ladder to my loft.

My mother hadn't yet turned the lights on, of course.

So I remember thinking: *Fine. Let it be night.* It was probably only eight thirty or nine, nearly the longest day, but the
cabin was already dark from being enveloped so completely on
all sides by pines. I remember Patra's headband pressing into my
skull as I rolled onto my mattress, and relishing the wonderful
ache of it. I remember the click of the lamp and my mother's
curse, before she went outside and fumbled behind the cabin
for the generator. I remember that when the lights came on it
was like a jolt to the skin, and that my mother stood breathing
for a moment at the foot of my ladder. "Madeline?" she asked
again. She jiggled one of the lower rungs, made the joints creak.

I burrowed into my sleeping bag, fully dressed.

"Have a good time in Duluth?"

'Night, I thought.

After a few minutes, I heard the pine boards groan as she
walked to the sink. I heard her swing open a cupboard, bite into
one of the pears I'd bought a week ago in town. Bite, then pause.
I imagined her pulling threads of wet peel through her teeth with
her fingers. I could hear her breathing loudly through her nose
and humming the same two lines from two totally different songs,
mixing them together. *Strange days have found us / Casting down
their crowns along the glassy sea.* My mother. That night as I lay
in bed, that night after going to Duluth and back, I remember
how loudly the moths buzzed around the lamp she'd turned on. I
remember the feathering of their wings against the bulb, and that
endless pear in her mouth, *crunch-crunch-crunching.* I remember
her humming, pushing out more air than sound, and how all
that—plus my pounding head—made it impossible to fall asleep.

HEALTH

12

"SHE'S A CORPORATE EXECUTIVE, I SWEAR TO GOD," my mom used to say to my father. "She's done an inventory of the pines on the hill. The pillows."

Twelve big pines, I'd think when she said this. *Two pillows and seven blankets.*

I was probably six or seven when my mom started calling me a CEO. I could still climb onto my father's lap in my cotton nightgown and pretend I was smaller, a little girl he could hold and protect— or better yet, a piece of equipment he could use, a wonderful worn tool that needed tending, like the tape measure he returned with such care to his leather belt. I curled up my legs inside my nightgown to try it out, put the tip of my thumb inside my mouth and began chewing the nail.

"Take care," my father warned me. "There's walls of wood nettles out by the—"

For a moment his arms were around me. He spoke into the back of my head, and it was almost, though not quite, like being petted. I could feel his breath on my scalp, his words before they were words in the rumble of his chest. Then he shifted, as if trying to scoot out from under me. He was tired. I know that now. He was tired in a way that made him seem absent, slow, hauling up some viscous thought he couldn't quite identify without putting everything else on hold for a moment. My mother and I waited for him.

"She's got such a pissy look," my mother finally said, laughing at me. "Look at that look."

"Just don't go counting things near the highway," my father finished.

I slid very slowly from the cliff of his lap. Since Tameka and the Big Kids left, I almost never even left sight of the bunkhouse and cabin. I let one leg go first, then the other, thinking my father might pull me back up. Then I lay on the floor, looked at the wormy brown laces of his boots.

"Seriously," my mother said. "She told me she wants to measure the cabin. And she's counted our dishes, apparently. We still have all sixteen spoons."

"Children like to count," my father said, knowingly.

"This one's got a talent for it."

On the floor, I bit into my father's bootlace, chewed for a moment. I could tell by the way he cleared his throat that he was getting ready to stand up, head for the shed.

There wasn't ever anywhere to go inside. There were only two rooms on the ground floor—the kitchen space and the bedroom—plus a stepladder to the loft, where I slept on a goose-feather mattress jammed against rafters. The loft was a particleboard platform. My bedding was a pile of army-issue sleeping bags that smelled of mildew and smoke. From the low ceiling hung a yellow cloth with black cats smoking cigarettes in an intricate, dizzying pattern. My mom drew this around my sleeping bags when I slept—unless it was too cold, unless it was winter. Then my father slung the old mattress over his shoulder like the body of a disheveled fat person he loved and wished to save. He hoisted it down the ladder and laid it by the stove. "Sleep," he told me, straightening the mattress creases with a wide red hand. "Get a good dream." He patted an old jacket into a pillow-like shape.

He was kind to objects. With people he was a little afraid.

Winters were especially confining. We were all tied—as if by rope—to that sooty black furnace. Which has a certain romance, I know, if you tell the story right, a certain Victorian ghost-story earnestness people like, and I've told the story that way to the delight of shark-tooth-wearing dates in coffee shops. So many people, even now, admire privation. They think it sharpens you, the way beauty does, into something that might hurt them. They calculate their own strengths against it, unconsciously, preparing to pity you or fight.

Like that mechanic I dated in Saint Paul. Eventually, he got tired of sneaking out of my bed in the morning; he made me come to his apartment to see him. He got me drunk one night, fed me burritos. He laid out tarot cards in rows on his blue carpet, pointed at the gargoyle face of the Fool and asked what I thought. Apparently, he'd been a psychology major before he was a mechanic. He had a thing for Carl Jung, as well as an intimate knowledge of carburetors. He wanted to excavate my past.

"Isn't this supposed to tell the future?" I asked, sitting cross-legged on his floor. I was just tipsy enough to give him a hard time.

"It's tea leaves, babe, not magic."

"Ah. You give me superstition, not the good stuff."

"I promise this'll be good." He scooted closer to me on his knees. Held up one finger. "Give me a second. What does this card make you think?"

"That Fool looks like pretty easy prey, if you ask me. His eyes are closed."

"Okay. That's perfect. What else?"

"Does he have, like, a pig on his stick?"

"I think that's a rucksack."

I narrowed my eyes. "Where'd you learn to read tarot again?"

He narrowed his eyes back—he was smiling though. "Who was easy prey in your childhood?"

"Did I ever tell you I know quite a lot about wolves?"

"Ha! The Girl Scout, I know her. The Girl Scout comes out whenever you're nervous."

"Like, I'm your wolf expert. Ask me anything."

"Who was easy prey, then?"

The truth was, that old woodstove was narcotic and banal to me as a child, so I was drawn to it without seeing it, and hated it without wondering why. The winter I was nine, I laid my cheek against it while I was reading *Mush, a Manual* on the floor. The burn made a bubble of clear skin—a round half globe like the air bladder of a fish—under my left eye. The bubble grew as the days passed, rose translucently from my face, obstructed my vision when I looked down. If my parents noticed, they didn't draw attention to it. At school I made excuses to go to the bathroom and poke at it in the mirror. Sometimes Sarah the Ice Skater would be there, too, leaving class early so she could change before practice. Sucking a Blow Pop, snapping a leotard

under her crotch. "Sick," she'd say, peering at my reflection in
the mirror and touching her own cheek.

And once, coming closer, getting curious, "Did your dad
do that to you? Is that the kind of thing they do to you?"

I had two chores to do with my dad: chop wood and clean fish.
By the time I was ten, I could chop whole logs on my own, so
my dad gave up that chore for me to do alone. But we did the
fish together until I was in high school, working quietly over a
pair of buckets in the shed. We used bleached fillet knives that
we scraped against the whetstone before starting—and that was
the best part, always, the gravelly, ringing drag of steel over rock.
The sound made the hairs on my arms prickle up, my teeth ache
pleasurably. Then there was just the sluice and slop of skins com
ing off. There were our two fist-size puffs of breath punching
the air side by side, my father's and mine. *Hu. Hu.*

The fish and wood only took a few hours, so I used to make
up extra chores for myself. When I was in fourth grade I started
writing down the good deals at Mr. Korhonen's on toothpaste
and toilet paper so we wouldn't run out, and I passed these lists
to my mom before she went into town. I took over care of the
dogs the winter I was eleven; I began feeding the stove in the
mornings because I woke so early for the dogs. Later, just before
I started middle school, I saw it as my responsibility to sit with
my dad on Sunday afternoons and listen to ball games and *A
Prairie Home Companion*. My dad told me once that he'd had a
class with Garrison Keillor in college, and for years I imagined
Garrison as one of the relatives I'd never met. I thought of him
as my dad's gregarious older brother, and my dad as the shy

younger one, who could handle himself better against loneliness and disaster.

I didn't have any regular chores to do for my mom. She
couldn't bear to have me around when she washed clothes or
cooked dinner. She said I was too slow, too judgmental. She
said I watched too closely for mistakes. "You act like I'm being
wasteful when I take off the littlest bit of potato with the peel."

My mother was inattentively industrious, full of ideas. She
had all kinds of do-gooder projects strewn on the table and
chairs, stations of interrupted activity. Quilting scraps for inmates, letters to protest chemical spills, Bible quotes she copied
onto index cards, thrift store mystery novels, a years-long scheme
that involved reading Russian fairy tales from a book she never
returned to the library. Her long hair always fingered the air as
she moved across the cabin. It clung with static electricity to
everything she touched—pot handles, broom handles, my face
when she bent over me.

"Are you still oiling the same old reel?" she'd demand. "How
is that possible?"

Her hair snapped when she moved away.

It bothered her that I wouldn't play her games, that I refused to read out loud or dress up as a dragon in the rags she
wound around my body and called a tail. "Roar!" she used to say,
coaxing, pulling my hair. She crossed her eyes, tried to provoke
me. She stuck out her tongue, and I could see a white film like
a layer of moss over the pink.

Then I would think: *We need toothpaste.*

I would add it mentally to my list: *toothpaste, mouthwash,
floss.*

"When *I* was your age, I wrote a novel," my mother told me.
"I put on *Macbeth* in my parents' backyard with a cast of twenty

characters! It was a funny version, actually." She scrunched up
her face and spoke with an exaggerated British accent: "*Out, out
damned Scot!*" She waited for me to laugh but I wasn't sure what
part was funny. "Here," she said then, sighing, and handed me a
wand she'd made from a birch branch rolled in glue and glitter.
She wanted very badly for me to cavort and pretend, to prove I
was unharmed, happy. During those years she went to church
on Saturdays as well as Sundays, to the Catholic and Lutheran
services as well as the interfaith one, to cover all her bases. She
never asked me to go along. She said she was a Religion Mutt.
She couldn't decide what mattered most: good works or God's
grace. She couldn't settle the sacrament of blood: man's flesh or
empty metaphor. "Both sort of suck," she said, when discour-
aged. What she did know, and believed with all her heart, was
that it was some combination of private school and television
that had corrupted her mind and cheapened her natural talents.

"Look at the *freedom* you have!" She said this when she
was the most exasperated with me, throwing open her arms. As
if all her rags and rocks and jars of sand were a form of rarest
treasure. As if she had saved up her whole life to acquire this
hoard of scraps.

Sometimes, to please her, I wore her dragon tail out to
train the dogs. The summer I was twelve I was transitioning
them from sled to search and rescue. They each had a different
reward: a broken paddle, a rubber hose, a tennis ball I'd found
at the high school courts. I'd unchain one dog at a time, tell
him to stay and duck behind a tree trunk. But that was too
easy. Each one found me every time. So one summer afternoon,
after trying all the familiar places, I dashed behind the house
and scaled the back of the shed, dragging my dragon's tail over
broken shingles. Then I gave the signal to look, a high-pitched

whistle, and watched Abe go for all the old pines, sniff upwind and down, run in frantic circles around the cabin. Abe wasn't an old dog then, but after twenty minutes, he was panting hard and flinging saliva in wide arcs across the yard. A half hour passed, forty-five minutes. The other dogs heaved on their chains, joining his distress. From above, I watched Abe's ribs swell and contract; I watched him try the same spots over and over again; I watched him stumble, once, in exhaustion.

I sat still on the roof of the shed. As an experiment, I put my own mouth on the scummy rubber fuzz of the tennis ball in my hand. The moment before I gagged, before I choked and spit it out, a queer euphoria lifted me up, as if by wings.

"Really, ask me anything," I said, pulling the extra tarot cards into a stack on the mechanic's carpet in St. Paul. His name was Rom. He had bright blue eyes, big muscly arms, a paunch. The stud in his tongue flashed at me when he yawned, so I poked him in the chest. "Ask me, how often do wolves eat? And I'll tell you, every four or five days. They straight-out starve. Then they gorge like—"

"I know this one! Teenage girls."

"They're never going to eat again. Now ask me, what do they eat? Ask it."

He shook his head but played along. "What do they eat?"

"White-tailed deer. Also worms and blueberries."

"Keep it coming, Girl Scout. Keep stuffing it all back down in the unconscious."

"And dogs! There was this little town in Alaska, Middleofnowheresville—"

"Isn't that where you're from?" He raised his eyebrows.

"And they came at night and got someone's Lab. Just chomp. Then the next night, it was a couple of huskies, who never even made a sound. The final blow was someone's pretty coonhound, one of those long-snouted things, a winner of dog shows. She was eaten right off her chain, just her collar left behind and, you know, her jawbone and tail."

"*Jawbone and Tail*. An album title."

"Wolves eat most of the bones, usually. That's a Girl Scout tip."

"So what happened in Nowheresville?" He was leaning in closer to me now, was murmuring into my neck. "Who saved the rest of the dogs?"

"No!" I pushed him back. "Who saved the *wolves*? They were all shot."

The fall I started middle school, my mom stopped calling me CEO and started calling me the Teenager. This was because I was always stealing magazines from the secretary's office at school, reading *People* or *Us* or *Glamour*. I read about procedures for blow-drying your hair so it looked like a tornado had come to town, and I studied tips for slicking down bangs so they looked wet. I never had any interest in trying these looks. What I liked seeing was something so mysterious broken down into steps, pieced together in charts and tables. Or, if there weren't any new magazines in the office, I got books from the library on ice age paleontology and the history of electricity. I coveted diagrams of hairstyles or skeletons, ink drawings of angles and equations I didn't understand. My mother didn't see me reading these things because I wasn't doing anything she found interesting. Instead she'd be setting out jars for jam—or copying a quote on a pink index card—and when she'd glance up, she'd look right through me. I didn't watch TV until I lived in Minneapolis with Ann, but when I did I recognized the feeling: to look at somebody who can't look back.

Occasionally, she'd see me reading and peer at the book over my shoulder. "Is that for homework?" she'd ask, shaking her head in amazement. I knew she wanted me to do well in school, but she wanted me to succeed the way she had—by disdaining the whole process. It bothered her to think I was trying. "Oh, you're becoming such a little professor, aren't you? We should get you one of those gowns." She was glancing down at a drawing of a velociraptor in my book, its bones labeled with arrows. She seemed one part surprised, maybe even pleased, but two parts disparaging and contemptuous.

"Don't give me that look!" she'd laugh.

I was twelve. My whole life I'd been unintentionally giving her looks she didn't like.

"You'd be impressive in one of those gowns, like a pope." She widened her eyes at me. "I'm kidding! Listen, I'm not saying there's no system at all. That's not what I'm saying. What I'm saying is that there's an order on a *higher* level than school, and it's worth paying attention to the relative elevation of things. God, man, bureaucracy, worksheets." She sighed. "When they say at school, do this worksheet, and the next one and on and on, you need to see, it's really important that you see, those aren't steps that go on up higher. It's just a fake kind of higher. Does that make sense?"

"What's this!" she asked me once, when she found a *People* magazine on the table, left open to an article about Princess Diana. I was fascinated by her sadness for a while, by how, pretty as she was, she could not keep it to herself. I read about her little boys, her husband's affairs, her eating disorder, her lipstick pairings, her stockings, her high heels. I found an article after her divorce in which she'd made a list of her morning routine, which included: Think Positively Even If You Have Bad Dreams. That seemed both pitiful and brave to me, poignant. My mother, however, turned the slick *People* pages in complete puzzlement, saying, "Did you read this whole article? I don't understand you. What is there in that thing to read?"

Once, near the beginning of seventh grade, I went to the bathroom and Sarah the Ice Skater was there with another girl, combing sparkly gel into her hair. It was Lily Holburn, who looked stricken. Her slick black hair came to a point like a stake behind her back. "Oh, the Freak," Sarah said when she saw me, but she seemed interested rather than disgusted, searching my face for a sign of the popped bubble. There wasn't any, except—maybe— the spot on my cheek that was less deeply tanned.

Lily squeezed one eye shut, a line of gel leaking down her forehead.

"Hey," I said, warily.

I knew Sarah was to be respected. I'd heard she had already landed a double axel, one footed, fully rotated, and I believed it. Her body was like a pulled wet branch, her taut muscles holding some weird snap that seemed mechanical and a little dangerous. Everyone assumed that triples hung in her future, that they followed her magically wherever she went, dangled just out of her reach. Triple Salchow, triple loop, triple flip, triple lutz. That meant Upper Great Lakes, Midwesterns, Nationals, Worlds.

Lily, on the other hand, was not what people considered athletic. Still, Sarah had befriended her in the months after her mother died and convinced her and two other medium-pretty girls, both blondes, to join synchronized skating. It wasn't charity, Sarah's interest. Though Lily wasn't called Indian anymore, no one was calling her retarded the way they once did either.

The Loonettes needed people with *poise* Sarah told her, all smiles.

Boobs, she meant.

Which was why Lily was standing in the seventh grade bathroom with Sarah's greasy hands in her hair, glitter everywhere, a gob of it now on her cheek. The Loonettes had a competition that afternoon in Duluth.

"Lil, don't look at the Freak," Sarah said, as I squeezed past them to get to the stall. "Her dad, you know, tortures her for fun. That's what they do in that cult where she grew up. They burn her face with wax. They force her to pee outside so she doesn't know how to use a toilet."

Lily's brown eyes met mine in the mirror. For an instant, I had the sensation I was looking at myself, and when I saw my own gaunt face beside hers I was startled.

"Her face looks okay to me," Lily hedged. She leaned forward, so Sarah pulled back on her hair like reins.

"I've seen what they do! Have you seen it? Have you?"

"No," Lily acknowledged.

I said nothing. On the floor of the stall lay the detritus of a quick change. Jeans, padded bras, a pair of off-white underwear in a wad. I nudged the pile out of the way with a toe, sat down but could squeeze nothing out.

Hiss-hiss went the hair spray—on and on, with no change. They were listening.

"Sorry," Lily mumbled when I came out, bladder full, humiliated. "About the clothes."

"Don't talk to Freaks." Sarah started spraying Lily's face. "Close your eyes!"

Lily did, but Sarah's eyes met mine as I rinsed the tips of my fingers under the faucet. It was the kind of look the dogs gave me when they had a meaty bone in the corner of the shed.

"Let's sing," Sarah said to Lily, who was cracking open her eyes. "Let's sing 'One Tin Soldier.'"

When Lily didn't join in, Sarah gave her a prodding kick in the shins.

"You need to *believe* in the song," she said.

"I wish I believed in this shit," my mother said the morning she baptized me. I was six, maybe seven years old. A slant of light from the doorway caught her face. Cold well water from the measuring cup trickled down my back.

"What shit?" I asked, shivering.

"Like *that*. Like, no more saying *shit*, okay? You're a new pot of rice, baby. I'm starting you all over from scratch."

"I'm not hungry yet," I told her.

She laughed, helped me out of the metal tub. "All you got to do, hon, all you got to do is be a kid. You do that, and I'll feel so much better."

"When's Tameka coming back?" I asked her.

"She's flown the coop with the others."

I thought about that, how we'd gone off together like loons with just our thoughts down the highway. We'd almost flown the coop then, but they'd sent a Big Boy after us.

"Hey, don't give me that look!" My mother turned me around by the shoulders, rubbed a rough towel over my back and neck. "Don't you feel clean, at least?"

"I'm cold," I said.

"Just feel clean for a second, okay? Just feel *good*." She was crying then, I could tell. I wasn't facing her, but I could hear her nose dragging with snot. "We're starting over, you and me. I'm trying to get God on our side, do things different. So you can be a happy little kid again, got it? Can you just be a regular little kid for one second? *Please*."

I wasn't sure what else I could be.

"How hard could it be to smile once?" she begged. Then she crawled around on her hands and knees so she was facing me again. She found the measuring cup, set it on the very top of her head, lifted up her hands. *Magic*, she breathed. She had tears on her face, a tight-lipped grin, hair that was getting wet from the cup. After a moment, her measuring hat clattered to the floor.

"Last resort," she warned.

She tickled under my armpits, so I squirmed away.

"Now, how hard was that?" she said, letting me go. I was breathing fast and faster, trying to get it going into a laugh.

"Why does the Fool carry a rucksack?" I asked Rom, pulling up on his blue carpet like grass, moving back and forth with my hand. It was late. All our beer bottles were empty, our burritos gone.

He shrugged. "He's a vagabond. A traveler."

"What's foolish about that?"

"Well, he's walking off a precipice, for one."

I hadn't seen that. I looked at the card again, and it was true. The Fool's right leg dangled over a cliff, but the Fool's eyes were closed. He was just walking along—*la-de-da.*

Rom leaned in closer so I could smell his burrito breath. "But it's not all bad to let yourself fall. Try it?" He kissed me, open-mouthed, pushing me back slowly to the carpet. The metal pin in his tongue roamed in and probed my gums. That felt good, I thought. That felt a lot like being wanted.

"Wait!" I said, figuring out what he meant. I got out from under him. "*I'm* not the Fool."

"But you're not staying, are you?"

I stood up, straightened my twisted jeans. "Not the whole night, if that's what you mean."

"I mean for good." There was an edge to his voice I didn't expect. "You're going back to Ass-crack Nowheresville. Eventually."

"No, no," I said.

But as I gathered my jacket from the floor, as I stuffed the burrito papers back in the soggy bag, I found myself adding, "My mom doesn't even know where I am. I split after my dad died without telling her anything."

"She's guilty," he said.

"My mom?" I turned around.

"No, the traveler. That girl there with her rucksack."

"Piss off," I said. "You don't know me."

He shrugged. "Go on, Fool."

The night I got back from the Tall Ships Festival in Duluth, I lay in my loft for a long time, the light from the lamp below drawing moths, flies, mosquitoes. They crawled in through cracks in the screens, through minute gaps in the door and window frames. My mother sat at the table below waiting for me to come and talk to her. I could hear her weight shifting, the pine floorboards groaning beneath her. I could sense that she wanted me to climb down the ladder, to let gravity take me by the ankles, to sit with her and tell her about Duluth. She wanted me to *want* to tell her about Patra and her family—at last—so she could deride them and their middle-class values, but at the same time be proud of me for getting along so well, for knowing how the world worked, for not fighting it like she had, and did. I could sense her waiting for this. And if I did that, if I told her about the Denny's soup and the maroon-and-white hotel, she'd make the Gardners seem trivial and bland, utterly ordinary. "Don't give me that look," she'd say. "What's that thing in your hair?" she'd ask. She'd notice the headband right away, and laugh at it, and call me a Teenager.

Which I was. What else could I be?

So I acted like one. There was a window in the loft, a small square of glass, which I sometimes propped open in the summer with a wedge of pine. After a long period of failing to sleep, I pushed that window open, shimmied out—I was wiry as anything back then—and pulled myself onto a slowly swaying pine near the back of the cabin. Then I swung myself around and leapt a few feet down onto the roof of the shed. My dad would hear that and think it was a branch falling, or a raccoon. He never took account of sounds like me: ninety-pound things blew down in the course of a regular night in the woods. It was nothing. I was nothing. I kept my gaze from traveling across the lake to the Gardners' place, whose lights would ruin my night vision. I let night do its work on my eyes. Gradually, objects transfigured in the darkness. Real tree branches emerged from the shadows of tree branches, and though clouds had come in, I found my way easily off the shed. At first I simply wanted to put distance between myself and the cabin, moving toward the lake out of habit. But once I got there, my dad's banged-up Wenonah was waiting for me to climb in.

For the thousandth time, I appreciated the waveless passage that was a canoe ride anywhere. I barely lifted the paddle. The boat moved all on its own.

"You wanna know what Jung would say?" Rom asked me. I stood in his doorway with my burrito bag. "The archetypal Fool is Pet-ah Pan." He used a British accent to say it. He scrunched his nose.

"Blah, blah, blah," I said.

"It's true. Girl Scout youth in gold-tipped shoes, with a pet and a lunch packed."

I zipped up my jacket, cradled my trash. I felt attacked, and at the same time sorry for him. "You said you'd do my *past*, not the fucking future."

"Same thing, in this case."

13

THAT THE HOUSE ACROSS THE LAKE WAS DARKER THAN I
THOUGHT IT WOULD BE, the night sky brighter, that true night
had yet to show itself—I noticed these things only gradually.
I dug my paddle deep into the leaf-flecked water. It was only
June, but fall it seemed had already come to ruin a few aspens.
I was still dressed for a day in Duluth. I hadn't taken off my
tennis shoes in the loft, or my good jeans, which were starting
to feel tight in the crotch as I shoved in with the paddle. Patra's
headband pulsed around my head, plaintively.

Please, please, please, it went, as I paddled along.

I didn't mean to go anywhere; I simply meant to leave. I
let the wind and the lake take me where they would. After a
few cool minutes, I set the wooden handle across my knees and
let myself glide. My temples were pounding. The ache in my
head had moved by then into my jaw and skull, making me
queasy, making me realize that we hadn't stopped for dinner
on the way home from Duluth. Breakfast and lunch combined
had been a few knotty strawberries. When this occurred to me,
when I realized I hadn't really eaten all day, I began to feel truly
sick. The sensation came over me in a pounce. I could tell the
feeling had been hovering over me for hours, just waiting till

I was out in the open, out on the lake, before bearing down. I was dizzy, lightheaded. By the time the canoe ran ashore, the whole world was swaying when I looked around. Still Lake, no longer still at all.

I climbed from the canoe carefully, gripping the sides with both hands. And though I hadn't planned on it, I wasn't surprised now to be clambering over the wet rocks below the Gardners' deck. I hardly had a thought in my head. I was just hungry and tired and fully dressed, unwilling to look back at the cabin where my mother sat, her hands sticky with pear.

I snuck around to the front door.

No, I wasn't, I told the police later, thinking of Paul. I was thinking about finding myself something to eat. I figured I could go right in the front door—I knew it was never locked—and scrounge around for some of Paul's pretzels in the cabinet. I knew I could do this without waking anyone up, chew without making a sound, leave without anyone noticing what had been taken. But once I had that thought—pretzels, maybe a granola bar—I realized I wanted more than that, that I would open the fridge and eat straight from the carton of cottage cheese, fish the last two pickles from the jar with my fingers, suck all Paul's leftover noodles from his bowl. I would do all that, and maybe I'd also go into the dark bathroom and pee (silently, trickling it out), slip their half-used bar of lavender soap into my pocket, take Patra's cell phone from the counter, push Leo's manuscript under my shirt. I felt almost giddy at the thought. Hadn't I planned this out long ago? It suddenly seemed I had. But of course it wasn't a true plan at all, only the pulsing in my head, that old yearning to take far more than was reasonable.

Fee-fi-fo-fum, I thought as I spun the cool doorknob, went in.

The main room was hard to make out in the dark. I saw the big triangular windows first, and through them the narrow strip of light I'd traveled from my parents' lit house. Out of habit, I wiggled out of my tennis shoes and set them against the wall.

I started toward the cupboard in my socks. I was thinking of snacks in crinkly packages. I was hoping for peanut butter granola bars, nestled snugly in boxes. The hinge on the cupboard made a throaty sound, and I no sooner had the box in my hands, the cupboard closed, when a tingling went up the back of my neck.

"Linda?"

I turned.

Patra sat in a shadow on the couch. She stood up slowly, a black silhouette against the window, and I had the fleeting, absurd belief that if I didn't say anything, if I froze in my tracks, she wouldn't see me.

"Is that you?"

I stayed quiet and didn't move.

"Oh, dear," she said. She was wearing just a T-shirt, and her bare legs looked pale as birch branches in the dark. She didn't bother tugging the hem over her thighs as she came across the room.

"What is it? Wait—Leo forgot to pay you, didn't he? Or did you forget your bag in the car? Good grief, Linda. I saw you coming across the lake, I watched you and I thought—I had this thought—she's come to rescue us, that girl in her boat. Isn't it weird the things you think in the dark? Isn't it funny how the mind goes flap-flap-flap, so you don't know if you're sleeping or not, and you think: That girl, that crazy girl in her canoe has come to row us all away somewhere."

"Paddle," I whispered.

"What?" she asked.

"You row a boat. Paddle a canoe."

"Whatever, yes." She put a hand on her head, so her T-shirt pulled up over her panties. "I'm talking nonsense. I must have dozed off before I looked out the window and saw you. Did Leo forget to write a check? Or did you come for something else?"

Why did I come? My stomach rumbled audibly, and as it did, I took in the room more fully. I saw the closed picnic basket on the counter, the cell phone in Patra's hand, and the way she stroked it compulsively while she watched my face, while she waited for an explanation. I looked over and saw that Paul's door was shut. A crack of light shone beneath it, and as Patra's head turned, as she followed my gaze, I became aware of Leo's voice behind it talking quietly.

Patra reached for the light switch, and an odd panic washed over me. "Wait—"

"We're all up, I guess. May as well admit it."

"But—" Some part of me still wanted to sneak away unseen.

"No one can sleep tonight—"

Paul's door opened and Leo came out. Patra flicked on the light, and the two of us were left squinting in the sudden brightness. Leo stood open-eyed, surprised—no, dismayed—to see me.

"What?" he said, and for an instant, a look of real fear passed over his face. I thought of that first morning when I'd met him with the hatchet as he came into the house. Then, he'd taken me as harmless, hardly worth noticing. He'd shaken my hand, introduced himself, poured glasses of juice for the both of us. Now he was acting as though I might be dangerous to him, and maybe I was—I *wanted* to be—but not in the way he thought. Discreetly, I set the box of granola bars on the counter behind the picnic basket. Crossed my arms.

"Linda?" he asked.

"You forgot to pay her," Patra said.

"Did I?" He was watching me intently. He seemed about to call me out for showing up unannounced, then appeared to think better of it. "I did. I guess I did forget." Like me, he was still wearing his clothes from the day—his khaki shorts and tucked-in shirt—but he also wore his black slippers. They flapped loose on his feet as he moved across the room to the table and began to write a check.

A sound came from the other room, a murmur or cry.

"He's hungry!" Leo explained, bending over the checkbook. "We'll have pancakes I think. That's one of those foods no one can turn down. He's ready for breakfast."

It couldn't have been much past eleven o'clock. The night sky had been bright when I paddled across the lake, the clouds a curdled gray over the moon. At the latest, it was just before midnight now, but for a moment it seemed possible I'd lost track of time, that the whole night had passed without my noticing. Had I fallen asleep in the loft? Was it dawn I'd seen in the sky?

"Breakfast?" Patra looked as confused as I, as muddled.

"Yep." He glanced up from his task. "It's early, but not *too*. And where is it that says you can't eat breakfast a little early? Who wrote that rule down?"

He ripped out the check and handed it to me. "Here," he said, and I saw that he'd written out One Hundred and Fifty Dollars. It was more money than I'd seen at once in my life, and yet so flimsy, so much less substantial than the ten-dollar bills Patra gave me. The line for my name he left blank. "Let's let Linda be on her way."

Patra unexpectedly grasped my arm. "Why not stay for breakfast?"

"It's been a long, long day for her," Leo warned.

"We should have *stopped* on the way home," Patra complained to him. "It wouldn't have *been* such a long day if we'd stopped."

"He was sleeping. It's good to let him sleep."

"But he's hungry now?"

"I think he could eat a horse," Leo told her. "And since he got to sleep all day, he's awake now. He's awake and telling stories."

"That's good?" Her voice splintered.

"That's *good*."

He took her by one hand, walked her to the couch, sat her down. Then he crouched in front of her, kissing her face—over and over. He kissed her cheeks, the wrinkles on her forehead, her freckled eyelids. She was still worrying the cell phone with a thumb, but I could sense something in her smoothing out, like a hand over bedcovers after a long bad night. I hadn't seen Leo like this before, and it was mesmerizing to watch. He brushed the hair from her face, the way I'd seen Patra brush the hair from Paul's. He said to her, softly, "So I figure, let's have breakfast, right? Let's start tomorrow early. It's not written anywhere that we can't do that."

"It's tomorrow?" Patra asked.

"Oh, yes. Oh, yes."

"And we're just having breakfast?"

"Pancakes and syrup and strawberries and milk."

At that, my mouth filled with saliva, and Leo went into the kitchen and started pulling out pots and pans. He paused to put in a CD. "A little music?" he asked over his shoulder. And then something classical with strings bloomed steadily into the room. Patra, who'd been glancing at Paul's open doorway, set her cell phone on the coffee table.

Once the phone was out of her hands, Leo started to relax. "Well, bye Linda!" he said to me across the kitchen island. Never looking in my direction, taking for granted that I was on my way out the door. His eyes were fixed on Patra, on her strange jittery walk from couch to hall.

"Maybe don't bother him now," he called to her, a pot in hand.

"But he's awake?"

"He's fine."

"He's awake?" She looked back at Leo.

"He woke up a few minutes ago. He must be hungry. He asked for *breakfast*."

So breakfast is what Leo made. He turned on all the lights in the main room and kitchen, went around flicking every switch. He filled a pot with water to warm the syrup bottle and, within a minute or two, had stirred a golden batter, which he ladled in bubbly, spreading pools onto the skillet. As he did this, as he dabbed at the pancakes with the tip of his spatula, he kept quietly suggesting that I leave. "There's your check, Linda," he said. "Thanks so much, again."

"No problem," I said, as the warm, doughy scent of pancakes filled the room.

"It was a huge help to have you, you know. So, thanks. A huge—huge—help."

He smiled without looking up, his forehead shining with steam.

"Let me do something," I offered. "Let me pour the milk."

"That's really nice of you! But I'm sure you're tired."

"Not really," I said.

"You've already done so much."

"You don't have enough batter for me?" I asked.

"It's not that. It's just that I bet your parents are waiting for you."

"I'm getting in the way?"

"No." A muscle in his jaw clenched. "Look, we'd *love* to have you stay, but—"

I met his bluff. I lined up four perfect glasses on the counter, opened the milk carton, and filled all four. I lifted a stack of plates from the cabinet and carried them to the table. As I did, the cats arrived from nowhere and bore down on my ankles with the sides of their faces. Steam from Leo's skillet fogged up all the windows. I could no longer see out.

Good-bye woods, I thought. *Good-bye world.* The pancakes were sizzling and the cats were meowing and the water was boiling rapidly around the glass syrup bottle. Classical music webbed back and forth through the air. I laid out knives and forks, paper napkins, a plate of sliced butter. When Leo's back was turned, Patra leaned into Paul's room, holding onto the molding with her hands. Then she pulled her head out, padded around the living room on bare feet, straightened pillows, restacked books, folded a blanket.

Abruptly, she turned to Leo and me in the kitchen. "What a good idea. Right? Breakfast."

"And Linda's here!" she added, coming over and giving me a hug, pushing herself in so I could feel her pointy chin tucked over my shoulder. Little Patra, shorter by an inch than I was—all limbs, all cool and clammy skin in her T-shirt. Then, fast as that, she moved away, kissed Leo on the back of the neck. "Leo, the Larger," she said on tiptoe, and I could see that some energy she could barely contain was coursing through her. All her movements had a jerky, outsize exuberance, as if she were struggling to contain something inside herself. She hastily rinsed the spatula

Leo had used for mixing. She washed the mixing bowl, swiped at the counter with a paper towel, and at some point she lifted an egg absentmindedly from the carton and squeezed until it cracked open.

"What am I doing?" she asked, holding up her glistening, gooey hand. But she seemed to be laughing. "What a mess!" she exclaimed, rubbing her hand with a dish towel, vigorously wiping each of her fingers. Then she took a deep, steadying breath and sat down at the table. "Okay, I'm starving," she said. "Where are those pancakes?"

I brought Patra her glass of milk and, while Leo went to get Paul, piled pancakes onto our plates. Leo returned only seconds later, smiling directly at Patra—smiling so wide that her lips curled up too, slightly—and said, "The little king wants his in bed!" So he turned to leave again with a plate and glass of milk.

Halfway across the room, his head swiveled around. "I got it, Patty. Eat."

I watched her sit back down.

Without speaking, she broke off a piece of pancake with her fingers and put it in her mouth. I did the same. I was so hungry, and the pancakes were so warm and soft, still gooey with batter in the middle. You could eat them without chewing much, you could get a lot into your mouth at once, you could nearly drink those pancakes down. I kept breaking off and pushing pieces in my mouth, and just when I thought I'd never get enough, never be filled up, I looked over and saw that Patra had stopped eating. Her lips were partway open, and I could see the half-chewed pancake wedged between her teeth and gums, balanced in a frothy mix on her lower lip. She sat there with her cheeks bulged out for ten seconds, twenty, and then, at last, she deliberately closed her eyes, carefully rotated her jaw, and forced that huge pancake wad down her throat. I saw it go.

"Patra?" I said, a low rumble of fear moving through me.

What was Paul like at that point? I was asked later.

I remember wondering if Patra would choke. I wondered if a person's windpipe could be blocked by something as harmless and soft as pancake. If that kind of crisis was possible.

"Ugh," Patra murmured. Then she stood up and went straight to the couch. She pulled her scrawny knees up inside her T-shirt, lay her head on a cushion. "That's enough of that," she whispered.

What time was it then? It was either very early or very late, and, as I looked across the table at the crumbs we'd made, at the pile of pancakes left, I felt suddenly drained. I made a ball of my napkin, drank the last gulp of milk from my glass. Then I went around the room flicking off the lights Leo had turned on. I found the blanket Patra had folded minutes before, shook it open over her curled form, and sat down at the other end of the couch.

Leo's music played on.

I didn't say anything to Patra. We looked out the window together. My parents' cabin across the lake was dark now, but the night sky was still bright. Perhaps, I thought, a full moon had risen—or perhaps true dawn had come at last. On the shore, my dad's Wenonah gleamed like a beached fish.

"You saw me coming?" I asked. I wanted to hear that story again.

"Oh, Linda."

"Have you ever been in a canoe?"

"Mmm. Once. But I'm not like you. I'm a city kid, you know?"

"I know."

She glanced at me across the couch. "At camp. They plopped me down in a canoe, and all I could think was I'm going to fall out. And the more I thought that, the more I was afraid I'd eventually tip the thing just because I'd imagined it so clearly. Splash."

"Everybody thinks that."

She exhaled slowly. "I need to get better at controlling my thoughts."

"Everyone eventually tips."

"Do they? Leo never thinks like that."

"Like what?"

"Like the worst thing, the very worst thing could happen."

I didn't say anything.

"He's a *good* dad."

"Yeah?"

"And Paul! My Paul is such a good kid."

"He is."

She seemed pleased to hear me say that. She lifted the blanket for me to come under, so I moved in closer and let her cover me up. "You know how Paul was born?" she asked, tucking the blanket around my legs.

No, I hadn't thought about that. I'd only ever thought of Paul as fully formed, as a four-year-old arrival from another planet. I never thought of him as an infant, as one of those hours-old, red-and-wet mounds of flesh—as coming out of Patra.

"Let me tell you something, Linda." And I wanted her to tell me something, I did. "After I got pregnant with Paul I was sick for so long. I had this belief I was doomed somehow, that everything that could go wrong would. I had such a bad feeling about it. Leo kept saying, you're afraid, that's all it is. You're afraid. And I was. I was so worried I'd made a huge mistake."

"You'd just finished college?"

"My friends were joining the peace corps, starting grad school."

"It makes sense, how you felt."

"It wasn't just that I was afraid. It felt really real, how sick I was during pregnancy. There were all these complications. Leo kept urging me to worry less, kept reading me all his books, but it was one thing after another. Low fetal weight, premature contractions, everything you could think of. Then during labor, I actually felt my heart stop. I actually heard it go *thump, thump, thump*"—she patted my leg as she said this—"then nothing else. And that's when I had this tiny thought, that I'd been wrong to be so scared of this, that God wouldn't do that. God wouldn't just stop my heart, would he?"

My throat closed up at the idea. "He wouldn't."

"Later Leo said that thought about God was Paul. That thought was him being born."

Through the window, the black trees stood stiff and un-yielding. Patra was quiet, her hand on my leg. She was quiet for such a long time I thought she'd drifted off, but then I felt her shift position, move closer to me so our heads almost touched on the couch cushions.

She was whispering. "I'd been resisting Leo's way of think-ing for such a long time. I kept telling him, I just don't have your kind of mind that believes one thing without question. But then

Paul was there and everything was fine. Paul was perfect, truly. And I was so happy after that, not fighting Leo anymore. Going his way seemed easy. There's nothing to say about happiness, you know? Nobody believes you when you talk about it." She was crying now, she was asking me: "I'm so happy, right? Don't we seem happy to you?"

"You do," I assured her. "You are."

I must have dozed off, because the next thing I knew I was half under the blanket and half under Patra's legs. I could barely move beneath her soft, warm weight. I could see Patra's head sticking out from the other side of the blanket, and I felt a deep body gladness suddenly, the same as when I used to curl up with Tameka in a sleeping bag in our shared bed. That old feeling came back to me hard, the way the sleeping bag had been like a second body we'd put on each night, the best body of all, so much more substantial than our separate ones. I nestled closer to Patra, let my hip sink into a crack in the cushions. Closed my eyes. Perhaps something did tug at the edge of my consciousness then, because I remember thinking there was nothing to be worried about—that worrying now was like worrying the canoe would tip because you'd imagined it would happen. That was impossible I told myself. It didn't work like that.

When I awoke next, I was sweating. Leo's CD was no longer playing, and a breeze was moving through my hair. I pushed a corner of the blanket back and let my damp neck grow chill in the cool air. What time was it? Patra, across the couch, was sleeping soundly. Somehow I stood without waking her, and it was only when I took a few steps that I realized the breeze I felt came from outside. I smelled a bit of woods blow in, the bright scent of pine needles. The sliding door to the deck was wide open, and a litter of pale leaves lay across the rug.

I stepped, shivering, across the threshold. True night had come at last. The sky: starless, dark, empty.

Someone was at the telescope, crouched.

"Paul?"

He looked up at me, and his face was bright and clear as anything. He looked stronger and healthier than I'd seen him in days, the whites of his eyes and the whites of his teeth flashing even in the dark. His hair had been worked by a finger into a sharp spoke that stood on the very top of his head. He was smiling.

"Oh, brother, another beaver," he giggled.

"Paul—" I felt relief then. I felt relief enough to scold him. "Come on inside."

"Let's play survival together," he suggested.

"Not now."

"Look! Here comes a bear."

He started running. He took off down the stairs and into the woods. For such a little kid, he moved far faster than I thought he could, scrambling over logs and under branches, pushing through pine boughs so they whipped back against my chest. I was running after him in my socks. Paul was in his footed pajamas. I could barely keep up, though the wet leaves and mossy rocks were all familiar to me. Then the last branch fell away and the trees opened up and the shore was in front of us. I saw, to my shock, that a silvery crust of early ice had congealed over the water. Paul looked back at me once, his hair horn bent double. He yelled, "Oh no, a bear!" The next thing

I knew, he was down on his belly, elbowing his way onto that thin sheet of ice, and I realized at last how cold it was, how the smell of snow thinned the air in my nostrils, how my fingertips were already going a little numb. "Paul!" I called out, taking a small step onto the ice, listening to it splinter under my weight, feeling the whole thing give way. My third step broke through to my ankles. As I stood in the bitter cold water, as I watched Paul drag himself across the ice by the elbows, pulling himself— snake-like—toward the center of the lake, it came to me finally that this was a dream.

Then it was dawn. Two gray triangles of sky shone through the big windows. Mist was rising off the lake, and I could just make out my parents' cabin through the haze. Bit by bit, I took in the shadowy room around me. Paul's light was off, Leo was snoring somewhere out of sight, and Patra was beside me on the couch, still sleeping. The sliding glass door was shut tight. Everything, everything was in its rightful place. I sat up more fully—and saw Drake pacing back and forth, back and forth, in front of Paul's closed door.

From the corner of my eye, I spotted Leo's manuscript on the easy chair. Unwilling to go back to sleep, but also unwilling to leave the couch, I leaned over and lifted the top page from the thick stack of papers. I was expecting a document about space, something about the misguided search for extraterrestrial life based on unexamined assumptions. I thought I had a feel for the way Leo would write. I expected jargon and equations mixed with deceptively simple questions. I hoped for diagrams.

Instead, the page on top was written in bland, square language. Once I had it in my hands, I noticed it used a different font than the manuscript beneath. I read the page twice through, first focusing on the typewritten words, and then on Patra's edits in purple pen. She'd crossed out a few phrases and scrawled a note in skinny cursive at the bottom.

Here's what Leo wrote:

Let me start by acknowledging the goodness that is the Church of Christ, Scientist and the inspired teachings of Mary Baker Eddy. I've written here of my son before but, today I want to give thanks for the omniscient, omnipotent grace of God, who shows Himself to the childlike nature in us all. My son, who has recently struggled with the belief of a stomachache, surprised me one night by asking me to read the Scientific Statement of Being instead of his favorite bedtime story. He is four years old, but his wisdom has long been a model to his mother and me. I read him the statement we all know so well, "There is no life, truth, intelligence, nor substance in matter . . ." After I finished, he asked me, "What is matter?" I was taken aback because he'd never asked this before. As a scientist, I thought of all the definitions my colleagues argue about and discuss, but as a Scientist, I was led to tell him, "Your stomachache and everything else that lies to you and tries to pretend it is real." "Out of the mouths of babes." He said to me then: "I'm not matter. I don't lie." So I saw that he knew better than I his own spiritual nature. By the morning after our conversation, my son's stomachache was entirely gone and he was able to prepare for a weekend trip we'd planned as a family. His demonstration was complete. As Mary Baker Eddy says, "Become conscious for a single moment that Life and intelligence are purely spiritual,—neither in nor of matter,—and the body will then utter no complaints." I'm so continually grateful to this church, which has sustained me and my family with the true teachings of Christ all these years.

Here's what Patra had added at the bottom:

> Maybe start with a little more description of Paul?
> Maybe add a little more about what he was struggling with?
> Re: "Out of the mouths of babes": Is that how he put it? Didn't he say, "I don't matter" instead of "I'm not matter"? Remember how he spooked me with that, and how you corrected him, and it was funny and sweet and everybody laughed? Remember how he was sitting with that old glove of yours pulled up to his elbow and he kept petting your chin as you talked to him? Details like those that will move people, I think. Don't forget to put a few details like that in. Or, remember how he was trying to fit both hands in that glove at once, like a fin? That was funny, too. Remember how when he took his hands out, all those little rocks from the lake came out on your lap? I'm not sure how that fits, but otherwise, of course, this is very beautiful.

14

I WROTE MR. GRIERSON A LETTER ONCE. He was living in Florida when I tracked him down, in a little town outside Tallahassee called Crawfordville, which was named for a doctor who'd lived there long ago. That's what the Internet said. I learned from online reports that Mr. Grierson kept a shop, a place that sold *Star Wars* lunchboxes and nineteenth-century rocking chairs and 1950s postcards of orange groves. The postcard oranges were a shiny balloon yellow, not really orange at all. *Junk*, people called it. The Treasure Chest the shop was called.

"Dear Mr. Grierson," I wrote.

Then I stopped. I was living in Minneapolis by then. I was eating my dinners with the mechanic and working days as an office temp and, when I couldn't sleep at night, I read biographies of explorers, stories about the sick drive to Everest where men with frost-bitten fingers dug in the ice with spoons. I read these books with a flashlight so as not to awaken Ann in her single bed across the room. I read for hours in a shadowy cave of blankets, leaning against the cold wall, growing impatient with the hopelessly boyish ploys for survival. When the climbers inevitably started up the mountain in a storm with just a pocketknife and a shovel, I tried writing Mr. Grierson instead.

I started the same letter again and again. Dawn grayed and regrayed the room.

"Dear Mr. Grierson," I wrote.

"Dear Adam." "To Adam Grierson." "To Mr. Adam Grierson." "Dear You." Then finally:

You may not remember me. I was your student in eighth grade American history in Loose River, Minnesota. I was the one by the window in the lumberjack shirt and the long braid and the hiking boots. You knew me as Mattie. You called me Miss Originality, for the prize I won in History Odyssey. I did wolves, remember? I did a history of wolves. I'm writing now because I've been thinking about something that has bothered me for a while. After you left Loose River and after Lily Holburn said the things she did, no one ever spoke one word about what you taught us in class. It was weird to me, like all those days never happened. But I guess you put a lot of energy into your lessons. I remember how you stood up and recited the whole Declaration of Independence by heart, which must have been a lot of work to memorize. I remember how you had us draw maps of the country as if we were Lewis and Clark, as if we only knew the shapes of the rivers by riding them. When you took me to History Odyssey, I admit, I thought you were laughing at my wolf idea, but later I thought about how you picked me to do it over everybody else. Maybe you saw me as less trouble for you than some other girl, but it seems to me now that the reasons you picked me matter less than the fact of it.

Did you know that when Lily Holburn came back to school the fall after you left, she had a surprise for us? People had been saying for a while she was sick. But no, she was pregnant, which sealed her fate and yours in town, though most people had heard by then that she'd taken back her testimony against you. The courtroom, people said, had spooked her. Can you imagine Lily pregnant? She was very beautiful, actually. She was even more beautiful than she was before. But then she got on a bus one day and went to Saint Paul, where there was a program for girls like her associated with the Catholic Church. She became a blood lab technician, I heard. The program gave her free career training, baby clothes and stuff, so it's not hard now to guess why she lied about you. Lots of animals in a trap will play dead. That's how I think of what she did. She found a sneaky way out of the little life she would have had if they'd made her stay and get married to the guy who knocked her up.

Lily wasn't as dumb as she looked. But probably you knew that already.

I thought once about moving to California. That's where you're from, right? I wanted to see the redwoods there. I wanted to feel miniature beside those big trees, to alter for good my sense of the scale of things. I've heard people say those trees can do that to you. But Minneapolis is more affordable. The trees here are a lot like the trees in Loose River, though there are fewer of them.

I've never been to Florida either. I think if I came into your shop I would buy the rocking chair with the high back and the bent oak runners. It looks comfortable in the picture on your website. It doesn't seem like junk. I've read what people say about you online, about how you shouldn't get to live in their town. What if a kid wanders into your store and so on. Maybe they have good reasons to write what they do, but I think you should hear this too: I think you're innocent. I think you should hear that from someone. I think someone should say that to you, and in case no one has, I'm that someone for you.

Sincerely,

Mattie Furston

Dawn is a free pass. I've always thought that. The hours between four and seven belong to a few fidgety birds and maybe a last bat charging mosquitoes. In Minneapolis, the traffic from the highway would grow louder and louder, and eventually a slant of light would work its way in through the curtain and crawl up my neck. That's when I put away my books and papers. At seven on the dot, I got out of bed, boiled water on the stove, and strained coffee for me and Ann. I wiggled into my pantyhose in the bathroom. When I stuck out my tongue to brush it, the girl in the mirror was gagging at me, earnestly. Eyes red.

That morning in the Gardner cabin, seven o'clock came and went without anyone stirring at all. This was a surprise to me I guess, but only because I'd assumed the Gardners were early risers. From my place on the couch beside Patra, I watched the lake silver gradually, and then I watched it net the first few bits of new sun. A loon surfaced on the far side and looked around. A motorboat sped past grumpily, calving the water, and when another boat followed in its wake, I remember wanting the morning to slow down, slow down. I wanted the morning to hold still, to take its time in coming.

Patra woke up reluctantly. She kept opening her eyes part-way and closing them again—as if reassured by my presence, as if my presence gave her permission to return to unconsciousness without guilt. When the early light caught her face, every freckle became vivid and precise. I watched two of them quiver together over her right eyelid. I noticed a slim white scar I'd never seen before, parting the down on her upper lip. I saw tiny flecks of dandruff riding a few hairs near her scalp.

Later, it would be impossible for me to tell anyone of the happiness of those hours, the exquisite sweetness of sitting there with her asleep beside me on the couch, and it was very hard for me to admit even to myself how much of that feeling had to do with Paul and Leo being safely out of the room. A slice of sunlight edged up her blanketed thigh. I remember how her breathing moved the natty yellow cotton up and down, how her eyeballs beneath the freckled lids shifted in her sleep. I noticed the palest blue vein in her neck. I didn't touch her. I sat cross-legged on the couch, the blanket covering us both, one of her small red knees poking out from a corner.

At the time, I did not question why she'd stayed with me in the living room—and not with Leo in their bed or with Paul in his room. I did not wonder why she chose to stay asleep so long, which seemed natural to me at the time, proof that everything was fine. That she was there with me after all those hours, that she was calmly sleeping still, was the only reassurance in the world I needed. Later, of course, I would wonder about it. Later, when I was asked about her actions, I wouldn't have a very good answer for why she hadn't gone in to check on Paul that night. The suggestion at the trial was that she'd remained with me in outright denial of the facts, that she'd aligned herself with a fifteen-year-old because she wanted to feel less responsible herself. A more generous interpretation was that she identified with me because we were both susceptible in a sense, young girls under the influence of a dogmatic older man. Leo, it was said, had kept Paul away from her on purpose. There's some truth to both theories advanced at the trial—I saw evidence for each—but even at the time I understood that they had missed something. They'd left something out. They didn't account for Patra's awareness of her own power, her disorganized but formidable determination. They didn't account for what made Patra *Patra*.

Didn't she always need someone to watch her and approve? And wasn't I better at that than anyone?

When at last she woke for good, when she sat up on the couch and pulled the blanket over her knees, she had a closed-lip smile waiting for me, like a reward for my vigil.

"So," she said. "Janet stayed all night."

"Janet?"

"Rochester's name for Jane Eyre. She was a governess, too. Like you." She brushed some hair out of her face. "You're both governesses." She smiled at the word. Then, as if catching herself: "What time is it?"

I shrugged.

She sat up straighter. "Where's Leo?"

I shrugged again.

She turned and shot a wild look down the hall. But instead of standing, as I thought she would, she closed her eyes. She appeared to be fighting something, summoning stillness through strength of will. Then she let out a deep breath through her white teeth, and I could smell it a foot away—the rot and decay, the remains of an undigested meal.

She opened her eyes again, squinting a little. "Did you read that?" She was looking at Leo's typed page on the chair beside me.

I waited a second before answering. "Yeah?"

"It's *okay*." She leaned forward in a gargoyle-like crouch. She set a damp palm on my arm. "It's *okay*, you know," she said, breathing it out, as if she were talking herself toward something.

Her fetid breath and her hand on my arm made something squirrel through my gut.

I leaned closer to smell her breath again, disgusted with myself—disgusted and interested, both.

When she spoke again her voice was lower than usual. "I keep telling myself, worry is the problem. That's the thing to work on, right?"

I hesitated. "I don't know."

"It's a problem with my mind."

"Well—" I thought about it. Something snagged. "What do you mean?"

"What *do* I mean?" She looked raked clean, purged for some reason, by the question. She stuck out her tongue— laughing? And I could see it, with its layer of white scum, slide back over her teeth. Between last night and now there was something looser about her, more disjointed, more tantalizing. She swallowed, grabbed my hand in hers. Her eyes were bouncing from thing to thing. "You're right, Linda. Of course you're right. It's stupid to worry about worry. Look, Drake's back, and Leo's here, and you're here, too. Everything's good."

"I'm here, too."

"Everything's fine."

"Everything is," I nodded. "I know, I know."

"Not even a cloud in the sky. And those are birds singing, right?"

"Chickadees."

"See, *you* know. I knew you'd know."

And because it seemed so easy to make her happy now, I added, "And purple martins."

"Purple martins, okay."

"Um, and"—I listened—"two loons." Though that was the whine of a motor, possibly. Maybe I was making things up, exaggerating slightly.

"Two loons, of course. I should know that. I should know. The thing is to let myself take things as they *really* are, like this—"

In a flash, I saw the white field of ice that was the lake last night.

"We just need to *know* the truth—" she said.

Here was the truth: everyone else was still sleeping—everyone but us. I nodded.

"Hey, you're wearing my headband," she said. Her eyes stopped on my face.

"Hmmm," I acknowledged, relishing the feel of her gaze. The old ache was still there, but it had changed. It had become part of my head—it had both affixed itself to me and disappeared.

"Looks good on you," she said.

Then Patra's phone rang. *Star Wars* did three notes before Leo appeared from the back room—instantly, like a grouse flushed from the bushes. Patra seized the phone and jumped up to get closer to the deck, saying: "Hello?" and "Thank you, yes!" I stood up too, holding onto the blanket that was still warm from our bodies. I kept my eye on Leo in the doorway, but he never once glanced in my direction. He was watching Patra, who was agreeing enthusiastically with the person on the phone as she paced up and down, nodding continuously. "Good, good, good." She paused midstep to take something in. "I'm trying to do that. I'm really, really trying. I *am*." She brightened. "I'm feeling so much better now it's morning. It's a turning point, maybe? Yes, he *is* perfect in God's eyes. That's what I've been thinking. And guess what? I didn't even tell you the most important part." She started pacing again, heading toward the table. "He had breakfast! What? Pancakes. What was that? So sorry about the connection, but absolutely, yes, that's true. Yes, we are! We are *so* grateful."

When she got off the phone, she turned to Leo with a huge, haphazard grin on her face, which gradually closed down as she stood there.

One look at Leo, and that smile went out of business.

Did they ever, to your knowledge, call a doctor? I was asked.

Patra said, "That was the practitioner, Mrs. Julien?"

"Yes," Leo confirmed. Though it had been Patra of course, not him, who spoke to her.

"She said we should be grateful?"

"We are," he told her.

There was a new stillness to him this morning, an economy of gesture, as if he'd realized how little movement was required to sustain himself. I watched him assemble some kind of smile on his face. There went his lips, pointing up.

To Patra, he said, "How about some hot cocoa? Can you put the kettle on, Pea?"

She shook her head once, and something strange was happening as she walked across the room toward him. All the braided rugs were sliding, then colliding under her bare feet. She was walking that fast.

He stopped her by opening up his arms and giving her a hug.

As he held onto her, his voice changed. It grew musical, full of highs and lows. "What are you doing, Patty Pea? Let's not backtrack now, Patty Cakes. Let's do what we always do, make the cocoa, clean the litter box, go about the morning. Can you do that for me?"

I watched him put his mouth against her ear.

Then, over her head and without the singing: "Linda, will you help me with something?"

I'd assumed he was ignoring me, so his question took me off guard. I frowned at him and prepared to shake my head. I felt my shoulders lift up defensively, but when he let go of Patra and turned, I found myself following him out.

I was curious. I couldn't help it.

"Patra," he said, when she started after us. "Some *cocoa*. Then the litter box, get dressed. Maybe read the lesson? It really is a beautiful day."

In my dream, Paul had been so wily and quick. He'd seemed both mischievous and manic, which had amused and irritated me in turns. In my dream, I'd become furious with him at last. There had been something very devious about the way he'd wiggled across the ice on his belly. So when I followed Leo into Paul's room, I felt some residue of resentment waiting for him. I took one look at him lying in bed and felt my resentment go dry. He was only a kid, after all. A little kid, sleeping. It was relieving to see him flat on his stomach, to see him tucked to his neck in covers, his golden head poking out. His chapped lips were open, his eyes closed.

"Now, Linda, don't be afraid," Leo murmured from behind, and it wasn't until he said it that I was.

"Now, Linda. It's okay." He seemed to want to pat my shoulder.

Leo closed the door behind us and my first thought was to back away. My second thought was to look for a way out. I wasn't sure what trap I'd been led into. I felt my calves tense up, my fingertips tingle.

Leo's face looked lopsided. He was pushing out one cheek with the tip of his tongue, and I knew without thinking it through that this was something he only did when alone.

"We're playing Candy Land," he told me, almost bashfully, gesturing toward the floor.

"What?" But it was clear enough. The pastel board was spread out over the carpet, a path of colored squares snaking across.

"Paul's blue. I'm red."

"Okay." But Paul was asleep.

"Just move his piece when it's his turn." Leo nodded at me, encouragingly. "I've got to use the bathroom, quick, and make one little call. If you could let me know if he—"

He was painfully apologetic about it. He was stacking a Bible and some other books on Paul's nightstand in a low embarrassed tower. He was glancing at the full plate of pancakes on the dresser, hastily and without turning his head, as if he didn't want me to notice it but couldn't keep from looking himself. Then he just stood there. Eyes bloodshot, tongue tenting one cheek. "Leo—?" I asked him.

He started tucking in his shirt with his fingertips.

"Don't be afraid," I found myself saying. Leo tucked in his shirt again—and again. He pushed the fabric down deep. He hitched up his shorts and shoved in his shirt. The fabric strained against his shoulders, and he looked like he wanted to tuck in his whole torso and his arms up to the elbows. He was going to tuck his whole self in.

To stop him, I knelt on the carpeted floor next to the Candy Land board.

"Paul," I said, to get Leo to leave. "It's your turn."

Actually, I didn't know how to play Candy Land. I'd never played games like this when I was a kid, so the rules, the way to move from square to square, eluded me. There were no dice or one of those arrows you spin. I could sense Paul in his lump of covers on the bed but I didn't try to wake him. Without thinking, I pulled a card from the stack. I moved Paul's blue Gingerbread Man toward the yellow square the card matched. Then Leo's red man. Blue, then red. With a sinking heart, it came to me that I didn't need to know how to play. It was obvious. It was a race. Gingerbread Leo plodded past the Crooked Old Peanut Brittle House. Gingerbread Paul took a shortcut through the Gumdrop Mountains. After only a few turns, I felt the deep drudgery of having played this game too many times before. I slid the pieces steadily along the pastel track. Leo wound through the Lollipop Woods, and Paul got stuck on a licorice space. Just when Leo's man was closing in on the Molasses Swamp, just when the outcome started to seem inevitable, though still a long way off, I happened to look up. "Paul?" He was watching me from his bed. His breathing deepened, then paused. Half his face was smashed against the pillow, but one eye looked out. Unblinking, blue as anything. "Paul?" I asked.

His pillowcase darkened with spittle as he started breathing again.

I cheated then: I set Gingerbread Paul on the final space.

The eye tracked over my shoulder and past my head.

I scrambled to my feet.

In the hallway, I ran into Leo, whose hands were dripping from the bathroom. "Umm?" he asked, still buckling his belt, leaving huge wet handprints on his blue cotton shirt.

I didn't know what to say. "He won" is what came out, and I felt my voice hack through a crust of panic to say it.

"He did?" Leo looked truly relieved to hear me say it—as if winning Candy Land were an achievement, as if watching someone else move your piece around a board counted now as victory. "That's a lucky break. He's *got* to be happy about that. He's got to be. He'll be back to his old self before we know it. It won't take much. He'll be ready for kindergarten in a few weeks."

"He's only four!" It felt like a protest to put it like that.

Leo took that in, then rejected it. "But he's got his head on straight. You know him. He's very, very advanced for his age. He'll be fine. He's going to be fine."

I shook my head. "He's still so—" *Defenseless*, I meant. "Such a little kid." I tried to corral some evidence to back me up. "He doesn't even know how to *read*."

Something about that, the fact that Paul couldn't even sound out "train" in his very favorite book, made tears spring to my eyes.

Leo didn't seem to see them. He put his wet hands on his hips, settled into the argument. He looked more comfortable now, back in terrain where he knew he could triumph. "Well now, that's not strictly true, Linda. You know that. He can read a little. He can read 'Paul.' And 'no.'"

"He's memorized those words!" I was veering far past the point.

"I'm sure that's not fair. What do you do when you read? Do you sound it out? What?"

I shook my head, bewildered. "Listen, Leo—"

"Now, Linda—" He reached out and cupped my hands in his wet palms. He was pressing them now, squeezing my fingers. His voice grew musical, the way it had with Patra. He'd gotten my hands wet, like his. He insisted, "You've been an enormous help. Now I'm just going to pop back in? See what he might be up for next? Excuse me a moment. All right?"

I left Leo and went into the main room, where the dishes from breakfast were still on the table. Drops of maple syrup had congealed to amber beads on the plates. Pancake crumbs were scattered in wide constellations across the wood table, the bamboo placemats, the maple floorboards.

Patra, still in her T-shirt, was cleaning the litter box. She was on her knees in the kitchen. With a blue plastic shovel in one hand and a white garbage bag in the other, she looked like a little kid playing in the sand. She glanced up at me, pushing hair from her eyes as I came around the kitchen island.

There must have been something in my face she didn't like, because she took one look at me and started scooting back on her knees across the tile.

"Patra," I said, coming forward.

She stood up, kitty litter embedded in her knees, pressed into her red skin in a gray mosaic. I took a step toward her, but she put the island between us. She held onto the white laminate counter.

I came around the island toward her, and she circled the same direction, moving away from me.

"Patra," I said again.

"It's okay?" she asked, pleading. As if I could do that for her, as if I could spare her.

"I think maybe—"

"Maybe?"

"He needs something. Like, from the drugstore, or—"

"Don't tell Leo," she interrupted.

I retreated from what I might have said. "Like Tylenol or something?"

"Leo says, control your thoughts. Think of Paul as a *new day.*"

"I can go to the drugstore for you, okay?"

"And who can stop a new day from coming?"

"I should go get something I think." I licked my dry lips. "Patra? Patra?"

I'd been creeping faster than she was moving away the whole time. Now I was just inches from her. There she stood, with her reeking morning breath and kitty-litter knees. I could tell by the look in her eye that she was riding just the surface of her brain, bobbing on that choppy surface of hope and worry, so on impulse I kissed her on the lips, hating her purely in that instant, wanting to do more than that, to hurt her, to slap her, to get something back. Her lips were cool and flat, unresponsive. They didn't seem like lips.

"Just the Tylenol," she said, stepping sideways. Not really taking me in—not really a mind at all, just a bobbing boat on a wave.

"This is fucked," I said softly.

"What?" she said.

She was too miserable to hurt though. Her T-shirt barely covered her panties. She was, every bit of her, limbs—gangly and thin, almost naked. The scar on her lip seemed to pulse red, then white. I was that close. I was close enough to see that.

"Fine, then," I told her.

I walked across the room and worked my socked feet into my tennis shoes on the skewed welcome mat. Then I spun the handle on the front door, opening it up to the harsh bright rectangle of summer. Looked back once at Patra, in her wrinkled T-shirt by the counter. She was soundlessly twisting her lips— slowly, weirdly—mouthing *thank you* in a way that made me want to turn back and force her to speak out loud. But then I was gone. Outside on the driveway it was hot already. I took a few steps into the woods, as if on my way home, and then, abruptly, squatted down and lifted the granite stone on the edge of the trail. Worms waved blindly up. Tiny, translucent beetles moved in stupid circles. Everything was squirming and pulsing piteously, but there were the bills Patra had left, weeks ago. They were sodden and damp, but they were real money. I stuffed them in my pocket and took off at a sprint.

15

FOR THREE YEARS AFTER HIGH SCHOOL I TOOK CLASSES AT
ITASCA COMMUNITY COLLEGE IN GRAND RAPIDS. I worked
at a pizzeria-bar called The Binge that had brown vinyl booths
and wine-bottle vases plugged with plastic carnations. The only
requirements for the job were to wear black shorts, even in
winter, and to keep the salad bar stocked with chopped lettuce
and shaved carrots. During that time I saved money for a down
payment on an '88 Chevy Corsica, and in the years after I bought
that car I lived in Duluth, where I worked retail and cleaned
houses on the side. Sometimes on my days off, I'd walk down
to the water and wait for the lift bridge to go up, for ore ships
and sailboats to slink out of the harbor. I didn't stand on the
grassy knoll with tourists but crossed the bridge and sat in stiff
baymouth sand. The fourth spring I was there my dad died. After
the funeral in Loose River, after I crashed my Corsica in the trees
and sold the car for parts, I found a job at a temp service in the
Cities. The temp service placed me at ManiCo Barge, where I
answered calls from hoarse-voiced men hauling scrap steel and
corn down the Mississippi. My job was to arrange their schedules,
give the anticipated arrival and departure times of their trips,
sometimes take calls from their wives and make their excuses. I

ate packed lunches in the break room with the other temps, and at the end of each day, I walked to the bus stop downtown on salt-strewn streets. Through the scratched windows of the bus I watched snow fall in fat orbs under lights, all across the river.

The mechanic's apartment was a basement walk-out in a once-grand Victorian. Students lived in the turrets. Bare poplar seedlings sprouted in all the gutters. "Hey there," I'd say to Rom when he opened his rickety back door—still in his mechanic's clothes, still in his greasy blue coveralls, his blue eyes watering at the cold I let in. I'd hold up a frozen pizza and a six-pack of Buds.

"Oh, man," he'd say. "Oh, really, a Tombstone? You shouldn't have."

If he was unimpressed it didn't stop him from drinking his three beers in the thirty minutes it took for the oven to heat up and cook the pizza. I kept him from my beers by whacking his hand every time he reached for one more. "Fair is fair," I'd say, so one night Rom went into the bedroom and brought back a fifth of whiskey. As he swigged from his bottle, he whipped up his standard salad from bulgur, mint, and a cucumber. He made me drink a glass of milk as we waited for the pizza to cook. He made me eat a few bites of the salad and half an orange, before allowing me one little sip of his ratty booze.

"Fair is *fair*," he mocked.

The pizza cheese burned the roofs of our mouths. When I went for another swig of whiskey, he pulled the bottle out of reach. "Eat your salad," he commanded.

That first winter I was in the Cities, Rom was big on vitamins. He thought I ate like shit and had an unresolved past and should go to the dentist. He wanted us to eat at his table, so he set out plates and squares of paper towels folded in half. He'd started pressing for a pet, a Labrador retriever, because he thought a dog would lead to a more regular schedule, a shared apartment, more exercise. Weekend trips to the North Shore, a fucking campfire. I don't know what. When I rolled my eyes at all that, he said, "If you're not going anywhere, Girl Scout, just shut up. Okay? Just shut up."

"I didn't say anything," I protested.

"You didn't have to."

Sometimes, after supper, we put on our mittens and hats and walked to the movie theater a few blocks down toward the capitol. We split the cost for two seats, two Cokes, and a bucket of popcorn. The movies Rom chose were always unrelentingly loud, full of cops shooting over the hoods of cars; still, I found it restful to sit there in the pulsing dark. The louder it was, the sooner I slept, my head against the seat back, my shoes sticking to the floor. I didn't mind missing the car chases, the explosions. It was reassuring to feel that something important just went on happening while I slept, something with guns.

Afterward, Rom would test me to see when I'd fallen asleep. "That guy with the face that turned into a fish?" he'd say, when we were walking out. "Did you see that?"

And I'd say, though I usually hadn't, "He was *incredible*."

When I'd been in the Cities for about eight months, when the holidays rolled around, I showed up at Rom's apartment on Christmas Eve carrying a little package I'd wrapped in red reindeer paper and a thin green bow. Rom opened it on his unmade bed, sitting cross-legged. His feet were bare, yellow nailed, but he was wearing stiff new jeans and a black button-up shirt, untucked. I watched as he broke the green ribbon with his teeth and lifted from the box a dog's spikey collar and heavy leather lead. It took a moment for him to unwind the leash, and it's weird how joy goes through a grown man's face, so that for a second you can see him the way he was as a kid: all smooth faced and unguarded. Then that look was gone, and he was squinting at me as I wiggled out of my jeans, as I unhooked my bra and got completely naked. I took the leather collar and fastened it around my neck. For an instant he looked so disheartened, so disappointed—like I'd done the one thing that could truly hurt him—but then I sniffed his crotch and handed him the leash, so we had a good time.

"Bad girl," he told me.

I pulled against the leash. I wouldn't go where he said.

"Down," he warned, a glint in his eyes. "Stay."

His present for me was a Swiss Army knife. "Fool's protection," he explained, looking a little nervous, leaning in so I could hear the stud in his tongue click against his teeth. This was after we'd gotten dressed again and were sipping eggnog in his bed straight from the carton. He waited until I said, "Cool. Thank you," before showing me all the things the knife could do. Peel an orange, scale a fish. I didn't tell him I had the exact same knife in my purse, though more banged up. I didn't tell him I already knew which metal slit to pull with my fingernail to get the wire stripper out, or the three-inch blade. It was like so many other things between us, that gift. It was exactly right and totally wrong for me.

That same winter, just after Christmas, I received a bright red envelope in the mail. Ann and I were sorting bills on a dark afternoon when she held up the envelope with a Santa stamp, a Florida return address. "Is this from your family?" she asked. I took it from her. Her pale, plucked eyebrows arched hopefully over the rims of her glasses. It bothered Ann—it broke her strict code of Canadian niceness—that I hadn't any formal holiday plans, that I wouldn't tell her even the littlest thing about where I'd come from.

I hesitated long enough to flip the envelope chestward before saying, "Yep."

I stood and carried the envelope to our kitchenette. Inside was a holiday card with reindeer and HO HO HO's in black cursive. When I opened the card, out winged a photograph of a white-haired man with his arm slung around a dog. It was creepy in a way, but also not. It was just a guy in a lawn chair, a guy with his hound— a palm tree shadow floating over his head.

I could feel Ann watching from across the room.

"Where in Florida does your family live?" she asked.

I couldn't look at her to answer. I couldn't bear to talk about Loose River, so I headed toward the doorway instead. "I want a snack. You want a Diet Coke from the corner store?" She always did. I whisked up my jacket, stuffed the photo and the card inside a pocket. Opened the door and rode the elevator down four floors, taking in all the jittery, stuttering sounds of invisible machinery. On the ground floor, there was a clank and a bounce. Why tell Ann I hadn't been in contact with my mother in more than eight months? Why tell her that? Outside the apartment, traffic crawled steadily over icy roads, exhaust and snow mixing in the air. The cold instantly tightened the skin on my cheeks, calmed me. After a moment, I circled back through the rotating door and stood in the warm foyer again, where the light was bright over the mailboxes.

"Dear Mattie," Mr. Grierson wrote in his card.

His cursive went *loop-loop-loop*.

"Thank you for your letter a few months back," he *loop*-said, slanting downward to the right. He went on:

What an unexpected thing, a real old-fashioned letter. I meant to write back right away, and then, after some time passed, it seemed likely I would not write at all. But Christmas is a good excuse, and it was a nice surprise to hear from you, I guess because I didn't expect to get a letter like that. Hearing from an old teacher, I worry, can only be a disappointment. I remember running into one of my professors a few years back, and we just stood around with nothing to say, so I guessed that he didn't remember me the way he said he did and was being nice. I vowed right there and then never to pretend to know an old student. What I'm saying is, please don't take it personally that my whole time in Minnesota is pretty much a blur to me now. I just don't have many memories of that year. Plus I'm not as young as I was, as I'm sure you know. Even so it's nice to know that someone got something out of my lessons. I did work hard, and it's good to feel that maybe all that work counted somehow.

I'm running out of room on this card! Florida's nowhere I'd recommend. It's like being squashed slowly by invisible hands. Ha, ha, ha. It's hot is what I'm saying. The days go by pretty fast, and lately I just want a shopping-list approach to things. That's about all I feel capable of at this point. Here's what I want, just sitting down at the end of the day and seeing that I can check off the items. I'm not in the least what you say I am, though your letter was kind. I've learned a little about these things in my time, that is, the kinds of people who take the trouble to write me. I've found that some people who've done something bad will just go ahead and condemn everyone else around them to avoid feeling shitty themselves. As if that even works. Other types of people, and I'm not saying you're this, necessarily, but I'm just putting it out there, will defend people like me on principle because when their turns come around, they want that so badly for themselves. My two cents, for what it's worth. California's awesome, though. Go, if you can.

Peace, God bless, and happy New Year!

Adam Grierson

On New Year's Day I got up early because I couldn't sleep, though I'd been out late the night before with Rom. I walked down the winding path that followed the Minnehaha Creek to Lake Nokomis. The sun never really rose. It was dark, and then it was just a little less so. When I got to the lake, I saw a hopeful fisherman pulling a red plastic sled of supplies across the ice. All the usual joggers and cross-country skiers had stayed home. They were sleeping in I guess, doing their resolutions on notecards, drinking their bright orange mimosas, getting laid. It was me and the sled man out in the world. His body made an acute angle with the ice; he was leaning that hard as he pulled. His sled had etched a long blue streak from one end of the lake to the other.

When the wind started picking up, I hurried through the trees to keep warm, peed in a brittle porta-potty without fully sitting down. Came out and left the lake behind, not looking back. Where did people in a city go to feel less trapped? On Cedar Avenue I stopped for a cup of coffee to warm my bare hands at a bakery that sold so many kinds of bread the loaves covered a whole wall. I stared at the bread for a while, then left without buying any. Instead I went to a bar I'd come to like, where the stools were painted to look like human legs. I let myself get drunk. I let myself slouch, like the sled man, at a very acute angle over the bar. Eventually I glanced at my watch and realized I needed to find a bus so I could meet Ann at our Laundromat—Ann who wanted to wash all our towels and rugs and curtains for the new year. "Fresh start," she'd said.

For three hours, until my buzz wore off and our quarters drained, we washed and dried and folded our linens.

By the time we started back it was almost dark again. Ann said she wanted to see the rich people's luminaries along the river, so we walked with our baskets the long way home, through an alley and down a winding line of shops. Between a closed camera store and a bank, we passed a crow pecking at a frozen breadstick in front of a lonely lit shop. The shop had SCIENCE AND HEALTH marked in blue chalk in the window, and inside a Victorian lady with a brooch smiled placidly from a poster. The sidewalk crow hauled its breadstick up to a telephone wire, and as it did, Ann paused with her basket and lingered by the glass. She had gone to camp with some Christian Scientists, years back, which made her think she was some kind of authority—and she stopped for a moment, reading silently through the window. "I thought they'd closed most of these reading rooms down. There's, like, hardly any churches left." Then she shook her head, shifting the weight of her basket from one hip to the other. "I mean, the thing I never understood, the thing that doesn't make any sense, is how you can have a religion that offers absolutely no explanation for the origin of evil."

I kept walking.

It was another dreary snowless night. Almost no one was out—we could have walked straight down the middle of the street. *Where were those luminaries?* I wondered. My arms were aching under the weight of our lemony-smelling towels. Had we gone too far? Had we missed them? But no. Within a block we caught sight of the first of several long lines of brown paper bags lit up, all flickering orangely with candles.

"Ah!" Ann cried, stopping short.

Hipping her basket so she could touch my arm. "Look-it that! Look."

At some point that year—maybe that night, maybe a few weeks later—I ended up telling Ann about Loose River. I told her about the competing nativity scenes at Christmas, the Lutherans' sand-bag Jesus and the Catholics' ice one. I told her about the gym roof that collapsed in eighth grade and about Mr. Adler, who loved the Russian monarchs more than anything, even America. I may have even told Ann about my parents eventually, and about beautiful Lily—Lily who left us to have her baby—but I never said a thing about Patra and Paul, and I never told her what I really thought about Christian Science, which is that from what I know, from what little I know, it offers one of the best accounts of the origin of human evil.

This is where it comes from, Ann.

I think, now: That's the story I'm trying to tell here.

When Paul was excited, he ran with big moon-landing steps. He always looked as if he were concentrating very hard, saying to himself *run, run,* and each time the word went through his head he'd take a slightly more determined leap into the air. When I told him to run faster, he'd just run *higher,* and his pace would slow way down. He'd do all this useless work, hiking up his knees, pumping his fists.

It was great to watch, and I was only a little cruel in provoking him.

"Run!" I'd say, and he'd slow down to a near crawl, almost stopping between each stride.

"Faster!" I'd say. His lips would pinch shut. He'd shunt one arm forward and one arm back. He was a kid who'd learned to run by watching dwarves in their mine, from TV, from cartoons.

"Race you to the house!" I said to him once, and, as if he'd finally figured it out—that day, at last—he'd stayed put on the dock. So I took a few exaggerated steps to encourage him. "I'm going to beat you!" I said, offering that irresistible threat, doing a *thump-thump-thump* with my boots on the planks. No dice. When I looked back again, he'd slunk to a lying position, belly down, his arms curled up under him on the boards.

"What's up?" I said.

I closed in on him, casually prodded him with the toe of my boot. "This bear has gone into hibernation, looks like."

After a moment: "I'm bored."

"The bear is bored?" I asked, mock incredulous.

"And—" He turned his neck so his face pressed into the boards, the skin of his lip pushing out in a loop. "My tummy—"

Something about the way he said it made me crouch down and look at him more closely. Then I pulled him up to sitting. I lavished on him all I had in my little reserve. "Then you don't know about the *wolf*."

"I don't *want* to pretend," he groaned.

"This one's *real*," I promised.

This was late May, maybe. The aspens and poplars were dropping their seeds in fluffy drifts that accumulated—the way

snow did—along the dirt driveway. I coaxed him into the garage
with a few pretzels and buckled him in the bike while he ate
them, slouched, helmeted, serenely disenchanted, looking big
headed and Buddha-like in his red plastic seat. I pulled the bike
out onto the driveway and swung it a little menacingly when
I climbed on. "Here we go!" I yelled, hoping to throw him off
balance, hoping to thrill him into acting more like a kid. It was
a long ride to the Nature Center, and the whole way there I told
him wolf facts, wolf statistics, wolf stories. I intended to impress
him with the taxidermy wolf in the lobby. I intended to point
out the yellowed canines under her blue-hooded lip, the cherry-
red drips of blood painted on her coral claws. I remembered the
first time I'd seen that wolf as a kid, how the feeling went beyond
love, how it made me hungry, hungry, hungry.

But Paul had no interest in the wolf at all. He looked at it
for a few seconds and shrugged. After eleven miles on the bike,
all he had to say was, "That's not real."

What he liked best at the center were puzzles. He found
one on a shelf in the corner that exactly matched one he had
at home. It was a bucolic winter woodland scene: a snowy owl
perched fatly on a black branch, eyes lidless and round as two
open black pots. Paul knew how to put this puzzle together by
heart, so instead of looking at the wolf or stuffed foxes, instead
of fingering the rubber scat or dipping his little hand into one of
the wooden boxes and guessing its contents, he sat cross-legged
on the floor in the corner, piecing together the same puzzle he'd
done dozens of times at home. I wandered around the center to
kill time, read about the tea you could make from pine needles,
watched goldfish circle Peg's aquarium. Eventually, nothing left
to do, I went over and squatted next to Paul, who was holding
a Swiss cheese slice of the owl's face in one hand.

At first it infuriated me that he didn't look up when I approached. That he didn't acknowledge me at all, or wonder what I was doing. He scooched over automatically, let his body flow into mine and work its way onto my lap. He never stopped studying the puzzle. He settled his body against mine, arranging leg over leg, till I finally had to sit down fully on the floor. He assumed I was available and interested; he always just assumed. He bent double at the waist to reach the puzzle from the perch he'd taken on my lap. And outside—outside the window and down the road—whole mountains of poplar fluff drifted past.

At first I was annoyed, but then I was less so. I felt his chest expand with each breath against his nylon jacket and against my ribs. I felt the heat of his body through my jeans. He moved his fingers very knowingly from piece to piece, leaning his head back into me occasionally to assess. When he'd finished, he broke the puzzle up to do it again.

"Nope," I said. Though I wasn't sure I meant it. By then the room was going golden in the early evening sun. It was something I thought I should say, though: "It's time. Time to go."

That's when he yawned, his skull stoppering up the breath between my clavicles. There was something about that that made me regret suggesting we leave—something about the simple gift of his body, its closeness and its heat—that made me want to stay a little longer.

Then we were at the door—me zipping his jacket up, Peg handing him three gummy bears—and I asked him, proddingly, for Peg, "Did you have a nice time?"

He nodded in a way that moved his whole body up and down. "That was a *great* puzzle," he said.

16

ACCORDING TO HER TESTIMONY, PATRA GREW UP IN A SUB-
DIVISION OUTSIDE MILWAUKEE. She was the youngest of five
children by almost a decade, raised in a household of adults. Her
father was an engineer, and her mother, who'd stayed home with
all her siblings, had gone back to school by the time Patra was
born and was getting a PhD in urban sociology. She had taken
little Patra to all the classes she TA'ed and to her field research
in a juvenile center in Waukesha. By the time Patra was in high
school, her mother was a tenured faculty member, her father
had died of colon cancer, and her siblings had teenage children
of their own. Patra finished high school a year early and left for
the University of Chicago, where she met Dr. Leonard Gardner
her junior year. The week she graduated they were married. He
bought a turn-of-the-century colonial for them in Oak Park,
with a vegetable garden and cats. A swing set, a gazebo.

After Paul was born, Patra took him to infant music classes,
then gymnastics for toddlers. She started him in preschool when
he was three, one of the best in town. She'd driven him to Mon-
tessori classes every day—Patra confirmed this on the stand—
even though she didn't like to drive, and even though she'd have
preferred to keep him home with her a little longer. Patra also

confirmed, when the DA pressed her, that when Paul's teacher had expressed concern one day in February about his health, she'd taken him secretly to see her mother's friend, who was a pediatric endocrinologist. The DA showed paperwork disclosing the doctor ordered tests that Patra never scheduled. Patra tried to explain that this was because Paul had seemed better after that, so she blamed her worry—and her decision to see the doctor—on overconcern with the natural fluctuations of a growing child. She was getting herself worked up, she said, losing a sense of perspective. It was around this point that she agreed to Leo's plan to spend some time at their newly built summer house in March. "To give us some mental space," she said. "To have a change of scenery."

I also learned during the trial that while I'd been in Loose River that day getting Tylenol, while I was on my way to and from town, Leo had decided it would be best to get "a change of scenery" again. He'd worked an unconscious Paul into a pair of pants, wedged his feet in shoes, filled his backpack with puzzles and trains, Handi Wipes and animal crackers, a coloring book of birds he'd bought in Duluth. He'd combed down Paul's hair, and when I returned with the bottle of pills in the afternoon, there they were on their way out the door through the kitchen. Patra came first and walked right past me—her face white and taut—then Leo. Then Paul in Leo's arms, Leo sidestepping the kitchen island like he was carrying a big bundle of wood, or a miniature bride. Leo's red eyes took me in, then moved on to other obstacles in his path. The table, the front door. "Thanks, Linda," he said, when I moved a chair out of the way for him. Paul's one white arm dangled behind him like a length of rope.

*   *   *

Did they tell you where they were going? I was asked.

They didn't say anything.

Did they tell you they would drive two and a half hours, and make two stops at private residences, in both Brainerd and St. Cloud—

They didn't say—

—neither of them medical professionals, before the victim expired from complications of cerebral edema at approximately seven thirty that night?

Leo just asked me to lock up behind them.

The last I saw of Patra, she was standing in the driveway, bent over double, the heel of her hand in her mouth like a hunk of bread. She had on unbuttoned jeans and slouchy moccasins, and when she straightened up, her whole face was slick. Her eyes were unfocused, her mouth open wider than it needed to be for breathing. She closed the car door without a word.

I stood in the doorway for a long time after they left. I still had the bottle of pills in my hand, and after a while I went back inside and set it down on the table. I didn't take my shoes off at the door. I could see tiny half-moons of dirt in a track I'd made across the floor. Back on the mat, I untied my tennis shoes and found a broom for the dirt, sweeping in my socks through the kitchen and down the hall.

Outside Paul's bedroom there was a fishy-sweet scent. I stood for a moment holding my breath. Then I went in and lifted Paul's full plate of pancakes from the dresser, gripped his full glass of milk—which looked viscous in my hand—and carried both back to the kitchen. I walked out to the deck and poached some pinecones and strips of bark from Europa's walls, carried them back in my arms. Arranged them just as they'd been outside right there on Paul's rug, in a half-circle around the dresser. The room smelled better then, like sap. I heaved open the window for good measure. Someone had already stripped the bed. I folded the Candy Land board, returned it to its box. I turned on Paul's caboose night-light, though it wasn't dark, though the late afternoon sun had hit an angle that allowed it to filter through the trees and shove a trapezoid of light across the floor. I sat on his little-kid bed, lay back. Willed my skin not to crawl when I felt the dampness of his bare mattress. I focused on the trapezoid of light as it bent in half, made a stage, then seeped up the wall. My feet in their socks dangled off the far edge of the bed.

You thought they'd come back?

The room began to darken. I could hear the clock ticking, a gutter creaking, the refrigerator humming. A loon called out twice, slicing at the evening, cutting all excess away. *This is this*, it said. *That is that.* A breeze shook the blinds. I didn't notice when the trapezoid of light disappeared. I didn't notice it was night until I heard a gravelly throat clear from the doorway.

I sat up. In the red glow of Paul's night-light I saw a man's silhouette. My first thought was that it was Leo, come back. I thought it was Leo, and a feeling of dread or relief—or both—went through me.

It wasn't Leo, though.

It was my dad. "Your mom sent me," he said. "I knocked?"

He must have come through the unlocked door, come hunting through the empty house while I'd been sleeping. Had I been sleeping? He looked at me sitting in Paul's bed, sitting guiltily mussed, like some teenage Goldilocks in droopy socks and a sweaty T-shirt.

"Madeline?" he asked.

I saw the room the way it must have looked to him. Red night-light in the corner, pinecones circling the dresser, bunnies and bears on the shelves overhead—and me, all by myself in bed, as if I'd made an elaborate fort in the woods, or something, as if I'd made everything up and he'd walked in on me playing dolls or pretend. For a second I felt like the littlest of little kids. I scooted to the edge of the bed, hooked my heels on the baseboard.

"Wouldn't've come in," he apologized. "But, I saw your tennis shoes by the door—"

He was wearing a shirt I'd worn myself, a soft gray flannel that was tight across his chest, but that had hung from my shoulders when I'd worn it to school last spring. His gray ponytail was threaded through the back of his Twins cap, as usual. He was blinking his eyes to adjust to the light.

"Everything okay?"

Maybe I was wrong to think that there was only one answer to that question that would keep me from walking straight over and setting my face against his chest.

"Yep."

"Your friend's family? They—?"

I could see how much it cost him to say even that much. Hadn't he always made it seem a great kindness—the greatest kindness of all—not to ask too many questions? Wasn't that something I'd always known? Hadn't he taught me that much?

"They just left. I'm on my way home now."

If that was overtly false, he didn't challenge me. "Okay" was all he said, setting his big palm over his mouth again, rubbing away whatever remains of an expression might have been there. Then he turned and headed out, me behind him.

He passed on about a decade after that. Two strokes in his last months made his face look softer, fatter. He became almost a fat man in the end, overnight it seemed, though he must have been gaining weight for years, slowly—as he walked less and drove his ATV more, as he stopped canoeing any farther than across the lake. I came home once that last year to help my mom winterize the place, and I saw that someone had hung a bird feeder from one of the front pines. All day long Dad watched birds come and go. I remember sitting with him one violet evening as the sun went down, watching birds congregate in the snow outside. At some point I lifted my hand and said, "Look, a nuthatch." I knew immediately I was wrong—the house finch hopped to a branch and shat. I knew he knew as well, and even so, he nodded.

That's the kind of person my dad was.

Here's what my mom was like. That same winter, as I stood on a stool tacking quilts over the window, as the birds fought for seed outside—and my dad slept in his chair—she went on and on about my father as a young man. "He would have followed me anywhere," she said, not bothering to whisper. "He didn't know if he wanted to start school or go to work for his daddy or go fishing. He just didn't know. He was turning circles, going nowhere! *I* knew what he should do."

She rested her elbows on an unfinished project on the kitchen table, open books on top of other open books. She was more restless that winter than usual. She stood up for more coffee but her mug was still full. "He needed direction," she said, sitting down, rimming her mug with a finger. "You wouldn't

know it from the way he was later, but he was just one of those
guitar-strumming kids at the time. Back then, all he could do
was pick a tune and catch a fish. That's it. He picked up everything else later."

It was 1982 when they set out, she told me, nobody's idea
of a revolutionary time. They were eight adults altogether, plus
three half-grown kids. Because my mother was older than the
rest, because *they* were good with talk and *she* was good with
plans, she'd been the one who'd arranged the timing of the departure, assigned jobs to the others, convinced my dad to lift a few
axes and rifles from a bait-and-tackle shop. "You understand?"
my mother asked me. I didn't answer. I'd heard most of these
stories before. I'd heard her describe that first winter in the cabin
many times when I was young: all the scrappy little crises, the
one fish they had to eat, the two new babies that came before
spring, the ex-nutritionist's kid who'd set one of the babies on
fire by accident one night and the frantic drive to the hospital
in a storm, the broken-down van on the road, the baby who was
fine after all, and the kid-turned-teenager who wouldn't speak
again after that. I'd heard the stories, but never quite like this,
never with this mix of bitterness and nostalgia. Before, she'd
always emphasized how young they'd been then, how ignorant
and misguided. But she *hadn't* been young she told me now. She
was thirty-three, long past her high school and college years.
Everything she did, she did when she should have known better.

"Listen," she told me. And she went through it all again
from the very beginning. The van stolen from her parents' garage
in the middle of the night, the perilous winter drive to her uncle's
abandoned fishing cabin, the big new bunkhouse they'd built
the first spring, the relief of summer, and summer again, the
commune charter they'd copied in calligraphy on parchment and

hung over the door—but then set on fire when everything fell apart six years in. "It was pretty bad at the end, sure. Everybody fighting everyone else, everyone jealous and getting confused about the kids. What to do with you guys. But not all the parts were bad, not most of the time. We had good ideas, good plans. We wanted kinship, not obligations." She paused. "We believed there should be more than the nuclear family. We really thought we could see something better—"

She glanced at my sleeping dad, his cheek smashed against his shoulder.

She went on: "We really thought we could do more with the world—"

I looked down at her from my stool and waited.

"But then everyone took off, and we started over with just you."

17

P.S. THE SEQUOIAS ARE MORE IMPRESSIVE THAN THE OTHER REDWOODS, IN CASE YOU EVER GET OUT TO CALIFORNIA. There's a difference just so you know. The coastal redwoods grow (obviously) on the coast and the sequoias are in the mountains. You can drive straight through a sequoia, right? That's one of the things people do. Plus the sequoias are older. I thought you'd appreciate knowing the difference. I used to go camping in the Sierra Nevada with my dad, and we'd eat canned soup and sleep in this tiny two-man tent he had from the army. It was great. Those trees really do seem permanent, they're so big. We stayed for weeks, never washed our hair, drank Tang. The woods look like The Time of Dinosaurs or something. Of course, things always seem more impressive when you're a little kid. That's one of the reasons I don't really want to go back. I mean, who wants to ruin one of the things you like thinking about most? Who gives that up on purpose?

Thank goodness for the back of the card but now I'm really out of room.

Bye again,
Mr. G.

18

THE SUMMER PASSED QUICKLY AFTER THE GARDNERS LEFT. Or, not quickly but in fragments. It was one of the hottest summers in a while. It was so hot some nights in July that I soaked my T-shirt in lake water before going to sleep. I wrung it out in the woods and wore it dripping through the dark house and up my ladder. Mornings, the sun coaxed steam off the lake and it was too humid in the afternoons to do anything at all. I remember waiting out the worst hours in some flickering patch of shade beneath the pines, brushing away flies with a fir branch, searching for ticks on the dogs—all four—who lay collapsed around me in the dust. Working my fingers through Abe's thick half-husky fur, I could feel each of his ribs in turn, convulsing as he panted. I could feel the way the bones separated and contracted again, making room for more oxygen. I could feel him scooching away, patiently, from the unfamiliar heaviness of my hand.

I remember bouncing one humid evening on the back of my dad's ATV to the police station in Whitewood, where they gave me a Coke poured so fast into a Styrofoam cup it overflowed on the table. This was a few days after an officer showed up at the bottom of the sumac trail and spoke with my dad over the hood of his black and white car. At the police station, they handed me a roll of brown paper towels to wipe the spilled Coke. They offered to get me another can, but I shook my head and sucked the froth from the top. Someone turned on a fan that blew warm air into my face, and as it dried out my nose and eyes, I remember wondering if this was where Lily had come. If this was where she'd sat last spring and had a Coke and said her piece against Mr. Grierson.

I never knew for sure.

I spent hours in that one little room that summer, in a green plastic lawn chair, answering questions from different people in uniforms and suits. I no longer remember who asked what, or when, or in what order. I know I drank lots of warm Coke. I chewed lots of lips off the smallish Styrofoam cups meant for coffee. I sprinkled the chewed white bits across the table, like clumpy snow, and eventually I learned to ask for the one cushioned folding chair they had, which was kept behind the front desk. By late July, I'd been prepped by a lady with a pouty face—the DA's assistant?—to cross my legs at the ankle and fold my hands and, if I remembered, to say "ma'am" to the judge and "sir" to the defense lawyer. "Don't let him scare you, now," she told me. "Don't bite your nails like that, don't look down, don't let it get to you. Think of yourself as floating or something? Like a fish? You like to fish, don't you? But not a dead fish, I don't mean float like that. I mean swimming? In the water? Get that image in your mind, remember you're not the one on trial."

I wasn't scared, though. I didn't need to think of myself as a walleye drifting along in a current somewhere, just waiting for my hook. I was yearning for it.

* * *

August came. The days grew hazier, ash scented. Forest fires
were going strong a few lakes north of us, and the air tasted of
it, though the worst of the blaze was more than fifty miles away.
"Safe by the skin of our teeth," people were saying. By then, by
the end of summer, all the deciduous trees—all the aspens and
birch—had gone crinkly and blond in the hot weather. The
pink geraniums in the window boxes of the Whitewood County
district courthouse lay slung over, and the grass along the front
walk was brown in strips. Brown, except for a square of emerald
sod laid down against the marble steps, like a tiny pricey carpet.
For weeks the heat had been oppressive, but now that summer
was ending, now that September was on the horizon and the first
geese were in flight, everyone was going on about how perfect the
season had been, how lucky we'd been all along, how blessed to
live in the north, in the woods, which was God's own country.

"What a doozy of a day!" I heard, as my mom and I filed
up the marble stairs to the courthouse.

"What a perfect ten!" was the reply—though it was ninety
degrees already.

Inside, I had to listen to the same conversation about the
weather again and again. I watched the DA's assistant flick a
finger in a glass of water and dampen her lips as she spoke
to a man who was painstakingly rolling up one of his sleeves,
inch-by-inch-by-inch. I watched them eyeing me in my thrift-
store dress—assessing me, and at the same time pretending they
weren't. When I glared back, they pinched their eyes into smiles,
looked at their watches, crossed their legs. Beside me, my mom
sat too close on the gallery bench, sweating and fanning herself
with one limp hand. My dad had decided not to come. He'd

said he was afraid that a shift in the wind would bring the fires closer, and though I'd hoped for more from him I knew better than to question this or ask him to reconsider. Someone shoved open a window at the back of the courtroom and a breeze trickled in, but it wasn't enough. At one point, my mom put her damp hand on my arm.

"Oh my, oh my," she said, so I followed her gaze.

Leo and Patra came in, single file. Patra's hair had grown out, I saw as they walked past. It no longer frizzed up around her ears, but hung gelled with product over her sweatered shoulders. She was wearing a baby-blue cardigan, and already, even before she got on the stand, navy crescents of sweat bloomed under each armpit.

I expected her to look over at me and give me a sign. A wave across the stuffy courtroom, a hello or a nod. Or, if she couldn't manage that, I thought I could understand. I'd take a glance in my direction, any indication at all that she saw me. But every time I looked her way, her eyes went somewhere else. She was whispering something in Leo's ear or examining the bracelet on her wrist. She took a sip of water from a bottle on the table where she sat. One knee jiggled under her black silk skirt, but her face was as calm as I'd ever seen it.

On the stand she kept her eyes down most of the time, her hands folded in her lap. When her lawyer asked about her childhood she answered in paragraphs. Back straight. She responded to the district attorney's questions when he addressed her with such precision—such mildness—that she might have been discussing weather, too, but with a touch more regret than everyone else in the room, perhaps even condescension. That's what the DA wanted the jury to resent her for most, I understood from my pretrial prep, her blitheness and her youth, her professor husband. He implied that these things made Patra the worst combination of snobbish and debased. "Speak up!" the DA said once when she folded a tissue to blow her nose, and she replied—with what might have been fear, but also might have been contempt—"I did not *say* anything."

It went on like that. The DA asking her to clarify or speak up, and Patra repeating herself in a small, breathy voice. She never once said my name, or Paul's. She said "the babysitter." She said "my son, whom I love." As she murmured her mild answers, I thought I could imagine the schoolteacher Patra might have been, the editor in her checking every word with her neat red pen. I could hear the grammar in her sentences. I could hear all her minute corrections. *My son* ~~who~~*, whom I love so much, told me he was feeling better.* ~~I was~~ *We were* ~~relieved~~ *overjoyed. We* ~~couldn't~~ *could not have been happier.* She sat up straighter and straighter as she spoke, and her neck seemed longer. In a short time, the blue fabric under her arms was nearly black.

"I'm trying to understand, Mrs. Gardner. I am." The DA put his hand to his chest so that his tie squished up a little under his chin. "You're saying you didn't see that something was wrong? Or that you did, and failed to seek treatment? It can only be one or the other. Please help us understand."

I watched Patra swallow. "He was being—treated."

"Yes, fine, your husband explained yesterday. We're all for prayer. We're not here to put anyone's religion on trial. But I need you to clarify something for us. The morning you were in Duluth, that is, the morning of June twentieth, didn't you tell your husband you were taking Paul to the store for—what was it—picnic supplies? When in fact you placed a call to the pediatrician you'd contacted months before, Dr.—"

The quickest of glances at Leo. "No one was there."

"But you thought something was wrong? You understood at that point something was wrong."

A swallow, the whole mechanism of her throat moving. "There was never a—diagnosis."

"Why was that?"

"People go to doctors all the time." For the first time all day I could hear the pleading in her voice. I could hear how much she wanted to convince him of this, or at least make him be nicer to her. She put her white hands on the railing in front of her. "Don't people go to doctors all the time? And they don't always get better?"

"Excuse me, Mrs. Gardner, you're changing the subject. Please don't make me remind you, again, to answer the question that's been asked. We've already heard that insulin and fluids might have saved him up to two hours before he suffered cardiac arrest. *Two hours.* The treatment is minimal and simple—"

"I'm his mother—" Patra interrupted.

"You *were* his mother," the DA interrupted back.

Something rushed into her face, then flowed out again like water. All the muscles in her face clenched—then let go. After that she waited patiently for the next question, eyes flat as two tiny blue screens. She repeated the same things she'd said before: *He was fine. He was resting in bed.* And when the DA dismissed her at last, frustrated, she moved across the courtroom with her TV eyes, holding her bottle of water upside down in both hands like a throttle.

That whole morning I kept waiting for her to look up at me so I could reassure her somehow. All I needed was the smallest sign from her, and I would have laid it all on Leo when my time came around. There he sat with his back to me—a Bible on his lap and a full bottle of water. Nodding ever so subtly at Patra.

He shifted in his seat when she sat down, recrossed his legs so his knee nudged hers. He'd grown a beard since I'd seen him last, one trimmed so close it was a half-mask of gray. I watched, but he didn't poke out his cheek with his tongue. He didn't look upset. He didn't look at all worried.

"It's going to be okay," he'd said to me that last day, after he'd loaded Paul in the car. I'd been standing stupidly on their front stair. Patra was hunched in the backseat, and Leo was circling around the hood when he saw me wavering in their open doorway. He'd paused then. Walked back across the driveway. "It's going to be okay," he'd said, hands coming at me through the air. He'd taken the time to reach out and hug me—*me*—saying, "You can't be anything but Good. Got that, Linda? You shouldn't feel bad about any of this."

Still, I would have accused him of bullying, of making us do his bidding, but Patra never gave me a sign. In the break before I was to take the stand, I went outside and smoked three cigarettes as fast as I could. I sat on the parking lot curb, and when the cigarettes were gone, I put my arms on my knees and my head on my arms. Closed my eyes. My heart felt like a black train chugging uphill through my body. I let the heat of the sun rise from the concrete and cook my skin, and when I opened my eyes, the dazzling white of the day emptied me out. A chainsaw buzzed in the distance. I heard branches splintering down.

Then—in a gust of hot wind—Patra came out. She pushed open the courthouse door and stood for a moment, taking in deep breaths. The wind blew her hair so she looked a little more herself. A little less combed. She uncapped her water bottle and sucked the water down—sucked so hard the plastic collapsed, and when she pulled her mouth away the bottle popped. I guess she didn't see me crouched on the curb between cars, because when she lifted the bottle to her mouth again, tilting back her head, she walked a few steps closer. She came close enough for me to catch a whiff of her coconut shampoo. Close enough, almost, to reach out and touch her black nyloned leg.

I could have left it like that. It felt like the sign I'd been hoping for. Just her leg and a big drop of water falling from her mouth and graying the concrete.

Thirty-seven, twenty-six, fifteen, I thought, watching another drip come down.

Twenty-six, fifteen, four.

I stood up the second before she turned.

Here's what her face did then. A mutant half smile formed on her lips, habitual friendliness mixed with undeniable loathing.

"I have nothing to say to you. Please." It sounded like a lawyer's line to me. She turned away.

"Patra."

"What?" She turned back, and her question seemed in earnest now. "*What?*"

"I—"

"Listen—" A muscle fluttered in her neck.

"I hate him," I blurted. "Leo." I hate him for *you,* I meant.

"Leo?" She seemed confused.

Another gust of wind had tossed hair in her eyes, and she pushed it back. As she did, as she palmed her hairline, I saw her freckles were disappearing in the red of her skin. Something new was turning in her eyes. "Leo?" she asked again, her voice dripping, soaked to the bone.

"Paul was just—" I whispered, more hesitant now. "It wasn't your fault."

"What are you *saying* to me?" She took a step forward.

I put my hand on her arm to calm her, and she started back as if stricken. She gave a peculiar shiver, and I saw then that I was just a part of the evil that took him, the one who arrived just in time for, and presided over, his disappearance. That's all I was to her now.

She bit out at me. "*You're* the one who thought of him that way. *You're* the one who looked at him and saw"—she sobbed— "a sick little boy!"

"No—"

"I know you did! And that's all you could see. Isn't it? Isn't it!"

"I should have gone earlier," I admitted—it was the only time I ever said it. "I should have gotten help for us." Us. We needed it.

"How could he get better with you thinking like that?" she spat. "How could he? I've thought about this. I've gone over it and over it. Leo told me, control your thoughts, but it was *your* mind—" She said it like she could barely get the words out. "*Your* mind. That was too small. To see beyond itself." She drew a ragged breath. "*Yours*. You saw him. As sick."

They'd made me wear my hair differently that day, combed and parted on one side, clipped with a single barrette. It kept getting in my face, so I had to hold it gathered in one fist, my bent arm across my chest. They insisted I wear a long, loose dress with a salady green floral pattern. I could feel my sweaty thighs slip against each other beneath the fabric. I could feel my cotton underwear droop down from my butt. Damp. I smelled like mothballs, cigarettes, and laundry detergent. I felt hideous, ridiculous. *The local teenager*, I was called by the defense attorney and the *North Star Gazette*.

Babysitter, Patra said on the stand.

So when she said what she did in the parking lot, I hunkered down and refused to say anything more. She didn't need or want a response. She screwed the lid back on her water bottle and turned around. After she left, I stayed in the parking lot until a bailiff or someone (my mom?) came to get me. I stood in the sun, which made my skin itch, made my face feel rigid and thick like it was stretched over my eyes, making it hard to see. I stood there and listened to the chainsaw as it brought down someone's bad tree: first the swishy leafy parts, then the clattering branch work, and finally the trunk in a thump.

Nobody believes you when you talk about happiness Patra told me once.

For months, I'd watched her blow into Paul's soup and kiss his perfect half-moon eyebrows. I'd watched her rush out in the rain before dinner, gather up books he had left by the lake, come back in dripping, elated. Run around the house rubbing her hands, trying to warm up again. Sing to him. Sing to us. I'd watched her slide in her socks from one side of the kitchen to the other, from counter to island, filling plates, stirring pots, pushing the frizz of her hair from her face with her hands. And all that time,

Paul had been fine. He was fine: he was better than that even. Hadn't Patra broken granola bars into bits to look like kibble, so he could eat like cats? Hadn't she warmed his apple juice in the microwave once, because he said it was too cold, it hurt his teeth? He was so entirely and evidently cherished: that's the truth. I could have said all that when I had my chance. I wanted to—I planned on it—but didn't.

Here's what I said on the stand when I was asked what Patra had done for her son: nothing.

She did nothing.

19

I REMEMBER THERE WAS THIS BIG FADED MURAL IN THE COURTHOUSE HALLWAY. It showed an Indian with a white guy in a canoe, both in chocolaty furs, both pointing into the woods at a bear on the shore. There were green trees and white fluffy clouds—everything nice and peaceful. You know, everybody getting along. But as I was leaving the courthouse that day with my mom, as we were walking out, I noticed the perspective on the mural in the hallway was a little off. The white guy was actually pointing at the bear's butt, and the Indian had a pointing arm but not another one, and the bear appeared to be levitating slightly. His paws were not quite on the ground, and he looked unsurprised to be floating off into the trees like that, bored and resigned to it, maybe, and also sort of terrifying.

I didn't know whether to push or pull the door, couldn't find the handle at first.

"Are you coming?" my mother asked, as I floated outside.

Somehow I found my way down the marble steps. Somehow I got myself and my dress back in the hot truck, and we were on the road again. The pickup was on loan from a church acquaintance of my mother's, someone who'd heard about the trial and wanted to show the difference between true Christians

and false ones. It had Mr. Yuk stickers in a line across the dash-
board, a dentist-office smell from the air freshener that spun
from the rearview mirror. My mother could only get her window
crank to work by leaning into it with her whole body, and even
then she could only slide the glass down a crack.

She focused exclusively on shifting gears in the busy streets
near downtown. She had recently renewed her license and was a
conscientious stopper at all the signs, a silent and focused merger
onto the highway. But then, when we hit the easy flat of Route
10, when the traffic vanished and woods returned, she started
easing her way from subject to subject. The heat. The judge's
drawl. The yellow toilet in the ladies' room. Mrs. Gardner's
sweater. She didn't know why anyone would wear a sweater in
August. It bothered her for some reason. She kept glancing at
me as she spoke, fishing for strands of her hair that had blown
out the window crack. "I mean, who would wake up and think,
hey, it's ninety degrees, I should go get my *cardigan*?"

She looked at me across the cab, where I was sort of slumped
against the far door.

"Earth to Madeline," she said.

Earth to me. Earth to me, I thought.

I was watching the way shadows and sun curtained the
black road in front of us, the way their movement seemed to
make the pavement undulate as we drove over it. I was wondering if the highway tar on the shoulder was actually melting or
just seeming to melt, if the little rodents and insects scrambling
across would get stuck in the mess, if it was a dangerous place
for them to be. I was mentally warning them all away, the toads
and the grasshoppers, and even as I was doing that, even as I
was creating a force field on both sides of the highway with my
mind, I could sense the appeal in my mother's glance, the way

it was almost physically painful for her to have to endure my silence now.

"Hel-lo?" she said after a moment, pretending to knock the air between us with her free hand. "Is the Teenager sleeping?"

I set my head against the window.

"I'm just saying it was an impractical thing to wear. It was impractical, wasn't it?" She was kneading the steering wheel with her hands. She was looking at me long enough for the truck to swerve, slightly, into the oncoming lane. "Just say yes, okay?" She got the truck back on course. She slowed down, or maybe the engine missed. "Just say, *yes*, that sweater was a strange thing to wear. You can add *fucking*. You're a teenager, so I don't care. Say it was a fucking ridiculous thing to wear, and then you can say that her explanation, her defense or whatever that was, was pretty much a load of bull, too."

I could hear the gumming of her palms against the plastic of the wheel.

Then she added, getting worried, "You know it's a load of bull, right?"

When I was eleven or twelve, I found this unexpected thing in the back of the shed. It was a wooden cradle wrapped in a clear plastic tarp, which I pulled open when I was looking for something else. The thing was hand painted with white daisies and blue lilacs, long-finned fish swimming through it all like golden grinning devils. It was filled to the brim with rotting firewood, mouse droppings, unfurling weevils. I remember covering it back up with the tarp, finding a stack of asphalt shingles to lay over it. I shooed the dogs outside and went back to my day, but later, when I was guiding the canoe through shallows or pulling some teeny thorns from Abe's paw—or working out a tedious math problem—the image of that cradle would occasionally come back to me. I'd see the grimy rim painted fresh with lilacs and fish, the maple runners creaking back and forth, some bald little thing wedged inside, wiggling.

I'd see a face hovering over it. Going, you know, *shh, shhh.*

The thing is I have no memory at all of my mother before the commune broke up. In my mind it was always just Tameka and a constantly shifting amalgamate of teenagers and adults—legs in jeans, legs in skirts—and I admit I wanted to bring her into focus, see her rocking a little baby I could imagine was me. But my mom never said much about my baby self. She didn't have any pictures of course, and she once said with a snort that my first word was "wah." She wouldn't even tell me what she'd chosen when the commune did the vote for my name. "Madeline's all your dad," she insisted, but I knew from stories that everybody wrote down the names they wanted and put them in a hat. For a while I thought about that a lot, the names she might have liked, such as Winter or Juniper or Ark. I thought about those baby days and maybe names (*Canidae,* I thought with longing, when I was doing my wolf project in eighth grade), until it dawned on me at some point that maybe my mother wouldn't say, not because she'd wanted something else, but because she'd suggested nothing at all. And then I began to wonder, who besides my dad had wanted Madeline? Who else had voted for that?

I'm not saying I ever consciously wished there'd been someone else. And I'm not saying this thinking happened all at once, because it didn't. It came over me gradually, almost unremarkably, in a way that seemed to move on a separate plane from all the other events in my life. I can't attach it to anything that happened, to a year in school or a particular thing my mother did or didn't do, but once the thought was there it didn't go away. "The CEO's doing her accounts!" she'd say, for instance, and my scalp would tighten like a cap above my ears. Or she'd dangle some decorative lure she was making in front of my nose while I was connecting dots in my workbook, and I'd have to lay my pencil down. I'd have to release that pencil like it was a match in a newly lit fire. Look up at her. "Hush!" she'd say to herself then, seeing the dark expression on my face, but not the plea, never the bald desire to be treated more gently. She'd whisper, "The Professor's at work! Shhh! Everyone be quiet."

Or she'd knock the air between us with the hand she wasn't using for driving. She knocked the air and kept her eye on the highway.

"Earth to Mad-e-line. Did you hear what I said—" And before I knew what I was doing that day in the truck, before I could stop myself, I was croaking out, "Did I do okay?"

"You mean—?"

I waited, felt the truck's engine churning us down the road. Missing, churning again.

She thought about it for a while before saying, "What happened probably would have happened whatever you'd done. If that's what you mean."

I returned my head to the lip of the door, watched clouds swell over other clouds that might have been smoke.

She tried again. "I'm not the judge of this one."

You only say that because I'm not your kid, I remember thinking, rolling my forehead grease against the window, making it look like some wide, unidentifiable insect had flown against

the glass. It's hard now to know how much of what I did and
wanted in those years came from some version of that thought.

What's the difference between what you want to believe and
what you do? That's what I should have asked Patra, that's the
question I wanted answered, but it didn't occur to me—or not
in that way—until after we'd talked that day in the courthouse
parking lot, until I was riding with my mother in the hot rumbling truck and she was parking between two vans behind Our
Lady. While my mom wrote a thank-you note to tuck under the
visor, I got down on my haunches in the gravel parking lot, my
salad dress pouffing around me, and started sifting through the
little stones. Then my mom came up, said okay, and we started
back. As we walked along the highway shoulder, I uncurled my
fingers and let the stones fall out. She didn't try to talk to me
anymore. She let me dawdle and lag behind, dropping rocks as
I went. She glanced back at me once at the turnoff to the lake,
but by the time I reached the sumac trail, by the time our cabin
chimney was visible again over treetops, she was out of sight.
She was a rustling of sumac branches, leaves moving in a pulse
as she passed underneath.

And what's the difference between what you think and what you
end up doing? That's what I should have asked Mr. Grierson
in my letter—Mr. Grierson, who, even after Lily took back her
accusation, was sentenced to seven years based on the pictures
and his courtroom confession. I read through his statements in
the months after his sentence, which he served first in Seago-
ville, Texas, then in Elkton, Ohio. The Gardners, who'd been

charged with manslaughter, were acquitted after three weeks
on the grounds they were protected by religious exemption. I
didn't follow them after the Whitewood trial ended. After I said
my piece in court, I went home with my mom in the borrowed
truck, ate three peanut butter sandwiches in a row, went fishing
for pike. Went fishing, got drunk for the first time, forgot. Their
cabin sat empty across the lake for months, and I never went
back, and I didn't stop to watch when the new owners set up
their grill and badminton net the next summer. But I tracked Mr.
Grierson around the country when he got out of jail, followed
his little red flag from state to state, from Florida to Montana
and back again. I watched him return to prison for violating
the terms of his parole, get out again after another year, set up
his shop in the marshes. By the time I wrote him my letter, by
the time I was living in Minneapolis with Ann, I'd read his official statement about Lily several times. "I thought about it, I
thought about it, I thought about it," he'd said. He went on a
few sentences farther down: "I wanted to, and when she said
that I *had*, I was like, yes. When all that stuff was found in my
apartment, I pretended I'd never seen it before. I did lie about
that. But when that girl Lily said what she said, I thought, all
right. Okay. Now my real life begins."

20

THE VIEW FROM MY DESK AT THE BARGE COMPANY IN MIN-NEAPOLIS WAS A WEATHERED CONCRETE PARKING RAMP. All day long I could see people puppeting out of their car windows, punching their tickets, waiting for the yellow arm to kick up. If I scooted my chair back from my desk and swiveled 180 degrees, I could also see a wedge of Mississippi between the ramp and a bank of willows.

Egrets, brown foam, white buoys.

After my first full year there, I was given my own cubicle and my own computer, so I could do what I wanted most of the time and no one bothered me. I could watch the egrets pluck fish from the river and the ferries of tourists head toward Saint Paul. Or, if I chose, I could look up things online while I input spreadsheets—cases of high-altitude cerebral edema on Everest or recent sales at the Treasure Chest. Though I was just a temp, I was at ManiCo Barge long enough to get a shelf for my lunch and a hook for my jacket in the break room. I was there long enough to become the go-to person for dealing with the distressed wives of deckhands. To everyone's surprise, I was good at calming these women down when they called. I'd say things

like: "Don't worry, your husband will be home again soon." I'd
promise: "He'll get to shore in Oquawka and call tonight." I'd
say this even when I knew he wouldn't get to shore for another
day, and when he did he'd probably hit the bar before calling
anyone. Still, the wives knew me by name and asked for me
every time. I kept track of the ages of all their kids, the names
of their dogs, the names of their babysitters.

I was used to them calling at the end of the day, so when
my phone rang at four one afternoon—one early spring my
second year there—I thought at first it was just another worried
wife. Right away I could hear irritation in the woman's voice,
the way her vowels squished up around her attempt to sound
friendly. "I'm so sorry to bother you at work," she said primly.
"Is this a bad time for you?" So then I was pretty sure it wasn't
a wife but a regular wrong number. I was about to hang up on
her. I was about to hang up and straighten my pantyhose and
get my last cup of coffee, when I heard whoever it was draw in
a sharp breath. "I'm very sorry to bother you," the woman said
again. Then: "Please don't hang up."

So even before she said she was from Loose River, even
before she explained who she was, I recognized something about
the way she spoke, about the way she apologized as a means to
express disapproval. That was a Loose River thing to do. When
I didn't say anything and didn't hang up either, the woman went
on. She said she'd found my number by calling my old job in
Duluth. She said she'd tracked down my old landlord, and that
he told her the name of the temp agency where he thought I'd
gone to work, but it took some doing before they gave out the
name of the barge company. I'd been pretty hard to find, she
said. She hadn't wanted to meddle this way, she went on, but

she wasn't sure how else to go about this. "I'm calling on behalf of your mom," she said—then paused. "She's stopped coming to church. She hasn't been to church for a few months. So I went out to visit her."

I waited.

"The place is getting . . . a bit run-down?"

I cleared my throat. "The cabin?"

"Actually, the cabin roof was taken off in a storm last year. Or that's what she said."

"The roof came off?"

"Um. I think she wintered in the shed. She moved a stove out there."

"To the shed? It's not insulated."

"She's tried insulating the walls with leaves and clothes. Newspapers."

I couldn't imagine it and then I could. "Okay."

"She nicked a finger chopping wood. I don't think she can see too good anymore."

"Who is this again?" I asked, feeling—not sick—but a slow pounding in my head.

"Liz Lundgren. I go to Our Lady with your mom."

"Ms. Lundgren." I stood up. I started pacing the length of the phone cord, chewing my lip, looking over the cubicle wall and out the window, where the brown water of the Mississippi was sliming steadily by on its way to the Gulf.

That's when something broke loose in my mind, drifted out. "Life Science," I said.

There was a pause. "Yes, a million years ago. Yes." Liz Lundgren bit down on something in her mouth, and I could hear relief flooding her voice when she spoke again. "I filled in before I retired. At the high school, yes. That's me. Listen, Linda. I'm not trying to meddle. I don't want to cause trouble, but I think I could arrange a call. I mean, I think she'd like me to arrange a call."

Heaven and hell are ways of thinking. Death is the false belief that anything could ever end. For Christian Scientists, there is only the next phase, which as far as I can tell is the same as this one, only maybe you see it differently. This much I got from the church service I went to one Wednesday night that spring. I went not long after Ms. Lundgren's call, on an evening after a happy hour that involved two vodka tonics and a couple of scummy warm beers. I paced the sidewalk outside the big church doors for a few minutes—pretty drunk, pretending I was going some-where else—before I finally pushed through the doors and went in. I walked as straight as possible to the nearest pew, sat down like I was in school again, looked around without moving my head. Whatever I'd been expecting to find inside, whatever I'd been avoiding for more than a dozen years, it wasn't what I saw that night. There were maybe eight people in a cream-colored sanctuary, which smelled like Pine-Sol, and whose white carpet was raked with deep vacuum lines between the pews. Everything was painted white and cream, white and beige, white and pink— the plaster walls and wooden pews and simple lectern in front.

The sermon, or whatever it was called, began. A smooth-faced elderly man leaned over the lectern and read from the Bible and *Science and Health with Key to the Scriptures*. Occasionally, he stopped to take sips of water from a glass that caught tiny panels of light and disco-balled them around the room. I must have dozed off because the next thing I knew someone two pews in front of me was speaking into a cordless mike. She was an old lady with a silver bun, and she held that big mike in her tiny hand like an ice-cream cone. Mumming it with her lips, fuzzing the room with static. She explained she had been healed of a toothache by being nicer to a neighbor who'd complained about her yard. Her toothache had been a false belief in mortal mind that had tricked her into feeling pain. But Mary Baker Eddy taught us, through Jesus, to love thy neighbor. She said she'd left a pot of tulips on her neighbor's driveway and the toothache disappeared.

A teenage kid went next. He wore polished leather shoes and a crisp white shirt rolled up to the elbows. He reminded me of the forensics boys from high school at first, except he had powerful tendons in his forearms and faint stubble, like someone who worked outside. He knew exactly how far to hold the microphone from his lips. When he paused, he smoothed a wrinkle in his pants very close to his crotch. He told a long, winding story about a test in school he hadn't been able to study for, an AP exam, and then, thanking Our Beloved Founder, Mary Baker Eddy, he explained how he'd done well anyhow.

After that it was quiet for a long time. The pews creaked like branches and my head began to ache. The night birds started to trill outside and I longed to slouch down in my seat, lay my head against the cool wood of the pew. But I didn't. I made myself sit straighter, pay attention. The last person to stand and take the microphone was another old woman. She said she'd been healed of the belief that her husband had died when she'd read this week's lesson. She smiled brightly and touched her snow-white hair with one hand as she spoke. She said she had given in to the false assumption that her husband was matter, and for months she'd been unable to part with any of his things, his shoes or books or soap. But she finally poured the last of his Old Spice shampoo down the toilet when it came to her that we are reflections of Life, Harold too. There was no death for any of us, ever. I remember exactly how she put the next part, because my palms started to sweat. "Harold's fine. Harold's fine always. It's not what you do but what you think that matters. Mary Baker Eddy tells us heaven and hell are ways of thinking. We need to know the truth of that, pray to understand that death is just the false belief that anything could ever end. There's no going anywhere for any of us, not in reality. There's only changing how you see things."

I was on my way out afterward when the woman with the snowy hair stopped me at the door. Up close, her eyes were a filmy, glistening blue. She was wearing a beige linen dress and a diamond on her ring finger. "Would you like to sign in as a guest? We're so happy to have you." She'd gotten a clipboard and a flyer from somewhere and was handing them to me.

"Excuse me——" I said.

As I moved around her, I could smell the peppermint on her breath, the lilac perfume on her wrists, the chemical detergent on her dress. She smelled elaborately and intimately produced, scented with a whole life's worth of good intentions. She must have been eighty years old at least, but there was something youthful in her face, enviably untroubled. I paused to study her more closely, despite myself. I wanted to hear more about the husband, Harold, and his shampoo. She must have seen my hesitation. "Are you new to the church?" She lifted the pen attached by a balled chain to her clipboard.

"Yes," I said. Then I instantly regretted it. She looked so avid. "I mean *this* church," I clarified, before stepping into the night. "I'm not—I mean, I'm not from around here."

*   *   *

This was probably around mid-April. I remember a glint of green had already started showing on the willows by the river. Not long after, the leaves on the sidewalk trees burst out—a wallop of bright green everywhere you looked—and I went to the credit union after work one day to see how much money I'd saved. Afterward, I went to the hardware store to buy a screw for the doorknob Ann had been complaining about for months. While I was fixing that, since I was already on my knees in the bathroom, I decided to repair the leaky bathtub faucet. I pinched a crimped nest of hair from the drain with two fingers and put a new roll of toilet paper in the dispenser and gathered up all the towels to wash at the Laundromat. I left the towels in the dryer until they were so hot they burned my arms when I hugged them out. Then I folded them into warm, leaning towers and carried them home with my chin resting on top.

On my last day in town I went to Rom's apartment at dawn.

Wind was battering the loose shingles on the old Victorian turrets. I used his key to get in, left my stuff by the door in a heap, and crept into his bed with my shoes and jacket on. He didn't wake up as he pulled me to him, as he sunk his face in my hair. "Good-bye," I said. I wanted him to wake up. I wanted to walk around on my hands and knees one more time, collared. But he barely stirred. He nestled his cock between my legs and fell into a deeper sleep.

The clock on his shelf shone its red numbers at me. Morning came in a single gray bar through a slat in the shades. I started to get hot in his arms in my jacket, sweaty. After a while I looked at the clock again and realized if I didn't hurry I was going to miss my bus. I was going to miss my transfer to the Greyhound station across town and my ride up to Whitewood, where my mother would be waiting with Ms. Lundgren at the Burger King near the bus terminal. She hadn't sounded especially happy to hear from me when I'd finally called. It had been two years since I'd spoken to her last, since my dad died, and all she said after a few stiff hellos, was, "It's looking like it's about time to sell some of the land." As the sun came through the high window in Rom's basement apartment, I wiggled my way out of his sleeping arms. I pulled out from under his grasp and that's when he woke up at last—when he felt me leaving.

"What're you doing here?"

"I'm *not* here."

"Who's this in my bed, then, Girl Scout?"

"Some fantasy of yours."

"Fuck you." I could feel his mouth smiling into my scalp.

"Okay," I whispered, pulling away. "Try."

As I was sliding out of his arms he pulled me back. He squeezed me tighter. I could feel my own ribs in his arms, even through my canvas jacket—the bones pushing back against his weight. I liked that. I liked how the more I fought, the more tightly he held on. I squirmed free of his grasp, half sitting up. I twisted around but before I could swing my legs to the floor, he grabbed me around the waist and pulled me back down. I wanted more. I wanted more. He started to pull open the buttons on my coat, and on impulse, I bent my leg and kneed him in the chest, hard, so he started coughing. Sitting back on his haunches in his boxers, he looked confused. I felt the chill of that moment hit my skin like a splash of water. Morning light caught the pores on his face, so it looked rough as sandpaper.

"What's going on?" he asked, now fully awake. His thin white shoulders looked rectangular against the wall. He'd taken the stud from his tongue so his words had no click to them. They sounded softer than usual, simpler, wetter.

"Nothing."

That's when he saw my big backpack at the door.

"What is this? Where're you going?"

"I came to say good-bye."

"Good-bye?" He blinked at me. "You're going back to Ass-crack Nowheresville. Right now."

I pushed off the bed, straightened my jacket. I went to the door where my backpack was waiting, and as I hoisted it to my shoulder, I turned back to look at him, huddled in bed across the room. He had one hand on his left eye, pirate-style.

"You're going to a place where the wolves eat the fucking dogs?"

I shook my head. "That was Alaska. An anecdote."

"It's been what, like, almost two years?"

"I talked to my mom. It's planned."

"We've been happy, right? What is it you think you did that you can't be happy?"

"Happy, happy, happy," I said.

"*Happy*," he flipped the word over, made it innocent again.

"*Don't be a baby*," I sneered.

He must have seen something ugly in my expression because he found his shirt and plunged his head inside it. For an instant, his face was a white cotton mask, blank indentations for mouth and eyes. Then his head was free and he was zipping up his pants. He was getting his cell phone from the dresser, and I found I could speak to him as myself again, more deliberately.

"Don't be childish about it. I came to say good-bye, okay? I came to say thank you and good-bye."

"*I'm* being childish? Listen, listen." He took a few steps forward, his T-shirt catching on the hill of his belly. "Do you remember when you told me about that little kid?"

"That little kid?" The thought of Paul went like a breeze right through me. I put up a hand to stop him from going on. "I didn't tell you about any kid."

"I mean *you*, Girl Scout. The easiest prey in the world. House of old hippies, girl left behind."

"That's not what I said. That's not what it was like."

"The Fool."

"No."

"Walking off a cliff every time you take a step. Poor little girl, with, like, no shoes and an empty belly. Who was taking care of you?"

"That's not how it was. I was fine. I was fine."

"What kid did you mean?"

I sucked in a breath. "Nobody. He died."

"Who did?"

"Nobody. He's fine." As I said it, I reached into my pocket, found the smoothness of the Swiss Army knife, and thrust it out toward Rom.

He stepped back. "What the—"

It was the one he'd given me for Christmas, shiny and red. All the blades were tucked in—but maybe he didn't see that. Maybe the memory of me kneeing him in the chest was too recent. He laced his fingers over the top of his head, and I could see the scraggly hair under his arms through the gaping sleeves of his T-shirt. After a moment, he let his arms fall to his sides.

"Whatever. Keep it." He shook out a breath. He slid his hands into his pockets. "Keep it, Fool Scout."

I found myself thinking of that church lady as I waited to board the bus. *Heaven and hell are ways of thinking. Death is just the false belief that anything could ever end.* I lingered till the last minute in the waiting area near a blind homeless man on his cardboard island—reluctant to get on, reluctant to climb the steep stairs onto the coach. *It's not what you do but what you think that matters.* I didn't want to board, but once I was on the bus I saw the windows were unexpectedly tall and wide, tinted against the bright morning sun, and I had the two-seat row to myself. The coach slid effortlessly through city traffic. It glided around the cloverleaf and onto the highway, passing even the semis going downhill. As the bus angled north, as we left the city behind, I watched the leaves on the trees through the window go from deep green to pale mint to nothing. I watched snow appear in banks on the roadsides again, and somewhere along the way—despite myself—I started to feel a sleepy, sweet, intoxicating calm. Perhaps it had to do with the speed and height of the bus, the feeling of soaring over the highway and going fast enough to kill somebody. Speed is one kind of magic. I've always felt that. But the wash of calm also came from seeing the lakes frozen over again at the shorelines, patches of bluish snow on the ground, black fields gone white and empty. After a few hours, I started seeing fish huts rise up from the lakes in compact, exact little cities. I could see crows circling the air above looking for scraps.

It came to me near Bemidji. We'd slowed for some teenagers crossing the road at a light, girls in huge puffy coats. How strange it must have been to move to a frigid place like this for the first time in middle age, to arrive from California in winter. But to him it must have seemed so forgiving at first. All the teenagers—all the girls—clomping through town in boots, in heavy wool sweaters and jackets. Everything up till then wouldn't count. All those pictures wouldn't count. It's not what you think but what you do that matters. I waited for Whitewood to appear over the next ridge, and the next, and then a new thought came to me. It came all at once: those pictures had been giftwrapped, purposely left below the sink for someone to find. To find and find out. That he'd wanted it to happen. It started to snow. Before we reached Whitewood, snow was blanketing the road. It happened so fast it was startling. Blacktop, yellow lines, median—all gone within minutes. I felt the disconnected parts of my brain snap piece by piece into place as fresh wet flakes flashed down outside. As the bus fishtailed and everybody gasped. As the wheels found traction and we barreled on.

21

NO, I DIDN'T THINK TO CALL 911. I admitted this on the stand. It did not occur to me to use the cell phone, or to go to my parents' house, or to take the bike into town. I didn't think about how it would have been faster to flag someone down on the road or go to the information booth at the National Forest Campground. I said: I didn't really have a plan. I said: I don't really know what I was thinking. When I told Patra I'd get the Tylenol that morning, I testified, I just put on my shoes and opened the door.

What I didn't say on the stand was that when I looked back at her from the doorway, Patra had been mouthing something. It had been strange to see, like she was yelling without sound. Like her whole face was contorting around each word. Going: THANKYOU. Going: HELPUS. HELPUSPLEASE. Did she think I would understand? I remember closing the door very gently, listening for the latch. Did she think I would do for her what she couldn't do herself? Having come this far, having accumulated everything that mattered to her at all through a series of little, irrevocable choices? I remember squinting into the hot morning, letting go of the knob. I remember lifting the rock in the woods, finding the money in its damp roll, taking off at a sprint. High summer sun hit from directly above. No breeze. No birds or clouds. Two tall walls of green rose up on either side of the highway.

I don't remember getting tired, but I do remember my chest starting to burn, and just as it did, a helicopter swooped directly overhead. It was one of those forest service copters, fitted with tanks and buckets, painted bright red. It churned the highest branches of the trees, and I stopped for a moment in the middle of the highway to look up at it. *Was there a fire?* I remember wondering. But only briefly, because the roar of the copter skimmed away all thoughts. Its wind whipped the loose strands of my hair and rippled like a spook through my T-shirt. By the time it was gone, I was walking along. My heart was still thudding, but some of the urgency had drained from my limbs. It was so much easier being outdoors again. In the woods, in the sun. I felt a little lighter as my T-shirt settled back over my sweaty skin. I felt chilled.

Let me be clear about something. The woods of my childhood are not the same woods I see today. When I was small, another name for Still Lake was Swamp Lake, because during dry years cattails ate up the shore and the lily pads were so thick they looked like solid ground. In wet years, the lake flooded its banks and we could almost dock the canoes at the cabin steps. Now, the association of homeowners has widened the channel between Still and Mill lakes, ensuring unvarying water levels year in, year out. There are twelve summer homes around the perimeter—not log houses so much as minichalets—with skylights and multiple decks and moored pontoon boats on beaches. In summer, it's a suburb. Most of the lakeshore pines have been cut down for sunbathers and flower beds. The water is crowded with little kids horsing around, with teenagers in black inner tubes bouncing behind bowriders. Dads in cabin cruisers skulk inlets and bays, hoping for some hoary walleye.

Sometimes, when I sit with my mother outside the re-habbed cabin on what's left of our lot, I try to remember how the woods looked to me when I was younger. I know better than to be wistful. It was never magical to me: I was never so young, nor so proprietary, as to see it like that. Year by year, the woods just kept unfurling and blooming and drying up, and its constant flux implied meanings half revealed, half withheld—mysteries, yes, but mysteries made rote by change itself, the woods covering and re-covering its tracks. When I was eight or nine, I used to go down to the shore and fill coffee cans with toads the size of dimes. I called these Zoos. My mother would want me to pray before I went to sleep, and so I said the same prayer every night: *Dear God, please help Mom, Dad, Tameka, Abe, Doctor, Jasper, Quiet, and all the animals in all the Zoos to be not too bored and not too lonely.* "Not *too*" was my mantra. I wanted very badly to keep the toads. I liked their many faces—their highly structural eyes, especially—but I worried about what I was keeping them from. After a few nights of swelling guilt, I would empty out the coffee cans in a speckled alder bush, and as the toads popped away on their tiny legs, I felt the power of the woods very keenly. I felt the way it chastised and corrected me, the way it always seemed to say: *See?*

Here's what I passed that day as I walked into town. First, the familiar spray-painted sign propped on the roadside, the one that promised LIQUOR AND GAS. For years Katerina the Communist ran that old place, selling bait and beer at a discount, vodka and gasoline at a premium. Katerina was fifty my whole life, a second-generation Czech from Iowa with the same hooded eyes as my toads. She sold my dad's blow-down wood in twined bundles and my mother's handmade lures reconfigured as ear-rings. As I got older, it dawned on me that she pitied us. Once, she gave me a pair of Adidas tennis shoes that had belonged to her niece. Saying, "Goddammit, Linda" when I wouldn't take them at first. Saying, "A high schooler does not wear hiking boots to school, period. Okay? Okay?" For years those were my very best shoes. I was wearing them that day.

I knew she kept a couple of dusty boxes of Band-Aids on the shelf, perhaps a bottle or two of Tylenol as well, but I skipped LIQUOR AND GAS that hot Monday morning, dreading Katerina's bustle and chewed nails, her greasy pity, which somehow infected me with her bad looks, which always made me feel as fetid and sweaty as she was.

The next thing I passed was the stop sign, which locals only occasionally obeyed, followed by the three bars and the three churches. On Monday morning, all six buildings were closed—the bars on one side of the road, the churches on the other. There were overturned empties on the grass next to Our Lady's wooden crucifix, Sunday bulletins blown into a paper mesh against the chain-link fence at the Hare and Fox. *All Are Welcome in God's House*, they said, again and again.

Then came the ice rink, with its shell-like hulk, its alu-minum siding and flat asphalt roof. It was the biggest building in town by far. Weekdays in the summer, it was packed with figure skaters and hockey players competing for ice time. When I passed the rink, I saw that the Zamboni had chased them all outdoors. They hobbled around the parking lot in their skate guards, the boys hoping to be the target of the girls' vitriol, the girls, in turn, hoping to be the target of chucked ice shavings.

Past the rink were the downtown shops with their old-timey facades in crumbling brick, their storefronts built during the timber boom last century. Bank, bait and tackle, hardware. Grandmas and veterans were already ordering their lunches at the diner, their white-bread sandwiches and wild rice soup. From the sun-bleached side of the building, the three painted walleye reared above a street lamp and waved. Closer to the river were the charred remains of the old timber mill, now so overgrown with summer trees and weeds you could hardly see it. Farther down Main, near the interstate, was the strip mall Pine Alley. After that, Whitewood was 21 miles east. In another 120 miles, Duluth. Then the lift bridge, the anchored tall ships, Lake Superior itself. I thought of it briefly, as I walked past the Pine Alley shops, as I fingered the four dirty tens in my pocket. It was almost longing I felt: Superior, with its 31,000 square miles of water and its thirty-nine-degree temperature year-round—with its sunken SS *Edmund Fitzgerald* and its piles of spilled taconite and its unrecovered bodies preserved facedown in silt in orange life jackets.

The drugstore was in the strip mall. I pushed the door and went in.

The air-conditioning sent a fast shudder up and down my skin. All the items on the shelves—the indecipherable bottles of vitamins, the cough syrups—were cold to the touch. I must have been extremely sweaty when I came in the door because after a minute or two my fingers were a splotchy white, and I had to wiggle them to draw blood back. In the back of the store, a sunburnt dad in flip-flops and bathing trunks was trying to pry the handle of a broom from a toddler's mouth.

He nodded at me, holding the baby's hand up in the air as if it were a prop.

"Do you need something in particular?" a girl's voice asked. I looked up and saw it was Sarah the Ice Skater. She was wearing a green smock and nibbling a red straw from the Frostie's next door.

I was too surprised to respond. Wasn't it summer? Didn't that mean Sarah had all day every day to work on her triples? Weren't the Olympics just a year away?

Then I remembered that Sarah's double axel had dried up last spring during Upper Great Lakes. Every time she went up in the air, people said, she had the determined terror of a suicide. She'd looked like she was throwing herself off a ledge.

"You need something special?" Sarah asked, approaching me, teething her straw. The baby in the back of the store was going GA-GA-GA.

"No."

As I scanned the bottles in the Wellness & Nutrition aisle, I felt the distance between us close. There was a medication called Human Health that claimed to close your pores. There was a multivitamin called IGGY that you squeezed into your nose with an eyedropper. I didn't see any Tylenol, but low-dose aspirin, I read, was for thinning the blood—as well as for preventing fever, stroke, pregnancy loss, pain, and possibly (promising studies showed) cancer.

Sarah asked, "Is it your time of the month?"

"No."

"You hungover?"

"No."

She watched me read the back of a clattery bottle of multivitamins. "You anemic?" She sucked again from her straw, never taking her eyes off me. "Are you, like, malnourished or something?"

"I've got a headache. A—" I searched for the word. "A migraine."

"Did you fall?" She lowered her voice. "Did somebody hit you?"

"I mean, a stomachache. Or a fever, possibly?"

She took a step back. "A fever? You better call Dr. Lord."

"You mean Lorn?"

"There's a *d* on the end of it, I'm pretty sure."

I was about to take issue with this point when the baby in the back of the store let out a wail. Something about that sound made me step forward and touch Sarah's wrist, briefly. "It might be a high fever. Is there something here for very high fevers?"

Though I'd barely touched her, I swear I could see Sarah's arm twitch. She narrowed her dark eyes. "Oh, God. You're contagious sick, aren't you? I've got a late-night shift! I've got to work late. Stay away from me, don't get too close. I'm serious."

I took a step forward. "I'm not that sick."

She shuffled away gracefully on her skating feet and stood with her back against a wall of tampons. "Don't come near me, okay? Just take what you need and put it on the counter."

At a loss, I grabbed the bottle of low-dose aspirin for $3.99 and put it in my basket. Then, on impulse, I added two Pixy Stix, a bag of tropical Skittles, and an Atomic Fireball. I set everything on the counter by the cash register, and Sarah motioned for me to back up while she came around, found a pair of green gardening gloves with the price tag still on, wedged her hand in one of them, and used that to ring everything up. It came to $5.39, and when I set one of my soiled tens on the counter—smeared with dirt and moss, folded at the corners—Sarah closed her eyes as if her worst fears were confirmed, as if visible disease clung to that bill in the form of actual mud, and she told me to take what I needed, she'd pay, whatever. Just go.

As I left, I saw the toddler in the back of the store had put a padded bra over his mouth like a bandit. He waved at me.

Once I was out on the street again, the real heat of the day slammed into me. I ambled up the hill toward the high school sucking one of my Maui Punch Pixy Stix, then down past the junior high working on the tropical Skittles. I went past city hall twice, three times, thinking somebody might stop and ask me why I was loitering on the steps. I sat for a minute on the curb where I saw an old lighter in the gutter, like it just wanted my fingers on it, and I lit the second of my Pixy Stix on fire. It burned slowly, smoking and dripping red goo on the sidewalk.

When nobody stopped me for arson or loitering, I stamped out the oozing straw and went to the hardware store. It occurred to me that I might see my dad there. He sometimes went in for nails and fishing line, but Mr. Ling, the owner, was alone, dozing with a Gophers cap over his eyes.

Next I went into the grocery store. It was empty except for Mr. Korhonen, who was reading the paper on the counter and didn't look up. Strangely, the door didn't make a sound when I entered or left—each time it caught a pocket of air and never quite closed. I poked my head in the diner, but Santa Anna, my old boss, was on vacation. She'd gone to the Laurel and Hardy Festival in Toronto and gotten her sister to fill in. "She'll be back in a week or so," the sister said, pushing long bangs from her eyes and pouring coffee for an old lady doing a crossword puzzle.

Down the road, I saw that the door to Unified Spirit was now open, and I went in, thinking I might see my mom at one of her many meetings. At the very least, I thought I might see Pastor Benson tending his rabbits in one of the cages in his office or the secretary folding Sunday bulletins in the multipurpose room in the back. But no one seemed to be there at all. The wooden pews in the sanctuary were set up in such a way that they blocked any reasonable route to the altar. I wound this way and that, moving through those maze-like pews, and in grim triumph arrived at the altar sucking on my Atomic Fireball. My mouth burned and, at the same time, felt finely and delicately needled through with shards of sugar.

By then, about twenty-four hours had passed since we'd left Duluth. By then, I later learned, Paul had an hour before he slipped into a coma, another four hours before cardiac arrest.

Dear God, I thought, when I got to the cross, though I knew it was a rinky-dink faith I possessed, of less use even than superstition. *Dear God, please help Mom, Dad, Tameka, Abe, Jasper, Doctor, Quiet, and Paul to be not too bored and not too lonely.* Not *too.* It was the only prayer I knew. As the heat from the atomic fireball filled my mouth—seeming to swell and lap at my tongue, seeming to enlarge the space inside me that could be burned—I thought of Patra, deliberately then, letting my mind return to her bit by bit. I thought about Patra with all that pancake in her mouth. I thought about Patra going to the hospital to give birth to Paul, of her hand tapping out the beat of her heart on my thigh, and when I thought of all that, I almost believed that by buying the aspirin and making no fuss, I had done something to please her. My eyes watered from the heat in my mouth. Relief came over me just that quick. I'd done exactly what Patra had asked, and no more, so it felt almost heroic then, valiant in its way, how little I'd accomplished.

I went up to the offering box on the altar and left the grubby tens with their folded black corners. At the last minute, I took off Patra's headband and left that as well, as a second thought, knowing the ache had settled in too deeply to dissipate anytime soon.

Then I wound my way through the pews and started back.

Here's how I remember the woods of my childhood. Every tree, even the pines planted in strict rows by the forest service years ago, seemed different: one with sap seeping out in blisters in the heat, another with a branch knocked down, leaving a gnome-like face in the wood. The woods were a kind of nursery for not thinking, for just seeing and walking along. I liked running my eyes over details, over twigs and pine needles, over roadkill with intestines like spilled baggage on the asphalt. There were certain things I knew about the woods, but always, too, there were things I was sure I'd never seen before in my life. A crow fighting with a snapping turtle over a fast-food bag on the shoulder, for instance. Or a carpenter ant, appearing from out of nowhere on my wrist, dragging a small green caterpillar up my arm like a prize.

Or this. Halfway back to the Gardner house, a car passed me by. Then a hundred feet ahead, it stopped and began to back up. By that time, the sun was much lower in the sky. A woman in a white sun visor was driving, craning her neck around, but it was the man in the passenger seat who rolled his window down and spoke to me. In the back of the car sat two little kids, a boy and a girl, staring out.

"Hey," the man said. "Everything okay?"

Their license plate said Illinois. Land of Lincoln.

I kept going.

The car, a station wagon with a canoe lashed to the roof, slowly followed along as I walked. Like one of those dogs you can't get rid of.

The man had furry eyebrows. "We're not trying to be creepy," he said. "And you're right to be wary, of course. But I think—"

The car drove over a fallen branch, which cracked very slowly and loudly.

The man went on. "I can't help but think you look like you could use a ride somewhere? Do you need a ride somewhere? The map says it's woods for fifty miles in this direction. Just lakes and woods." He held the map out the window to show me. As if I didn't know this already, as if this was news to me.

But he was watching my face very closely.

"Okay," I said finally. Late afternoon was settling in around us. The bottle of aspirin was still in my hand. I felt calm, delivered. "It's not far," I promised.

In the backseat, the little kids in their shorts and T-shirts helped me buckle my seat belt.

I had to direct the car. I had to say "slow down" at the turnoff to Still Lake and then point the way in the shadows toward the narrow road that led to the Gardner cabin. The visored woman was a good driver, and she took it easy on the gravel roads. The woods passed by languidly, the branches a blue-green slurry through the windows. I wondered how long I could keep the woman driving—she was very trusting, I could tell. I had the feeling I could point down any backwoods road, any rutted path, no matter how remote, and she'd go where I said. When I found myself enjoying this thought, it felt like a betrayal of something, though I wasn't sure what, so I urged the careful woman driver forward. I tried to warn her of bumps in the road, of future dangers. "Sometimes it's hard to see deer. You gotta watch out if you're driving at dusk. Keep that in mind for later. There's no streetlights or anything."

The woman gave me a little smile in the rearview mirror. Like: *I know.*

The man was into small talk, but not like Leo, who liked facts, or my dad who only did baseball, weather, and fish. He asked me where I was going. I said "home"—which I guess sounded about right to him, because he left it at that and started telling me about their campsite up near Turquoise Lake.

"Ever been there?"

I couldn't help rolling my eyes. "A million times."

"Any tips?"

I thought about it. "There's a bald eagle's nest on the north shore."

One of the little kids, the girl, said with all earnestness, "Cool." She had out a notebook, and she wrote it down. *Eagels Nest.* At the top of that page it said *Plans*, and next to that was a second list for *Memories.* Here's what she'd written down under that: *Dead deer on the road. Girl who looks like a boy. Doesn't know how to use a seet belt.*

"S-E-A-T," I told her.

She made the correction, rubbing at her paper with the eraser.

The father up front said, "We'd *love* to see a bald eagle."

The mother said, "We've seen some hawks, but not any eagles. That would be great."

I almost told them then: There's something wrong with Paul.

I almost said it. I think I need some help.

But I didn't because I knew they *would* help, and I didn't want Patra squinting at them through the front door in her T-shirt, her panties exposed, or Leo shooing this other father away with a sweaty handshake. I didn't want to see Patra shushed by Leo, sent back inside, or Leo tucking in his shirt and blinking his bloodshot eyes as he explained the way back to the highway. And I knew that if I somehow got this visored woman inside, if I somehow got her past Leo and into Paul's room, it would mean the end of Janet and Europa for good, the end of everything worthwhile. So I had the woman take the slow way around the lake, going down the one-lane logging road that was almost never used, that was overgrown with shrubs and young aspen. I had her take the boat access road to the shore and double back. As she drove, I could see the woman watching me very closely in the rearview mirror. She was driving and watching me both, but I broke her gaze and looked down at my lap.

Beside me, the boy reached out and touched Paul's aspirin bottle. "What's that you got in your hand?"

"I got a headache," I said.

Though I no longer did. It was gone.

We were going so slowly and the woods were so shaded and dark it seemed the trees, not the car, were moving. They were sliding past the windows, mechanically, and it was the car that seemed fragile and hesitant.

Then the Gardner cabin appeared. Car in the driveway, front shades closed, white cat peeping out one window.

"Oh!" the woman driver exclaimed, surprised. Plainly relieved to have reached a real destination. She rolled down her window to get a better look. "What a nice little house! Just hidden away back here."

I could see the little girl writing it down. *Cottage.*
She wrote it down carefully. *Deep in the woods.*

At some point—not long after that summer ended—the woods started to seem different to me for good. Let me be clear. This feeling started long before the twenty acres on the east shore of Still Lake was subdivided, and subdivided again, by developers from the Cities. It started long before the channel was widened between our lake and the next, before the aspens and pines were cleared and all the new houses built. Those were only the most obvious changes. What I'm talking about is something else. I remember watching the wind scuttling through a branch near the beginning of tenth grade, and thinking I could see the earth's orbit setting up a chain reaction of weather that made the blowing branch inevitable. I looked up at the foliage and saw electrons from a not-so-distant (and not-so-spectacular) star turning carbon dioxide into a yellow-green leaf. Abe died later that fall, and as I dug a hole for him beneath the pines, I started to think about what would happen if we never found humans or humanoids or intelligence or cells or life of any sort anywhere else in the universe. I started to think maybe all those astronomers were wrongheaded in their quest, that the difference between life and nonlife was minimal at best, probably beside the point. We'd gotten it backward. We'd pointed our telescopes into space in hopes of seeing ourselves, and seen so many clumps of chemicals reflected back. There was no helping the boredom I thought. After Abe died, after Leo and Patra left. There was no changing the loneliness.

22

THE FIRST DAY OF TENTH GRADE I GOT UP EARLIER THAN I NEEDED TO. As my parents slept in the room behind the kitchen, I got dressed—jeans, green wool sweater, boots—and pumped the little propane stove next to the sink. At first, the blue light of the gas was all I could see by, but as the water began to thrum in the pot, a bit of the gray September day showed itself through the one window. Pines shivered in the wind off the water. I filtered coffee through a wet cloth, poured the oily black brew into my dad's thermos. Nestled the thermos in my backpack. The dogs whined even after I let them out of the shed, pulling on their stakes, dropping dew from their chains. They'd become accustomed to me again over the summer. They'd come to expect more than a pat or two, though I didn't have time for that now. I poured their kibble sloppily, shoved their four bowls against the woodpile. They were always hungrier than they were affectionate, anyhow. They didn't look up again once they got their breakfast.

The highway was empty, still. Early fall fog clung to the trees on the edges, muffling sounds, making the five-mile walk into town a long slide from one four-foot patch of asphalt to the next. I swung my arms against the chill. I got my heart going, and once I did I couldn't slow it down again. When I got to Main, I took a sharp right behind Katerina's gas station. It didn't look like she'd opened the place up yet. The Plexiglas window on the side of the shop was still dark. Out back, she had the hides of two bucks strung up on poles, which would have interested me usually, but I was in a hurry and didn't stop. I followed the wet woods path past the old timber mill, whose charred black boards rose higher than the pines and got lost in the fog overhead. I kept going. I went around to the bank of Gone Lake, where I knew Katerina kept a second aluminum canoe, unused for years.

After a few minutes of searching, I found the battered canoe sunk in cattails and mud a little way down from the creek mouth. Wading into the mud, I turned the thing over—first draining the water—and cleaned the mucky seats with the sleeve of my sweater. The sun was burning the fog off the lake now. The surface dimpled with minnows below and water striders above. I dipped the paddles in the cold creek water to rinse them clean, then propped them up against the beached canoe. All ready to go. All ready for Lily.

Back in town, back at the baseball field behind the school, I sat down on the batters' bench and waited. I knew Lily's dad usually dropped her off not far from here on his way to the forest service station. If she was coming to school, if she was coming at all, I meant to head her off on the way to the door. I had something to give her, and I wanted to give it to her in the canoe. My idea was to tell her I'd gotten a letter in the mail from Mr. Grierson. And if she didn't believe that, I'd explain how close we were, Mr. Grierson and I—closer than it seemed—because of History Odyssey. I'd written the letter myself the night before. I'd snuck a beer from the shed and a good ink pen from my mom's craft supplies beneath the sink. Sitting cross-legged in my loft after my parents went to sleep, I'd written on a yellow legal pad in careful block letters. I'd only had to think of Patra kneeling in front of Leo in the hotel to get the picture I needed in my head. After that the words came easy.

I had this letter for Lily, sealed. I wanted to take her somewhere she couldn't get away while I watched her read it. The canoe in Gone Lake would be perfect, but if that made Lily suspicious then it could be the woods behind the gas station where Katerina kept her buckskins and bloody axes in pails. Or I could do it here at school, if she wouldn't go with me to the lake, here in the stiff grass with the hockey players watching. They could watch if they wanted. In the end I didn't care. Somewhere between home and the baseball field I'd gotten angry. Somewhere between August and September I'd grown a pins-and-needles feeling on my neck and scalp, a tightness in my chest that almost never went away. I couldn't bear to walk down Main Street anymore, even to get tackle at Bob's shop, because that's where the bank was with my babysitting money inside. I couldn't go by the elementary school or even to the Forest Service Nature Center, which used to be my favorite place in the world. I couldn't go anywhere or be anyone. I was trembling as I waited in the baseball field. I was hoping Lily would arrive before the final bell rang.

I saw her dad's pickup a few minutes after the last busses took off. He did a little half turn against the curb, so a mess of two-by-fours and an open cooler slid around in the bed. I stood up and shakily drew the letter from my pocket. Seeing that pickup arrive when I wasn't sure she'd come at all—seeing Lily open the passenger door—made everything else I would do to her seem inevitable. Now things would simply run their course. Now, one way or another, she would see this was not playing, what she'd said, that you couldn't just do whatever you wanted to someone and get away with it.

When she climbed out of the cab, I saw her hair was wet. It swung in clumped ropes on either side of her head, and she was strangely unsteady. She had to hold the pickup door with two hands as she got out, and for a second I thought, *Oh no, she's drunk*, but then I saw she had a belly so big that her red hoodie didn't quite cover it. So big, I could almost see the baby inside her when the sun hit her skin, the outline of a terrible tiny person there, I swear—

—but no, it was just her veins, a branchwork of purple lines that were covered again when she pulled down her shirt.

I didn't step forward and say her name. I didn't approach because of that belly of hers, and because I saw—as she waddled toward me—she was wearing the black suede boots I'd left at her house three months ago. She was wearing my boots, which shone a dark plum color in the morning sun. I just nodded at her as she passed, as she glanced once in my direction and then on to the next thing. The door. The crowd of hockey players in their white caps on the curb who'd caught sight of her, now, and were staring outright. School. Tenth grade.

Dear Lily,

I've been wanting to write you a note for a very long time. I'm having Mattie give you this letter because everybody will be watching you for correspondence from me, and nobody will be watching her. What I need to tell you is I can't stop thinking about what you said last spring. I think about your fantasy of Gone Lake all the time, every day, every minute. I think about it so much that it's all very clear to me now, like something

that actually happened. Like something we really did. Did you
intend that? I think maybe you did. I think about the feeling
of your lips on my skin in that boat. I think about the feeling
of my dick in the back of your throat, you sucking me down,
and then your sweet look of surprise when I finish. Can you
imagine how deep it went, how good it was, how long I lasted,
how I drew it out for you at just the right moment—did you
feel all that, Lily, you fucking pervert?

Even now—in the murky moments before sleep—I sometimes
think about what it would have been like to have taken Lily
out on Gone Lake that day in the canoe. I think about it when
nothing else works, when I can't find a way to jostle myself from
the overwhelming sense of quiet in my new little room in the
rehabbed cabin. In my mind, I go through the ritual preparations
methodically, staving off all feeling of any sort, heating a kettle
on the stove, filling a thermos with coffee in the early morning
and slipping it in my backpack, ambushing Lily when her dad
drops her off in the schoolyard. Saying to her, "Let's cut class, this
once." Saying, "Let's have a smoke, catch a few crappie, okay?"
She's reluctant, in my dream of her, but then, magically, we're
out on the boat, out in the bright center of Gone Lake. The
waves are shushing the boat around, and it's early fall, a couple
of hours past dawn, and Lily's wet hair hangs in cords down her
back. Her teeth are chattering and her lips are white, and she's
only wearing one of her sheer sweaters, no jacket or gloves. I see
the cold curl her thin shoulders in. But I cannot feel it myself.
No cold, no wind. I feel nothing. When she turns around to
flick out her cigarette, the one I lit for her, I lunge and take her
paddle from her. She gives me a confused look, so I tell her,

quietly, "You knew what was going to come next." Then I creep from the back of the canoe toward her. I feel the boat like my whole body going under me, the thing rocking back and forth, shuddering and tipping us both off balance. I say to her when I get close, warningly, menacingly perhaps, but also with tender commiseration: "Just a kiss." It feels almost like a benediction, giving her this. The violence in me is almost overwhelming. "That's what you wanted, right? Just a kiss."

And then there's this. Even now, when those words move through my mind, like a curse or a wish, I *become* Lily. It happens just like that. I have to go through all the preparations for it to work: I have to heat the coffee, fill the thermos, wipe down the wet canoe seats with my sleeve. I have to paddle through the rolling water for a long time, and do it silently, and let Lily ride silently in the front. I have to be patient. I have to do all the steps. But by the time the shore is a huge ring of horizon around us, by the time I've taken her paddle, and seen the look of recognition on her face, I find *I'm* the one stranded in the boat, I'm the one shivering with cold, I feel everything and I'm the one wanted more than anyone else.

ACKNOWLEDGMENTS

My deepest gratitude goes to Aimee Bender, who read this novel with such generosity and insight in its earliest of drafts. I am very grateful to Elisabeth Schmitz for championing this book and guiding it toward publication. Many people at Grove Atlantic have gone above and beyond with their time and care: thank you Julia Berner-Tobin, Paula Cooper Hughes, Kirsten Giebutowski, Judy Hottensen, Gretchen Mergenthaler, Katie Raissian, Deb Seager, Chin-Yee Lai, and everyone else who helped this book find its way into the world. My profound thanks to my agent Nicole Aragi, who responded to this novel with more enthusiasm than I could have hoped for, and also to Duvall Osteen for keeping things organized behind the scenes. Thank you, too, to *Southwest Review* for publishing the first chapter in 2013 and honoring it with the McGinnis-Ritchie Award for Fiction. A special thanks to the Barbara Deming Memorial Fund for recognizing the value of supporting feminist projects. I also thank T. C. Boyle and the students in his workshop at the University of Southern California, who were the first readers of what became the opening chapter of this novel. Let me extend my heartfelt appreciation to all the teachers over the years who have provided me with such superb models of thinking and writing, especially Bill Handley and Natania Meeker at the University of Southern California and Marshall Klimasewiski and Kellie Wells at Washington University in St. Louis. My sincere thanks to both of these institutions for financial support and for offering wonderful communities in which to grow as a writer. I will always be immensely indebted to the colleagues and friends in these writing communities who provoked such influential conversations about books. On a more practical level, thank you to Janalynn Bliss at USC for printing off chapters of this novel when I was no longer on campus. More recently, I owe Cornell University my thanks for providing a teaching home as I revised *History of Wolves*.

I want to acknowledge, too, some of the books that inspired the writing of this one. In chapter 1, Linda quotes in her presentation from Barry Lopez's *Of Wolves and Men*. The full passage reads: "But the term *alpha*—evolved to describe captive animals—is still misleading. Alpha animals do not always lead the hunt, break trail in snow, or eat before the others do. An alpha animal may be alpha only at certain times for a specific reason, and, it should be noted, is alpha at the deference of the other wolves in the pack." In chapter 8 there is a reference to Maurice Sendak's *Where the Wild Things Are*. I am indebted to many sources for information about flora, fauna, and life in northern Minnesota, but two stand out: Sigurd Olson's *The Singing Wilderness* and Helen Hoover's *The Years of the Forest*. I was grateful to have Caroline Fraser's excellent and harrowing book *God's Perfect Child: Living and Dying in the Christian Science Church* by my side, along with Barbara Wilson's *Blue Windows: A Christian Science Childhood* and Lucia Greenhouse's *fathermothergod: My Journey Out of Christian Science*. It should be said that Paul's case is a fictionalized composite of many around the country, and it reflects neither a specific child nor the particulars of any one court case in any actual place or time. Caroline Fraser's book offers an especially powerful nonfictional record of children and their families in Christian Science—including detailed religious, legal, and social histories—for those interested. I am grateful to Sharon Ostfeld-Johns for offering medical advice on the manuscript and pointing me to UpToDate, a physician-authored online resource, where I learned about some of the symptoms of diabetic ketoacidosis and cerebral edema.

This novel owes a great deal to all the time I've spent wandering around in the woods: thank you to my parents for this legacy of woods-haunting (to modify a phrase from Virginia Woolf), and thank you, particularly, to the establishments that fed me and put me up when I was traveling in the summer of 2012 in northern Minnesota. In addition, and though my vein of gratitude runs more obliquely than I can easily express, let me acknowledge here those who were kind to me when I was very young at Principia College.

Finally, I am grateful to my family for being there through the years, for their patience and openheartedness at every odd turn in my own story. And my most humble thanks go to Nick Admussen, who believed in the value of this project from the beginning and kept my head above water all along the way. This novel is dedicated to him.